# PUBLIC GARDEN

# PUBLIC

James P. Moran

CROWN PUBLISHERS, INC.
NEW YORK

# GARDEN

*To Lisa*

Copyright © 1994 by James P. Moran

All rights reserved. No part of this book may be reproduced or transmitted in any form or by any means, electronic or mechanical, including photocopying, recording, or by any information storage and retrieval system, without permission in writing from the publisher.

Published by Crown Publishers, Inc., 201 East 50th Street, New York, New York 10022.

CROWN is a trademark of Crown Publishers, Inc.

Manufactured in the United States of America

Book design by June Bennett-Tantillo

Library of Congress Cataloging in Publication Data
Moran, James P.
    Public garden / James P. Moran.
        p.    cm.
        1. Women lawyers—United States—
Fiction.  I. Title.
    PS3563.0765P8   1994
    813'.54—dc20                                    93-6221
                                                        CIP

ISBN: 0-517-59606-7

10  9  8  7  6  5  4  3  2  1

First Edition

# Acknowledgments

*For their generous advice and support,*
*I wish to thank the following persons:*
*Nick Ellison, my agent; Tony Ardizzone;*
*Jack McNamara; and Kathryn Haight Meyer.*

*Ye are confounded for the gardens
ye have chosen.*

*—Isaiah 1:29*

et your *Herald*. Get your *Globe* here," the news vendor shouted to commuters passing in and out of Park Street station. He folded and slapped papers into customers' hands, collecting coins in his till. Jack watched him from the top of the stairway inside the station door and lit a cigarette, his fingers in a steady tremor. He pulled the lapels of his camel-hair coat under his chin and blew on his hands for warmth.

It was a blustery October day. Brown, green, and yellow leaves glided in the air and slammed against the door like naive birds. The foliage was supposed to be at its peak. Jack thought of the trip to New Hampshire he and Alison had recently planned, how they carefully researched the bed and breakfasts, mapped out the preferred route, anticipated a romantic getaway. All plans were off now.

Jack heard a voice from below, felt a hand touching his pants leg. "Excuse me, sir." A man dressed in a torn gray overcoat, his white, grizzled face partially hidden beneath an upraised collar, lay sprawled at his feet. A crumbled brown lunch bag was stuffed in his pocket. Blackened fingers stuck through his tattered mittens, extended upward, flexing back and forth. He gestured to the cigarette with a queer smile, revealing his reddened, sore gums and yellow teeth.

Never give them an opening, Jack thought with a sigh. Cigarettes are a conversation starter. From there it's a quarter for a cup of coffee, a couple bucks for a bus ticket, a full-length recitation on the purpose of your charity. Jack was jostled toward the man by a crowd streaming up the stairs from the station below, and he fought to maintain his balance.

Jack bent over and handed the man a cigarette. A stale urine smell clung to the man's clothes. Nodding in appreciation, he pawed the cigarette in his thick palm. He pulled himself up against the wall, sitting with his legs outstretched, and fumbled through his pockets in an absentminded search for a match, as if he had lost something of importance.

Frustrated by this deliberation, Jack flicked a lighter in front of the man's face. Startled, the man snapped his head back and hit the wall. He grabbed Jack's hand and steadied it before the end of the cigarette. Sucking in, he coughed hoarsely, nodded again to Jack, and averted his face to the side.

Jack walked out the door to avoid further contact, cursing Alison under his breath. She was late, he thought with irritation. The hourly bells rang from the Park Street Church, and he realized that he had actually been early.

She crossed the street toward him, dressed in a black turtleneck sweater, a short skirt, white nylons and flat shoes, a faded blue-jean jacket. Over her shoulder she carried a large black bag. Her straight light brown hair tossed in the wind, and she brushed away errant bangs. The sight of her added a further chill to his bones. His stomach was queasy.

"Hi," he said quietly. She looked up at him with dark cold eyes. Her small oval face was flush from the wind, fixed into a pout. She offered none of the charm that he had learned to expect and anticipate. He played with the loose button on his overcoat, absorbed by the thread, running his finger up and down. He just wanted it all to be over, the whole sorry episode.

"Alison," he said, reaching for her hand, attempting sympathy, but she drew back.

They walked down the steep stairway to the subway platform. She held on to the railing, and he fought the urge to assist. He wondered why he had agreed to come with her, except out of some perverse sense of duty to see a thing all the way through, to live with the consequences of his behavior. At the bottom of the stairs, he bought their tokens. She remained silent as he passed one to her, never moving her eyes from the ground.

The platform was dense with waiting passengers. There had been a delay. When they boarded the Green Line train to Brookline, it was jammed with people. They were crushed in the car, against the door. The car smelled of sour breath, cologne, perfume, hairspray. A large man, his stomach protruding over his waistband, was reading *TV Guide*. College students with backpacks listened to silent radios, their ears plugged. A red-faced drunk mumbled to himself. An old woman with white hair and wrinkled face sat clutching her black purse and a Filene's bag, a look of trepidation etched on her face. The train wheels screeched as the train hit a curve.

Jack stared out at the dark walls, wires, and beams in the tunnel. Each stop was a struggle as people pushed their way on and off. Along the way, he lost Alison in the interchange. He saw her sitting down at the end of the car, forlorn. He remained standing near the door.

The train came up from below onto Beacon Street, the gray sunlight bathing the car. As Alison and Jack stepped off, he was conscious of a commotion across Beacon Street. A crowd was gathered in front of the clinic. There was shouting intermixed with chanting and singing. Fists were raised in the air; posters on sticks bobbed up and down in rhythm. One group stood behind a barricade fronted by police caressing nightsticks. A caravan of police cars lined the street in front of the clinic. Swirling blue and white lights bounced off the surrounding buildings.

Alison turned from the action and into Jack. He started to put his arms around her, but she spun to face the crowd, her mouth clenched with determination. She began walking across the street, treading slowly through the stalled traffic. Horns blared.

They negotiated a serpentine path through the cars. Behind the barricades, rows of women ranging in age, some dressed in blue jeans and sweatshirts, others in long coats and knitted caps, shook coat hangers at people in front of the clinic. The police stood impassively, blocking their way. The crowd was packed tight against the police cars, holding up posters: FREE TO CHOOSE; IF MEN COULD GET PREGNANT, ABORTION WOULD BE A SACRAMENT; MOTHERS FOR CHOICE.

Jack grabbed Alison's hand and pulled her with him around the barricade to the right of the crowd. They stood to the side watching the scene.

"Just a minute, Jimmy," a blond woman standing next to them said to a man with a large camera hoisted on his shoulder. She removed a compact from her purse, balancing it on her left hand, and deftly wound her lipstick with her right. She pursed her lips, applied a thin layer of pink, and smiled.

"How's the visual?" she asked, twisting her elbow into Jack

and sneering at him. "Excuse me. We're trying to set something up here, okay?" She picked up a steno pad from the bag lying at her feet and flipped the pages, licking her fingers and examining her fine, long nails. The man removed the camera from his shoulder and lit a cigarette. He leaned against the TV truck. The woman walked over and took a drag from his cigarette.

"Maybe we should try another day," Jack said.

"There'll never be a good time," Alison said. "I want to get this over with."

The group immediately in front of the clinic was waving pictures of aborted fetuses, and chanting, "Murderers! Murderers!" There was a rustling in the crowd. A black-haired, plump woman fell on top of another woman holding a coat hanger. She hit her on the head and chest, and the crowd gathered around, enclosed them in a circle, still chanting. The police broke through the crowd. The barricade collapsed and the crowd swelled. One of the cops ran to his car and pulled a radio out.

"Send them in, Charlie." He paused, laughing. "No, we can skip the dogs. I see some press. Fucking junkies. Yeah, right. Ten, fifteen, maybe. One meat wagon for these wackos is enough. Don't want them comfortable. Yeah. Great fuckin' duty. The bitches killing themselves."

The reporter and cameraman leaped into action as the crowd pushed itself further onto the street. Sirens wailed. On the steps of the clinic, a group of six people lay prone on the sidewalk, silently praying. Officers came running down the street. They wore white elastic gloves.

A cop stood in the middle of the street, urging cars to move on. Other officers pushed the crowd back to the sidewalk. A young cop with thin white arms and pale face struggled to place the plump woman in handcuffs. She spat on the ground. In reaction, the cop tripped her and she slammed against the door of the patrol car. He opened the door and shoved her head down into the seat. The cameraman fought through to get a good shot, but someone elbowed him and he fell back.

The reporter stood on the outskirts, near Jack and Alison, stamping her feet like a little girl who had lost a favorite doll. "Freedom of the press. What the fuck are you doing? Can you believe that? Did you see it?" she said to herself, gesturing her arm toward the crowd.

The police officers attempted to lift the demonstrators on the steps, but they went limp, remaining prone. A man dressed in black and a priest's white collar stood reading from a small Bible, the gilded pages flapping in the wind.

The officers dragged the bodies from the entrance and down the sidewalk. Half of the crowd began cheering and clapping, the other half stood in silence. The crowd began to disperse, leaving placards and coat hangers strewn in their wake. Two women walked up to the reporter. She picked up her microphone.

"Jimmy. Hey, Jimmy, get over here," she said to the cameraman, who sat on the curb checking his equipment for damage. "We're getting statements. Okay." She turned to the women. "What we're going to do is to get you to stand over here. Like this." She stood with the clinic at her back. "And I'll ask you, like, the obvious, you know. What's this about? What your positions are. That kind of thing. Okay?"

"Let's go," Alison said to Jack.

"Go?" he asked, surprised.

"You don't have to, you know," she said. "Do what you want."

"No, no. I promised."

"Yeah," she said and began walking toward the front of the clinic.

"This is Wendy Thomas reporting from the Beacon Street clinic, where today . . ." the reporter began.

Jack stopped at the door and removed his wallet from his back pocket. He took two one-hundred-dollar bills out and folded them neatly, as if about to hand her a gratuity. Alison stared at the money and looked away. He tried to stuff it discreetly into her black bag, but she turned sharply and grabbed his arm. The bills fell to the ground and he retrieved them. The warmth of shame hit his face as he bent over before her on his knee. The soles of her tennis shoes were blackened with soot. He placed the bills in her dangling hand and stood up, dizzy, holding the railing. She walked in without him, the door closing in his face.

"These people should be prosecuted," he heard one of the women say into the camera. She was dressed in a floral-print dress and flat shoes. "They're interfering with lawful activity." She tried to continue but the other woman put her face before the microphone.

"We're like the civil rights groups in the Sixties," she said.

"You would have hosed the blacks down if you were there," the other replied.

When Jack walked inside, Alison was standing at the counter, registering, reading the consent form. A gray-haired woman in a white nurse's dress and a cardigan sweater watched them from a chair encased in a clear plastic booth. Bland music came from a portable radio next to her.

"Yeah, ever since they started coming around, business has been slow," the nurse said. "Sorry for the inconvenience. Can I help you, sir?" she asked Jack.

"Oh, no," he mumbled. "I'm with her."

The waiting room walls were painted in a light orange and the room was furnished with plastic padded chairs. A butcher-block table was covered with medical magazines, tattered issues of *People* and *Time*, pamphlets on birth control from Planned Parenthood, postcards to send to congressmen and senators. In one corner, a young woman sat with legs crossed delicately, flipping through a magazine. A younger girl sat huddled next to her boyfriend, a man with dark eyes and hair and a menacing mouth. She appeared frightened, like a hostage, looking to Jack and Alison for reassurance that the assault was over. The young man gave Jack a quick glare and patted his girlfriend's hand. The girl's thick coat of black mascara had smeared from crying, and she wiped her eyes with a tissue from the box on the table.

Alison took a seat and clutched the bag on her lap. She rocked back and forth, biting her lips with a touch of her teeth. Jack stood anxiously beside her, hands shoved in pockets, fidgeting. Alison's eyes remained blank, staring ahead at the landscape painting on the far wall, above a woman primly dressed in a blue suit, her legs in brown nylons. Jack tried to imagine the circumstances that brought these people together in this room. They all shared something unpleasant, and they were there to rid themselves of it. Jack detested being there, implicated in the process, all those present aware of his intimacies and mistakes.

The doctor, a tall, middle-aged man dressed in a white jacket, a stethoscope wrapped around his neck, walked up to the glass booth and picked up the clipboard. He glanced down the list of names.

"Full slate today, Judy. They gone yet?" he asked, nodding toward the outside.

"It's died down," she assured him.

A nurse came out from the hallway, her thick-soled shoes squeaking on the linoleum floor.

"Alison Moore," she said.

Alison jumped up. Jack walked behind her.

"You can wait out here," the nurse said, stopping in her tracks. "It'll be about a half-hour before you can see her." She pointed back to the waiting area with a schoolteacher's stern direction. He watched Alison make her way down the hallway. She never looked back at him, and he had nothing to say.

"I'm going out," he told the receptionist. She was rifling through files with exasperation.

There was no evidence of the demonstration outside. The news people were gone and traffic moved steadily down Beacon Street. Jack strode quickly to Coolidge Corner, buttoning his jacket against the wind, to the front of the Red Lion Lounge. He checked his watch. It was early, perhaps too early for a man of his position to be seen in a lounge, but he needed a drink.

The nurse led Alison into the operating room and left her. Alison removed her clothes and hung them carefully on the rack, smoothing the creases on the skirt, folding the white nylons into a square. She shivered, her feet chilled on the floor, goosebumps forming on her breasts, legs, and arms. She lifted the pale blue-spotted smock over her head and sat down on the hard surface of the examining table. At one end were metal stirrups. Next to the examining table was a shorter table with steel instruments arranged in a row like a place setting, a syringe and needle, and a pair of stiff rubber gloves. A sink and mirror were set along the wall.

She told herself that it would soon be over, and she would be free of Jack. Instead of the purpose of her visit, which was too awesome to contemplate in its particulars, she focused on her anger and resentment toward him, toward the position he had put her in. All those sophisticated birth-control devices, all her so-called knowledge, lost and forgotten in recklessness.

"Did you understand the forms?" the nurse asked when she reentered. "You read about the possible complications?" She paused. "Are you all right?"

"Yes."

"It'll all be over soon. In an instant. Could you roll up the sleeve?" She picked up the syringe full of Valium and Demerol, examining the levels inside. The needle sprayed a spot onto the towel on the table.

"This'll just pinch a bit," she said with a smile, inserting the needle. Alison twinged slightly. The nurse applied a piece of frayed cotton to the spot, wiping away residue.

"You'll start to feel it in a few minutes. The doctor will be right in."

7

The interior of the Red Lion was decorated in a dark rich crimson. The lights were dim. No other customers were visible. The television set was tuned to a black-and-white rerun of a sitcom Jack didn't recognize. He heard the clinking of glasses being washed in a sink in back. The bartender came out of the kitchen, wearing a red vest and black bow tie.

"It's wicked cold out there," Jack said, sitting on a stool in the center of the bar, setting his briefcase on the floor.

"So I hear," the man said.

"You're open, aren't you?"

"Sure. Sure. What's your pleasure?"

"I mean, it's after noon," Jack said with a sad, painful smile.

He ordered a draft beer, and the bartender left him alone. Jack gulped it down.

Alison lay down on the table. The nurse stood to the side as the doctor snapped on rubber gloves. Alison placed her heels in the stirrups and spread her legs. As she grew drowsy, the doctor and nurse became muffled presences. The aspirator began to hum, and the doctor inserted its tip inside her. After he was through, the doctor removed the gloves and tossed them in a garbage can. He washed his hands, and Alison breathed in the pink liquid soap. It roused her like smelling salts.

"It's all over," the nurse said, wiping the beads of sweat on Alison's brow with a cool, wet towel.

Jack sat in a booth, papers spread before him on the table. He worked on a summary judgment motion for the Microtech case. He had called the office and checked his voice mail—Hal's secretary reminding him of the meeting at four o'clock; a younger associate who had finished a memo on the statute of limitations issue; Hal's secretary again asking if he wanted roast beef or turkey for the litigation lunch on Friday. Jack had told Sally, his secretary, that he had a dental appointment and would be back in a couple of hours. Nothing serious, he assured her. Just a cavity.

After the second beer, he went to the bathroom and washed his hands in the sink. His face appeared ashen under the pale light. The smell of his cologne mixed with sweat under his white oxford shirt. He touched the wet spot as it spread across the middle of his chest, adjusted the gold stickpin under his red paisley tie. He lit a cigarette and blew a cloud into the mirror.

Alison sat up on a stretcher in the recovery room, sipping a glass of orange juice. She had slept for twenty minutes but was still drowsy, her eyes drooping, her hair flattened. She stood up, attempting to fix her bangs back in place, out of her eyes.

"You really should relax more," the nurse said, running toward her. "We recommend you rest awhile."

"I'm okay," Alison said, curling her toes on the floor. She wanted desperately to leave.

"You should have someone take you home. Remember, there may be some spotting. Be sure and call if you have any problems. We encourage you to attend the counseling sessions."

Alison ignored the nurse's words and moved gingerly down the hallway to retrieve her clothes.


Sunlight burned Jack's eyes when he came outside. His head rung dully. Alison was waiting for him when he returned, sitting on the steps, smoking a cigarette. She flicked the ashes on the sidewalk. Seeing her there, he trotted the remainder of the block.

"Sorry I'm late," he said, reaching for her arm. "How are you?"

"Fine," she said, her eyes wet, opaque, and cold. She stood and began walking back to the subway stop in a quick determined stride. He followed with hunched shoulders.

On the train ride back, she sat by the window peering at the dark walls. A man reeking of gin stumbled down next to Jack and removed a small, clear vial from his pocket. He removed the cap, inhaled the potion in his nose, and sighed deeply.

When the train lurched to an uneasy stop at Arlington, Alison went to the door, and he followed. It was their old habit. They usually walked through the Public Garden, past the memorial of the Pope's visit to Boston, the statues of historical figures, and up through the Common. On weekends, they would head up Charles Street for a stroll past the antique shops, the bookstores, the cafés, and to Sevens, the cozy, dark bar where they first met. To Jack, those days seemed long past. There was no desire left. He hadn't known where it came from and why it had been so ephemeral.

They stood in the center of the platform. A tall, frail woman with a plastic beanie on her head played "Magic Carpet Ride" on a toy organ. A coffee can beside her contained loose change and crumpled bills. Alison tossed some coins in the cup.

"So, I guess, um, what," Jack stammered. "I got to meet with Hal at four." He tapped the crystal on his watch, then put his hands in his pants pockets. He wondered where she intended to take him now.

Alison hitched her bag to prevent it from slipping off her shoulder. "Just walk with me for a few minutes," she said. They walked upstairs to the outside.

On this day, the Garden had none of its usual charm. Empty beds of dirt were the only evidence of a vanished summer. The grass was hidden beneath fallen leaves. Branches extended from large trees like withered arms. The wind whipped, adding a further chill to the air. The Garden was empty; no other pedestrians were visible.

They went down the walk to the bridge over the pond. Below the bridge, the swan boats were tethered by chains next to the gazebo, bouncing against one another and the platform with the breeze. Alison stopped at the center of the bridge and leaned against the pale green corrugated railing, peering into the water. The sun was breaking tentatively through the clouds, throwing faint shadows across the bridge.

Alison wiped her nose, putting her free hand in the bag. Jack wondered why they had stopped.

"Remember the swan boats," she said, not as a question, but a declaration. He turned and faced her. She appeared ready for an embrace and he moved toward her. She removed a pistol from her bag and pointed it at his chest, the barrel jumping in her trembling hand.

"What is this? A joke, right?" he said. Her face was clenched. Dimples formed on her chin and the corners of her mouth. Her eyes were dark and narrowed.

"Alison," he said, looking over her shoulder to see if anybody had observed her. Down the bridge path, a man was taking pictures with a video camera, but Jack feared that signaling him would force her hand. Should he lunge and grab the gun? "Come on," he said, stretching out his hand. He had provoked her, he clearly saw. His body shook with fear. The suddenness of events had left him unprepared. She pulled the trigger.

He leaned to the side. The bullet grazed his right arm. He missed the bridge railing with his arm and spun facedown on the pavement.

A jogger ran toward Alison. He threw her to the ground, landing on top of her, keeping his legs between hers. She cried out. She began to bleed, the blood staining her underwear and trickling down her thighs. The jogger slammed her arm, and she let go of the gun, which fell into the river. She began to sob.

The man with the video camera had watched Alison remove the gun from her purse and point it at Jack. His hand held the button steady. When the jogger pinned her, he moved in for a close-up, catching the fear and confusion on their faces. Then he continued over to Jack.

Jack was sprawled on the ground, his face smashed on the concrete, blood leaking from his nose and smearing his cheeks. The images before him were fuzzy. He tried to sit up, touched his wound, and fell back on the pavement.

"Hey!" the jogger screamed to the other man. "Get the police. Ambulance. The guy's been shot." He ran over toward Jack. The man with the camera resumed filming. The jogger bent over and removed Jack's coat, seeing the bullet hole, the blood tearing through the shirt. He threw a glance at Alison and then back at Jack's quiet face.

A few moments later, the police arrived. The jogger ran up to them. "She did it. She shot him," he said, pointing an urgent finger at Alison's sprawled figure.

"I'm bleeding," Alison said to the officer. She rubbed her hand on the stain; her face was caked with dried tears. The officer signaled to a paramedic. Her arms were pulled behind her and handcuffs snapped to her wrists. The officer began reciting her rights, words she knew from law school.

"Complications," she said to the paramedic, remembering the form at the clinic. He looked puzzled and accompanied her to the patrol car. "I want a lawyer," she said to the officer.

The paramedics placed Jack on a stretcher and carried him to the back of the ambulance. He saw Alison sitting in the backseat of the police car, people behind a yellow ribbon line, policemen scouring the bridge. The ambulance doors closed behind him and he was safe inside the white and steel walls, grateful that her aim was as unsteady as her mind.

AWYER ARRESTED IN PUBLIC GARDEN SHOOTING, the headline blared in thick black bold print on the front page of the next morning's *Herald*. Below the print was a misty picture of the bridge. Andy Gottlieb, a fellow associate at the firm, held the paper in his hands in front of Jack like a newsboy desperate for a sale.

"You're famous," he said.

"Shit," Jack replied, grabbing for the paper. He sat up in the bed uneasily, his body aching. He was light-headed from painkillers and antibiotics. The sunlight sneaking through the blinds stung his eyes.

He opened the paper and read to himself: "Jack Donnelly, a lawyer at Adelman and Kaplan, was shot in the Public Garden late yesterday afternoon. Alison Moore, a fellow lawyer at the law firm, is being held on charges of attempted murder. Hospital sources describe Donnelly's wounds as superficial. He is in good condition. Motives for the shooting are unclear. A spokesman for the law firm, one of Boston's most venerable and distinguished, refused to comment on the incident."

Jack closed the paper and put it facedown on his lap, then fell back on the pillow.

"I told you she was a dangerous bitch," Andy said.

"You did not." Jack coughed, needing a cigarette. For the

first time since the shooting, his body tingled with the desire for nicotine. During the night, he had awoken with a nightmare of the gun barrel and a vision of Alison's clenched mouth as she pulled the trigger.

He could tell Andy none of this. He never expressed any real fears to him. "I'd never date a law crack," Andy had once said, shoving a handful of cheddar goldfish in his mouth at the Purple Shamrock. Jack never listened to Andy's theorizing about women lawyers, found his attitudes tiresome.

Andy was dressed for work, his blond hair cut sharp around his ears, his blue double-breasted suit fitting neatly around his body. Andy worked out in the firm's weight room early in the morning and was proud of his physique. Alison said that if he spent half as much energy on developing his mind, he'd still be an idiot.

"Well, I thought it, anyway. The point is, this is not that surprising."

"What isn't surprising?" Jack shouted, but the words came out weak.

"Well, I mean," Andy said, retreating, "what did you do to the poor girl?"

"None of your fucking business."

"Maybe so, but with this play it'll be everybody's business soon."

Jack shook his head, rejecting Andy's suggestion. He was surprised by how little he had thought about the shooting. Sitting in his bed, filled with the hospital's antiseptic smells, the bustle of the nurses and doctors, and the patients, with their slow walks and intravenous tubes filing past his room, he played nothing in his mind. There was no recounting of a horror, besides the brief nightmare. He wasn't quite ready to absorb what had happened to him.

"What's the line at A and K?" Jack asked.

"No comment."

"Come on, you can tell me."

"No. No. I'm not hiding anything. I haven't been in since the story came out. But I can tell you what it'll be. Everybody thinks she's nuts. I guess this takes her off the partnership track." Andy laughed, a weak attempt at humor.

The Mommy Track, too, Jack thought. Alison's pregnancy had been a secret up until now, and Jack was not about to reveal it to Andy. Although everyone in their litigation group was aware of the edginess that had been growing in their relationship—the petty criticisms they directed toward each other at meetings, Alison storming out of the conference room with angry tears beginning to form,

Jack's reddened, shamed face, their barely concealed fights in the library—the nature of their troubles was unknown.

In an attempt to exonerate himself during those difficult times, Jack had consciously cultivated an attitude, as if to say, It's a mystery to me. Andy was confirming that it had worked, that Alison was seen as unsteady. But to Detective Hardy earlier that morning Jack had said he had no previous evidence of Alison's instability, that he only felt sorry he was responsible for her actions. Jack didn't know if this was how he really felt or if it was what was expected, like comments after the death of a despised relative. After all, it was her escalating instability due to the pregnancy that had given him the reason to end their relationship. She was harming his chances for advancement in the firm. He wanted to call Hardy back with clarifications.

"What do you think's going to happen, really?"

"My honest opinion?" Andy asked, as if giving Jack a chance to withdraw the question. "It've been better if her aim was sharper. You're both going to be tubed." He hesitated. "That's just one man's view. I could be wrong."

"Thanks for the encouragement."

Jack feigned tiredness and yawned, shutting his eyes tight like a child wishing away an imagined demon underneath the bed, and when he opened them again Andy was gone.

he heels of Lee Klein's black pumps clicked rhythmically on the marble floor of the Suffolk County courthouse. She bounded down the hallway, the flaps of her lime-green jacket billowing, her brown frizzled hair, speckled with traces of gray, bouncing off her shoulders. She was a tall, angular woman, her arms and legs toned from workouts.

At the end of the hallway, outside the lockup, she recognized the metro beat reporters chatting with one another. They paced anxiously, unnaturally, she thought, with artificial pressures.

Their heads shot up at the sound of her approach. She felt exposed.

"You representing the Moore woman, Lee?"

"No comment," she said, whisking by them and slamming the door behind her.

Inside, an officer sat slumped behind the counter, staring at television screens with views of hallways, the outer wings of judges' chambers and courtrooms, the lobby, the cafeteria. The screens were a blurry black and white and the shots seemed exaggerated, blown up. Lee saw the back of a judge heading down the hallway, his black robes like a vampire's cape, disappearing behind a door hidden from the camera's view.

She signed the sheet on the clipboard, waiting for the officer to notice her.

"Excuse me," she said, exasperated.

"Yeah," he said, turning from the screen.

"I'm here to see Alison Moore."

"You her lawyer?" he asked with evident surprise, perusing the sign-in sheet with mild suspicion.

"No, her beautician."

"It's just a question. We can't let just anybody back there, you know. Security problems and all. Good luck," he said as she moved toward the door.

"Why do you say that?"

"She was a bloody mess when she got here. A little . . ." He made circles with his finger around his forehead. "She won't talk to nobody."

He pressed the button behind the counter and the steel door clicked open. Lee walked in with trepidation. Alison had called her at the office, her voice edgy and distressed, telling her no details. The only facts Lee knew were those from the newspaper. She had met Alison almost a year before at a Women's Bar Association meeting. Lee recalled that Alison had been mostly silent during the meetings, only offering suggestions intermittently, as if there out of obligation and not commitment. Her impression of Alison was that she seemed to find all the mild feminist solidarity fraudulent, like the League of Women Voters, quaint and ineffective.

Lee admitted to herself that she had no real affection for women like Alison. She was part of the second generation of women lawyers and didn't have to face the same obstacles as the first. She was accepted, and she took it for granted. These women were termed postfeminist, pejoratively. At the meetings Alison attended, she appeared diffident, difficult, a loner. Lee remembered she seemed proud to be at Adelman and Kaplan, one of those Boston firms Lee despised for their former exclusionary policies.

This was a sticking point. Since Lee had left the public defender's office, after six years, her only criminal cases were ones she was sympathetic to, concerning clients she thought were innocent or not so guilty, or causes she could believe in—battered wives, civil disobedience cases. She'd left the public sector to have the freedom to turn down the vicious killer, rapist, or petty thief, whose only nobility was his poverty. She no longer believed the myth that had sustained her—that making the system work fairly was all that mattered. It was only a game. Everybody involved—the prosecutor, the judge, and the defense lawyer—was there for the excitement, not the constitutional principles.

Lee was respected for her courtroom style, which was slyly aggressive and subtly seductive, but she also knew she was ridiculed for her empathy for clients. Prosecutors and fellow defense lawyers never forgot her weeping after a guilty verdict in a cocaine case. On the steps of the courthouse after the verdict, Lee was caught by a *Herald* photographer sobbing for her client. Weeping Willow, they called her around the courthouse, and despite her many subsequent successes and reputation as an effective advocate, the label stuck.

Alison was in the first cell on the left. She sat on the white enamel slab, her arms folded around her knees, dressed in a beige smock with matching pants. The walls were painted a decaying yellow. The cell was empty except for the bench. Alison stared at the floor, her face drained of color, her hair in disarray. After the bleeding had stopped, she was taken to the jail, searched, fingerprinted, and photographed. She was told to undress; it seemed she had been ordered to change clothes all day, in empty, antiseptic rooms.

She sat quietly in the cell, overcome periodically with chills. She remembered that Trabor's deposition was scheduled for one o'clock today, and she hoped it was being covered by someone good. She had anticipated his testimony. With the documents the firm received in discovery, she knew Trabor had to contradict himself, that great cross-examination material would be available for trial, or the plaintiffs would be forced to discuss settlement seriously.

"You'll eat his lunch," Jack had said one night, a couple of weeks ago now, she figured. She was sitting up in bed with a legal pad on her thighs, biting a pencil between her teeth, jotting down areas to cover, possible questions. "You'll do great. I can't believe you're actually worried about it." He reached across the bed and landed a light, moist kiss on her cheek.

"Alison," Lee said softly, breaking the trance.

Alison walked over to her quickly, shook her hand and smiled. "Thanks for coming." She was weak from the brief movement and sat back down on the bench, close to the bars.

"How you feeling, okay?"

Alison nodded. "Lee—"

"You don't have to say anything about it yet."

"You're going to take it, though, aren't you?"

"Uh ... sure," Lee said, although until then she hadn't decided.

"Good."

"The guy up front said you were bleeding."

"It's nothing. From the fall, I think."

Lee was unaccustomed to this type of muted, dispassionate reaction from clients. Most had been through the system before and were voluble, not about the crime for which they were accused, but about what she thought the bond might be, or how brutal the police had been in arresting them.

"Did you give a statement to the police?"

"No."

"Good. Now listen, we'll talk about the facts later. The first thing is we have to get you out of here. I have to know a few things for the bond hearing."

Lee took notes. Born and raised in Indiana. Attended Wellesley College and Harvard Law. Former actress. Father, history professor, Wallace College. Brother Peter, a former student at Berklee School of Music, now living on Cape Cod. Six months at Adelman and Kaplan. Prior to that, an associate at Perkins and Gray in Washington, D.C. A short biography that said nothing. She was reduced to these facts; the system could digest them. It was like a rap sheet— cold, devoid of content. Charge: Attempted Murder. Not something she'd put on her resumé, a career gap she would have to explain to interviewers.

"Assets?" Lee asked.

"I have some savings. The condo's paid up. A trust fund from my grandfather. My parents can't know," she added.

"Okay. Um, I should tell you. It's in the *Herald*."

"What?"

"The shooting. It's being covered."

"That ought to piss Jack off," Alison laughed, and then her forehead furrowed. She hadn't figured on this. Actually, as she thought about it, nothing was really planned. Even the shooting itself.

"It'll probably die down. Slow news day, I bet," Lee said, although she knew such a public event was bound to keep the *Herald*'s interest.

"I'll get out, won't I?" Alison said, gripping the bars with her small hands like a child in a crib.

"Sure. No priors. Good family ties. An isolated incident. That's how we'll play it."

She eyed the floor, whispering, "I don't know why."

"One step at a time. Try not to think about it. I'll talk to the D.A. beforehand. Grease the wheels, so to speak. I have to go. I'll see you in the courtroom. Hang in there."

Alison just nodded, listening to the sound of the door lock. She eyed her chipped, bitten nails with chagrin. Her arms were pink from constant scratching, a nervous tic. She saw herself walking out of Saks Fifth Avenue after a facial and manicure, while Jack rebuffed a street vendor's attempt to sell off some costume jewelry. The unplanned romantic weekend in New York. He said she looked sexy, beautiful, and they skipped the boat to the Statue of Liberty and Ellis Island for an afternoon of tumbled sheets and sweat, the sunlight coursing through the gauze of the white drapes, as in a perfume advertisement. Sex, maybe the perfume would be called. Sex, the fragrance you can't get enough of.

She tried to shut her mind off, but it kept humming along, on its own track, a runaway train.

unkin waited impatiently for Ray Ballard to place the dish on the floor. She stared up at him with opaque green eyes. Ray peered at the tin can. Deluxe Fish Platter. Did Purina think cats could read these labels? Or was the owner supposed to feel proud of satisfying his cat's fondness for gourmet cuisine? Ray imagined a whole line of fine products: pastas, soufflés, chow mein. "Hey, honey, I feel like seafood tonight," he said to Punkin, a scrawny black kitten with a half-shut left eye and limping back leg. She meowed and rubbed against Ray's leg, and ignored him when dinner was delivered.

Gray shadows flickered through the bars on his windows. From his vantage point, he only saw soles, thick black ones from wingtips, white ones from tennis shoes, the tips of heels, and a glimpse of nylon. They called it a garden apartment, he figured, because you got a corpse's-eye view of plants and flowers. Pushing up the daisies. The outside weather was a mystery. Every day seemed the same; no changes in fronts, highs or lows, just a steady dampness. Sunlight never penetrated.

He placed the remainder of the can in the refrigerator, which was empty, except for a box of leftover pizza from Gino's down the street and a can of Pepsi. In the sink sat a week's worth of saucers and coffee cups. Besides the cramped, narrow kitchen, there was the main room, with his mattress, beanbag chair, and equipment: a thirty-two-inch color television, a videocassette recorder, a compact disc player, a video camera, all bought at discount from the trunk of a car. A stack of tapes crawled up to the ceiling. Tools of his unappreciated trade. He was a video artist, producing the docudramas of his time.

He was ill-suited for his vocation. He went out into the world unwillingly, as if on a mission not of his choosing, a martyr to a cause. He hated the crush of people on the subway and on the streets, the rude jostling and sneers, the smells of obnoxious colognes and perfumes, the idle chitchat about weather and sports. But he also loved the city scene in his own perverse way. He reveled in it. Sitting for hours in the Common watching the young professionals glide by with their finely pressed suits and dresses and oxblood valises, the wretched homeless aggressively panhandling, shuffling from bench to bench, urinating on the tree trunks, Ray derived a vague discomfort that validated his worldview.

Watching the vagrants, he marveled at their ability to survive. Did they wake up in the morning, fearful of the weather forecast, dreading autumn winds, the onset of winter, celebrating the spring like returning migratory birds with chirps of glee? Ray didn't know. He kept his distance. Communion with them was no more inviting or possible than with the briefcase-laden, neurotic professionals who were insidiously taking over the city, razing burned-out neighborhoods, turning the waterfront into a playground for their diversions.

After a day of wandering and stopping for cups of coffee, he shuffled down the steps, past the sooty red-bricked walls, past the overflowing dented garbage cans, and entered his room with a sense of relief. He was safe here in his hibernation. His migraines eased, the knots of his stomach unwound.

Punkin finished her meal, jumped onto the mattress, and began washing herself with loud licks of her paws. Ray sat beside her and lit a cigarette, picking up the television remote control with his free hand.

He saw his reflection in the television screen. Thin white arms protruded from his khaki T-shirt. His flat snub-nose precariously supported wire-rim glasses above. He was skinny and sickly, coughing from the constant ingestion of cigarettes and the dampness of his room.

He was a twenty-seven-year-old college dropout and thought himself an inventor of a new genre. He made his living money cleaning dishes at Von's, a coffee shop off Harvard Square. During the day, he stalked the streets with the video camera on his shoulder like a trained monkey, recording scenes. String quartets in front of the Coop. Couples arguing over politics and then kissing. Students in Harvard Yard traipsing by with their backpacks. Intense young men playing chess on a makeshift board in front of Von's. The homeless and cops in the subway. He was an urban guerrilla, conducting warfare through video. Isn't this how true artists did it, exploring the depths of the realities around them haphazardly, and one day, click, you were there, you had found your subject, your text, and you were a star?

Yesterday, he had made a foray into the Public Garden. There he captured the urban madness at its best. When that chick shot the guy, he couldn't believe his luck. In broad daylight! One moment Ray was photographing the statue of Washington on his horse, then he turned, and there it was. The man and woman leaning over the bridge, pondering thoughts of their future together. But not her. No, she was thinking of killing him. Ray didn't know why. And he didn't care. The rest could be worked out in rehearsals, rewrites, and editing.

The noon news would be on shortly. He longed to see Channel 4's Wendy Thomas on location. He adored her dancing light blue eyes, hated his desire for her. She really wasn't his type, too prim, without substance.

Ray filled a glass with ice coffee. Punkin curled up in a ball for a nap. The screaming headline of the *Herald* lay on the floor before the beanbag chair. He scanned the sports section. The Bruins were four points down in the division. The Celtics were in third place behind the Knicks and Nets. Ray held no hope they would ever catch up.

He turned on the news.

". . . as of yet, the police have no motive for the shooting." The camera panned the bridge, focusing on the spot where Jack fell. In the corner, Ray could see the pedestal of the Washington statue.

"I got it, Punkin. I got the video of the goddamn thing. We're going to be sitting pretty. It's my Zapruder."

Wendy came on the screen. She appeared disheveled, but nevertheless ravishing, wetting her dry bottom lip with her tongue.

"Yesterday's protest outside the Beacon Street clinic erupted into violence. The sit-in and counter-demonstration led to the arrest of four persons. Our cameraman was injured in the melee. Both sides claim the other is to blame for the violence." She glanced down at her notepad. "Pro-choice spokesperson Sarah Barnett, of the Center for Reproductive Freedom, said that this showed what the anti-abortion people were all about: violence against women. Karen Hill, representing the anti-abortion forces, said civil disobedience was a valid response to the murder of what she called, quote, human life, unquote. She said protests would continue across the country.

"The protests are in response to the Supreme Court's latest statement on the abortion question. It continues to be a divisive issue among the American people. This is Wendy Thomas reporting."

"Thank you, Wendy," Ray said. "Love that blouse."

He picked up the black cassette and gave it a kiss. Earlier, he had inserted it in the recorder, fearful that what he had seen would be too crude for distribution. But it was a clean, crisp piece of work. The black-and-white film provided the perfect texture, the urban violence and alienation he had been seeking for months with limited success. Only the redness of the blood was lost.

Then there was the hero of the piece, the brave jogger slamming the girl to the ground. Ray had all the nuances of the situation, his cast of characters. The poor sap with his petty wound, that expressionless look. There was a small smile on the woman's face or it could have been a grimace of regret, that she didn't get him in the heart point blank. If it was Ray's story, that would be his angle: that she regretted not killing the bastard. The written text was all Ray's to create. He wasn't bound by the truth. Pictures spoke louder than words and it didn't really matter what the words said. Their little sordid story, whatever it was—maybe she was just crazy, maybe it was a lesson that all human entanglements led to violence—was recorded.

He stuffed the cassette back underneath the mattress, undecided what to do next. Maybe give Wendy the video. It's a come-on, a starter. She was ambitious and was floundering at the station. Although he was bursting with anticipation, Ray would wait out the developments, look for his opening, maximize exposure and profit, deliver to the highest bidder. One day he would explode into the public eye, get out of this hellhole, live like the true artist he was. Punkin could eat richly every night. Chicks like Wendy would flock to him.

isten, Danny. Listen . . . You gonna stop a minute? This is the thing. The thing is your client's a scumbag, and I got him by the balls. You see . . ." Michael Hurley sighed deeply into the receiver and parted the blind. ". . . Oh, Jesus. The guy's had some tough breaks, huh. I'm playin' the world's smallest violin here. You hear it? . . . Compassion? I got your fucking compassion right here."

He picked up his mug from a pile of papers on his desk. Drops of coffee fell on his white wrinkled shirt, and he wiped the stain with the back of his tie. His chipped mahogany desk was littered with police reports, case files, and legal pads. File cabinets overflowed against the wall. The floor was sticky with stale coffee, gum wrappers, the stains from twenty years of shoes. On the bulletin board behind his desk was pinned a photograph of him with the mayor five years ago after the conviction of the Brighton arsonist.

Hurley was chief deputy district attorney for Suffolk County. His specialty was violent crimes. He couldn't get enough of them. Around the office, he was known as Mad Dog. He regarded the moniker as affectionate, complimentary. And he looked the part. Hurley was a heavyset man with a large broad face, prematurely lined with age and weathered storms. He was thirty-six years old, with sparse balding hair which he tugged incessantly. He stood five feet six inches tall but looked shorter, dressed with his shirttails out, his tie loosened. Since giving up cigarettes three months ago, he chewed on pencils, bent paper clips with amazing dexterity, and shredded napkins into strips.

Despite the seeming chaos of his office and his disheveled physical appearance, Hurley's mind was directed and orderly. Too much so, others thought, including fellow district attorneys and judges. He only saw one side to an issue. If the sign of genius was the ability to conceive two opposing ideas in one's mind simultaneously, then Hurley was an idiot. He was a trial lawyer of a particular type—the hyperactive, jugular-grabbing bully.

"You're gonna stick your neck out for this guy, Danny? Pick your battles carefully, pal. Save them for a rainy day. The jury'll be out ten minutes."

Hurley was bluffing. The case against Danny's client was weak and was complicated by the dubious constitutionality of the cops' search of his house. The only way to save face on the case was to bully his lawyer into a plea.

"Okay. Okay. To show you I'm not a totally unreasonable guy, I'll tell you what. Simple possession . . . No. No deferred. This isn't no altar boy we have here. . . . Deal. I'll call Cicerilli's chambers this morning."

"Shit," Hurley said to himself. He stared down at his desk. On the top of the pile were police reports from yesterday's arrests. Every morning, he pored through them and decided assignments. He had discretion to choose his own cases. The initial press on the shooting in the Public Garden left him undecided. At first glance, the case had little to offer except the obvious publicity. Too bad the victim had not suffered more serious wounds.

But it wasn't the facts as reflected in the report that intrigued him. It was that the defendant and victim were both lawyers. Not just any lawyers. Associates at Adelman and Kaplan, one of those high-paying, big firms, full of graduates from Harvard Law. Hurley resented them. They thought they were better than the government hacks, that public-sector lawyers were people who couldn't make it in the "real" law. Hurley had always been a prosecutor, since graduating in the middle of his class at Boston University Law School, and he loved his work.

Outside his office, he could hear typewriters, the hum of computer terminals, the ringing of telephones. The sounds were soothing. He read Jack's statement to Detective Hardy, and then picked up the phone.

"Hardy . . . Yeah, Hurley. I'm looking over . . . What's with this Public Garden thing? . . . Uh-huh. She asked for a lawyer. Surprise. Surprise. Even the corporate law types remember *Miranda*. Let's get Donnelly in here right away. I want the straight shit on this. Not this mea culpa stuff. And Hardy. What you think? . . . Yeah. Who knows? . . . You shitting me, the Weeping Willow's got it." He laughed. "This'll be fun. . . . Yeah, later. Call me when you get him. He's the fucking victim, for Christ's sake. . . . Hold on," he said, covering the phone, reacting to a knock at his door. "Yeah."

"Mr. Hurley." It was Julie Bellamy, his latest hire, who handled initial bond hearings.

"Yeah, Julie, come in," he said. She was a recent graduate of law school. She had none of the emotional toughness he expected in assistants, but he saw promise in her.

"Get back to me," he said into the phone and hung up. He took his feet off the desk.

"What's up?"

"I was looking for the Moore file. The hearing's in ten minutes."

"I'm gonna handle the case," he said, reaching for his jacket on the chair.

"Really. Can I—"

"What do we know about her? Nothing? Come on, talk as we go."

He marched out of the office, Julie following.

"Summa cum laude, Wellesley," she began. "Law review, Harvard. No priors."

"You want to nominate her for sainthood?" He touched her shoulders with one of his large hands and gave her a wink. His assistants took those gestures—the Irish wink, the pat on the back—as a sign that they were among the favored. But Julie knew she could only get so far with Hurley. She wasn't Irish, she was a woman, and she realized that despite his relatively young age, Hurley found the presence of women at his work unnatural.

"Well, there's the abortion."

Hurley stopped in his tracks. "What?"

"Didn't you see it in the report? She had massive bleeding when she came in."

"I thought it was from the fall on the bridge."

"I don't think so. She was taken to the hospital first. Complications from the abortion."

"An abortion? Yesterday? Why don't I know this?"

Julie shrugged. "How does this help us now?"

"Get me the hospital records ASAP." The case was developing potential in his mind; adrenaline flowed.

"Now?" she asked, disappointed.

"What you think, tomorrow?"

He started down the steps. "And call Hardy. Tell him to start tracking down the guy with the video camera. You know—"

"The guy on the bridge."

"Yeah. And listen, maybe you can second-chair this one."

"That would be great," she said, too eager. He arched his eyebrows.

"We'll see," he said, leaving her at the top of the stairs, ready to eye his latest prey, the baby-killer and attempted murderess. He needed to develop a hatred for a defendant in a case he really cared about, or he couldn't perform well. He represented the civilized world against the barbarians. He brought a moral righteousness to his endeavor.

But when he saw Alison standing in the defendant's box in the middle of the courtroom, he was momentarily deflated. She appeared pathetic, with her pale, pained face, the look of a child. She turned when he walked in and threw him an indifferent stare, as if he were invisible, a noise outside the window.

The courtroom pews were filled with newspaper and television people, gluttons for bad news. All faces turned to Hurley when he entered, and he flashed a feeble smile. His instincts were correct. This was going to be a major story.

"Are you doing this case?" Lee whispered to him as he walked through the small swinging doors and headed to the prosecution's side.

"Good morning to you, too, Miss Klein," he said.

"Glad you could make it, Mr. Hurley," Judge Kaufman said. There was hostility between them. Judge Kaufman saw Hurley as too aggressive a prosecutor. Hurley thought the judge was one of those liberals appointed in the mid-1960s, who clung, too stubbornly, to the edicts of the Warren court. He was the most anti-government judge on the Suffolk County bench.

Kaufman was a short, irritable man who ran his courtroom with the ferocity of a Dickensian schoolmaster. He screamed at the lawyers, reducing some to tears. Despite his size, Kaufman loomed large from the bench, with an angry scowl, blazing white hair, and a mustache that drooped, disguising his mouth. Kaufman treated defense lawyers with uncharacteristic patience, if only as punishment to the prosecutor. As one of Hurley's assistants once said, "I feel like telling him I'm not the one who committed the crime, Your fucking Honor."

"Ms. Moore," the judge said gingerly, like a grandfather reciting a fairy tale, "you have been charged with attempted murder. You have the right to remain silent. You have the right to an attorney. I see you have Ms. Klein as your attorney."

"Yes, Your Honor," Lee said. She gave the judge a thin smile. With Hurley on the case, she knew a favorable plea bargain was out of the question. The trial would be brutal. That Judge Kaufman was presiding she took as a favorable sign.

"Do you have a recommendation on bond, Mr. Hurley?"

"Yes we do, Your Honor. This is a truly hideous crime. Premeditated. The defendant tried to kill a man in a public place—"

"Save it for the jury, Mr. Hurley. I can read the papers. What's the bottom line?"

Asshole, Hurley thought. "We believe the defendant is a danger to the community and should be detained pending trial."

"Ms. Klein."

"Your Honor, my client has no prior criminal record. She has extensive family ties. She's lived in the community for a number of years. She has a good steady job with a law firm."

"Your Honor," Hurley said.

"I've heard enough. Ten-thousand-dollar bond, either property or cash will be fine. We'll see you back here for arraignment after the grand jury meets. If there's nothing further, the court's in recess."

He pounded the gavel.

"What a gem," Hurley said to the air. The bailiff escorted Alison back to her cell. Lee began gathering her papers when Hurley came over to the table. She smelled his stale coffee breath and a large dose of cologne.

"What's she, a nut case? It's your only hope."

"We'll see," she mumbled, thinking to herself that he was right. Based on what she knew, Alison didn't have a chance to beat the charge. Maybe there was some mitigating circumstance or maybe she was crazy. Temporarily. It was an option.

"Possession of a dangerous weapon?" she ventured.

"Are you shitting me, or what?" He laughed. "This is premeditated, cold-blooded stuff. You got yourself a trial." He walked past her. The reporters followed him out.

Lee stared in front of her. The sun splintered through the windows and made patches on the floor. The courtroom was eerily quiet and had a musty, humid feel. She inhaled heavily, remembering why she had given up criminal defense. The good, unfortunate clients you couldn't do enough for. The habitual ones were ungrateful, either second-guessing or numbed to their fate. When she walked into court that day, she was uncertain where Alison fell on the scale. But nobody deserved the treatment Hurley would hand out. Lee hated his type, the overaggressive prosecutor who thought nothing about the human beings they affected. Alison needed protection from him, whether she warranted it or not.

In the hallway, a small group of reporters surrounded Hurley. The three local networks had cameras trained on him, and the lights made him squint. "I think the crime speaks for itself. The Commonwealth will prove that Miss Moore is guilty of attempted murder."

"What's the condition of Mr. Donnelly?"

"Reports are that he's doing fine physically. Mentally, I'm sure it will be a long recovery process. Can you imagine what he went through? What he's still going through? It's tragic. That's all." He walked away while they continued to pepper questions.

Lee attempted to duck them, but they saw her and the entourage shifted to her side, trapping her against the marble wall. She touched the wall with the palm of her hand to steady herself. She saw a mass of faces, nothing distinctly in view. She barely heard their questions and responded "No comment" to multiple variations of the same inquiry. From the back, pointing his finger with a stubbed pencil above the shoulder of another, the *Herald* reporter's thick Worcester accent shouted over the others.

"What about reports that your client had an abortion the day of the shooting?"

Lee's cheeks flushed. "No comment," she mumbled, outraged at being caught off guard. Why hadn't Alison told her? She thought of the jailer who mentioned the blood. They all know. Everyone except me, her lawyer.

"Guess she was going for two in one day," the reporter said. They all laughed uneasily. Lee glared at them.

"Let me remind you all," she said, "of the presumption—"

They groaned.

"—of innocence. My client intends to fight these charges. We'll find out who's really guilty."

"Would you care to elaborate?"

She gave them nothing more, slipping through a narrow space and down the hallway.

delman and Kaplan attracted some of the best legal talent from around the country. The firm was founded in 1917 by Herman Adelman and Benjamin Kaplan. It had been one of the first predominantly Jewish firms to penetrate the Brahmin establishment. By 1980, it had grown into a bloated bureaucracy, top-heavy with senior partners, stuffy, conservative, lacking in vision.

With the elevation of Martin Kaplan, the leader of the family's third generation, to managing partner, the firm changed course. Martin was grandson of one of the founders, fifty-six years old, considered a maverick when he arrived. A Yale Law School graduate, he worked on Wall Street for four years at Reade and Rifkin before returning to the family firm. He had risen to the top, earning his place on the merits of his fine legal skills and business acumen.

In an age when long-term loyalty to a firm was disintegrating, Martin knew changes were necessary. He set about refurbishing the firm's image. It began with cosmetic changes. The firm was moved from State Street, the center of Boston's legal community, to Copley Square, where it occupied the top two floors of the John Hancock Building. The interior was full of chrome moldings and glass, giving the offices a more open, airy feel. Contemporary paintings and sculptures lined the walls and entrances. All the offices were paneled in a dark, fine oak, and all were the same size, a symbol of democracy.

The firm's litigation style became more aggressive. Whereas

his predecessors had worked to cultivate a gentlemanly approach to legal matters, Martin knew the law was essentially a business. He wanted bold, imaginative approaches to trial work. The deferential, conciliatory approach that epitomized prior generations was inappropriate and unproductive. Associates were encouraged to be more confrontational, to take cases to trial. The firm represented corporations, banks, and savings and loans in employment disputes, business contracts, patent and copyright infringements, and antitrust.

Martin's style and changes were successful. The firm aggressively recruited from other firms, expanded its client base, and, by fiscal year 1990, had amassed 225 lawyers and earned $185 million in revenues.


"The true measure of an Irishman's success," his father had said the night Jack announced he had received an offer from the firm. "Working for the Hebes. Congratulations." He raised a glass half in mock salute, half in genuine pride. "Did you hear that, honey?" he said to his wife. "Your baby boy's really made it now."

"I'm happy for you, Jack," she said. "Are *you* happy?"

"Of course he's happy," his father said. "He's making fifty goddamn Gs, how could he not be happy? I'll never see that kind of money."

Jack's father hated lawyers because, he said, they didn't work for a living and preyed on other people's misfortune. But he understood one thing: Law was a moneymaker. Frank Donnelly was a salesman of security systems, a father who had no room in his life for anything but his trafficking in hope and confidence. He had never reached the heights he imagined for himself, and he blamed his failure on his territory. "They give me the nigger neighborhoods. What you expect?"

Frank had told Mary they would eventually escape South Boston and get a place somewhere in the suburbs, but they never moved from the predominantly Irish Catholic neighborhood in which they were raised.

Their house was located at the end of a street that terminated at the railroad tracks. Its porch was caked with a steady layer of soot. When Jack was a child, he heard the train whistles passing by every morning, and he was accustomed to the house's shudders and shakes. The sounds helped drown out his father's drunken outbursts, the rage directed at Jack and his mother. Jack would open his bedroom window, feel the cold, dirty, sulfur air brush his face. He yearned to crawl out, enter the warmth and silence of the dark open cave of a freight car heading to a destination unknown. But the trains moved on without him.

Six months after joining the firm, his mother called him from a telephone inside a Stop & Shop.

"What's going on, Mom?" Jack had asked.

"Oh, nothing special."

"It's Dad, isn't it?"

"He's just having one of his phases."

He imagined his father drunk and yelling insults.

"Business not going good?"

"Not really. You know, ups and downs. Listen, honey, I gotta go. Someone wants to use the phone." She hung up without a formal good-bye.

Jack abandoned the pile of books on his desk and left the office. When he walked up the driveway to the house, he heard a scratchy Sinatra record and thought of turning around. Inside, his father lay asleep on the couch, his necktie loosened, his white shirt wrinkled over his ample belly. On the coffee table next to him was a half-empty glass of Dewar's. Sweat was dried on his forehead and streaked down his cheeks.

His mother was not there. She must be out shopping again, Jack thought. He walked past the couch to the kitchen and poured himself a drink. The remaining scotch dribbled out of the bottle, filling only half a glass. He returned to the living room. The Sinatra record had ended.

"Hey, Dad," he said, noticing for the first time that his father's body was still. Jack shook his father's shoulders. He could see the combination of scotch and disappointment etched in his forehead, on his cheeks, in his pale lazy lower lip.

Jack unbuttoned the shirt and checked his father's heart, feeling nothing. There was no movement, and Jack knew there would never be.

He called for an ambulance, then sat on the couch for twenty minutes, staring outside the screen door. What followed became a series of images clashing together. The swirling red lights from the ambulance; the neighbors with folded arms standing on their front lawns, sidewalks, and driveways, gawking; the medics pushing the stretcher through the narrow front doorway; his mother, burdened with two grocery bags, letting them fall to the ground as she ran toward the house; a can of tomato paste rolling back and forth on the crack of the sidewalk.

His mother adapted well to her widow status. She had been alone for years and accepted death as inevitable. She went to early mass every morning and lit a candle in her husband's memory. She became more active in the church, was made a lay minister, and served communion on Sundays.

She sold the old house and moved into a smaller place, closer to the church. At Jack's request, one of the real-estate lawyers at the firm handled the transaction. The furniture, the coffee table, lamps, and couch, were donated to the St. Vincent de Paul Society. Mary lived off the meager life insurance money.

Jack never returned to the neighborhood, avoided any hint of the street. He telephoned his mother on holidays to exchange ritual greetings and queries about each other's health.

With his father gone, Jack thought a great burden would be lifted, that he would begin to finally live for himself, by his standards, but the opposite occurred. He began to unravel during his first solo deposition. The deponent was Bob Andrus, a former janitor at the Mayflower Nuclear Power Plant in Plymouth. One day, Andrus was ordered by his supervisor to clean a room in the reactor. When he finished, he was fired because he had exposed himself to an intolerable level of radiation. He filed suit against the company. The firm represented Mayflower. Around the office, it was known as the "Mop & Glow" case.

Andrus was in his mid-forties, with large, callused hands that he displayed to Jack like battle scars. "That's all I got, Mr. Donnelly. These hands. Why they want to take them away, I don't know." To Jack, Andrus was a failure, like Jack's father. Jack's throat became dry and constricted with pity and disgust. He was unable to speak. He terminated the deposition and walked back to his office, closing the door behind him.

Chills ran through his body and then sweat seeped through his shirt and off his forehead. A cold fear hard as steel gripped him, and he longed for his pillow to cover his ears from the pounding in his head. He envisioned himself slumped on a tattered sofa waiting for death, wailing at his wasted life. He placed his head between his folded arms on the desk.

He didn't know what the feeling was. Certainly not mourning. Not grief. He had no tears for his father. Jack's heart was racing, he sensed its pounding, and his entire body pumped with adrenaline.

Later that day, Jack found himself sitting in an underground bar at Quincy Market. The place was virtually empty. A group of foreign students, Scandinavian or Swiss, sat at a table talking loudly in a language he did not recognize. A young teenager, dressed in a black leather jacket, his hair over his collar, stood enraptured in front of a video game, only taking time out to sip his beer. A truant, like himself. Jack stared at a basketball game on the screen, a repeat on ESPN of a game from the previous night, even though he knew the final score. Until the first beers were consumed, Jack always felt uncomfortable alone at a bar.

All afternoon he drank draft beers and then staggered over to the Purple Shamrock to continue. After midnight, he began to order Jameson whiskey shots until he could no longer form the words to order one.

Somehow, he navigated his way to his third-floor Beacon Hill apartment. He lay in bed for three days, staring at the ceiling, and out the window to the Charles River, eyeing the Red Line heading for Cambridge. He listened to the beeps and messages on the answering machine. First Sally, then Andy. Then Kaplan's secretary. Finally, Martin himself.

He felt himself spiraling deeper and deeper inside himself, like a tumble down a stairwell. He began to fear himself, began to think that there were two souls competing for him, one urging him to snap out of it and another to end it all.

After three days, it was over. He stood for fifteen minutes in a hot shower, the steam rising around him, the water soothing stiff muscles. He shaved. A spot of blood formed, and he extinguished it with a tissue. There was no color in his face, and he smiled peculiarly.

He went back to work. His absence was well-noticed, although not its cause. He staved off his colleagues' coy attempts to extract confidences. At an early age, he had learned to put his best face to the world, to hide his hurts and fears.


When Jack entered the firm the day after leaving the hospital, it was with the same feeling of shame and humiliation he had returning to work after his breakdown, a grim spotlight poised on him. He ignored the whispers and the mumbled greetings.

Sally was chatting on the phone. She covered her mouth with her fake red nails and abruptly terminated the call.

"Morning, Sally," he said, smiling. "Any messages?"

She shook her head. He signaled her to follow him into his office and closed the door behind them.

"How you feeling?" she asked.

"Fine. Just a scratch. Superficial wound, they say." He laughed ruefully. "Glad she wasn't an expert marksman."

"Oh, Jack."

"What's the poop around here?"

"I don't know," she said.

"Sally."

"It's so awful. I can't believe it." She bit her lip. "I mean, what did you do to her?"

He jolted up and leaned across the desk.

"What did *I* do? She shot at me. Don't you read the papers?"

He was as startled by his anger, the heat rising up his neck, as he was by her remark. Until now, he had not summoned any rage at Alison or the situation, just numbness and shock, and a nagging guilt.

"Shit," he said. "I'm sorry."

"No, no. I'm sorry. I didn't mean it. It's just so hard to understand. I guess you never know with people. It's like one of those stories you read in the paper about the happiest kid on the block who kills himself and his family one day. And everybody says, 'He always smiled. He always took his mother to the grocery store. He was an Eagle Scout.' You know what I mean?"

"What's everybody saying? Anything?"

"Well, you know this place. Gossip Central. Nobody liked her. Except you."

To himself, he echoed the sentiment. He first met Alison in early March at Sevens, a smoky, cramped bar on Charles Street. Associates in the complex litigation group congregated there regularly. Alison had just started work, a lateral from a firm in Washington. Given the competition for partnership slots, she was resented. Members of the litigation group, including Jack, wondered what impact her hiring would have on them. She was the subject of much conversation. The word inside the firm was that she was sharp, forbidding, and, worst of all, well-recommended. Since Jack had been out of the office most of the week examining documents at Microtech's plant in Needham, he had not seen her.

When Jack entered Sevens, Andy was standing in the aisle between the bar and tables. He raised his glass to Jack.

"There's our Microtech man, come in from the dungeon," he said. Jack walked toward him and ordered a beer.

"So, did she show?" Jack asked.

"Yep. Second to the last table."

"What you think?"

"I'd do her."

"You say that about everything that doesn't bark."

"Yeah, but I'm kidding."

"Would it be worth it?"

"For a while. She looks like one of those strong, silent types. The best ones in the sack are."

"Available?"

"Hey, I'm a happily going-steady guy, how would I know?" He slapped Jack on the back. It must have been Andy's third or fourth beer, given his chumminess and his choice of subject matter. "No rock at least," he added. "You're not going to screw yourself to the top, are you?"

"I haven't even met her yet."

"Since when are *you* interested? I thought you were a monk."

"No, I'm a fag. It's no crime to look."

"Too much for you. She'd kill you."

"You going to introduce me, or what?"

"I'm not your social director."

Alison was at a table separate from other lawyers from the firm.

"Jack Donnelly. How you doing?" he said, extending his hand. She eyed him curiously, and said in a raspy, throaty voice, "Alison Moore." She curled her hair behind her ears, revealing large gold hoop earrings. She was dressed in a white blouse and black-pleated skirt, white nylons and black flat shoes, like ballet slippers. Her legs were crossed and she hunched over the table. A half-empty martini glass was set before her.

He sipped his beer and admired her elegance, the smoothness of her skin, the deep-set dark eyes, the light shining off her brown hair. The rim of her martini glass was lined with red spots of lipstick. He had never met anyone his age who actually drank them. It was old-fashioned, a sign of wealth or perhaps sophistication. Watching her, he was stirred slightly with arousal.

Alison appeared to have a strange mixture of elements—self-assured, yet demure, possessing some hidden passion. At that moment he wanted her to a degree he knew was disturbing, irrational. Not in a physical or sexual sense, he thought, but to have her for himself, to be entranced by her, to observe her in an intimate way.

What they said, after he sat down and after her two martinis, he could not recall. He did most of the talking, priming her with meaningless details about the firm, superficial facts about himself. Afterward, he walked with her in the rain to the Massachusetts

General subway stop. After she had purchased her token, he shook her hand formally. She thanked him for the escort. He watched her climb the stairway to the platform, admiring her slender ankles. On the way home, up Charles Street, he bought a bottle of red wine, which he put in the kitchen for a special occasion.

"Just give me the lowdown. What's everybody saying?" he asked Sally.

"Oh, you know, everybody's in a kinda shock or something."

There was a knock at the door. It was Susan, Martin Kaplan's secretary. "Excuse me," she said officiously. "Martin would like to see you when you get a free moment."

"I'll be right there. Thanks, Susan."

That can't be good news, he thought, and his stomach absorbed a sharp punch. Sally stood up quickly. "I'm glad you're back," she said.


Martin Kaplan's corner office was down the hall from Jack's. It was wide, expansive, excessively neat. Not one piece of paper cluttered his large glass-top desk. He was a distinguished-looking middle-aged man, of medium build, white haired, balding on top, his skin finely, evenly tanned from outings to Palm Beach.

"Jack, Jack, how are you?" he said, coming out from behind the desk, his hand extended.

"Fine, Martin."

"Sit down. Sit down. How's the arm feeling?"

"Fine. Just a nick." Jack took a seat on the couch against the wall and fell deep within it. The scene reminded him of his initial interview with Martin, when, apprehensive about the impression he was making, he was unable to get comfortable. With his watchful stare and formal manner, Martin was no less forbidding now.

"Jack." Martin grinned and sat down at his desk. "Let me first say for everybody at the firm how sorry we are about this. As you can imagine, we're all pretty shook up. Not the usual kind of problem, you know what I mean?"

Jack knew what was coming, and he had no way to stop it. Martin was renowned for his gentle diplomacy, his pleasing manner. Now, as a victim of it, Jack was annoyed. It all was so unjust. He fought against an emotional outburst or sign of weakness.

"That's assumed, I'm sure. I mean, our concern. But let's get down to brass tacks. Let's be frank. Can we? You know that I've always been very supportive of you. I've brought you along. I liked your gumption. I liked your willingness to work. You've developed into a fine, fine lawyer. When your father died, remember? Who stuck by you? Some firms, they would've let you go. Not us. But let's not get into that now. It's nothing personal. You know that. I'm thinking of your good. Alison's good. The firm's good. I'm not making any judgment, mind you. That wouldn't be fair. Presumption of innocence and all that. Two sides to every story."

"Martin." Jack tried to speak.

"Let me finish," he said. "This isn't easy for me either. But I have responsibilities. To the firm. Can you imagine one of our clients waking up this morning and reading the papers? Well, I can. I've been getting calls. The press is bad. No question. Something's got to be done.

"Now, before you jump the gun, listen. It's not as bad as you think. I'm suggesting— What I'm suggesting, Jack, is a sabbatical. Six months maybe. Hey, maybe it'll blow over before then. Who knows?" He shrugged and the sleeves of his jacket lifted.

"But we're in the middle of the Microtech discovery," Jack said.

"Don't you worry about it, okay? It'll get done. You've got more important matters to worry about."

"But I want to work. I have to work." He stopped. This tack would never work. Take your medicine and get out.

Martin stood up and shook Jack's hand again.

"It'll be for the best. You'll see. You'll come back as my young tiger again."

I'm dead, Jack thought, leaving Martin's office. That fucking cunt did it. She could have killed me and didn't. This is worse.

In his message slot on Sally's desk, he saw two pink slips of paper: one from his mother, the other, marked "urgent," from Detective Hardy. "Terrific," he said aloud.

Sally came toward her desk. In her hand, she held a coffee mug.

"It looks like it's vacation time," he said, winking at her. "I'll be in touch. I'm sure Martin or Susan or somebody will tell you about reassignments. And don't believe anything you read and only half of what you see."

He left her there, staring at his departing figure. A few beers at the Purple Shamrock was what he needed now. His mother could wait. So could Detective Hardy.

didn't want to get involved with anyone at that point. The last thing I wanted was a man. A relationship."

Alison sat in Lee's office, dressed in a conservative brown suit, her face and hair freshly washed. In her shower, after she had been released on bail, the water felt cleansing, she thought, in a too obvious metaphor, as if she were wiping the grime of Jack from her. It was odd that she sensed freedom from him at a time when her actions were ensnaring her further in his life.

Alison wondered if all defendants had a similar sense of relief and release prior to trial. In the jail, she was protected from all hope. She thought of it as an appropriate punishment; she was stripped down to her essence. She didn't want to leave it. The cell was safe, away from everything. Standing in court, she sensed the eyes of the reporters on her back, and felt naked, accused, ashamed.

"God, I feel like I'm with my therapist," she sighed.

"Have you seen one?" Lee asked, jotting notes on a yellow legal pad.

"What?"

"I have to know."

"Oh." Alison waved her hand as if brushing a fly from her face. "That was years ago. I had some shit to go through."

"Uh-huh. What kind of, ah . . . shit?"

"Man problems. No big deal. Nothing really traumatic. I just needed someone to talk to. I wasn't depressed or suicidal."

"More like counseling than therapy, then?"

"Right. Is this necessary?" Alison strolled over to the side wall and examined Lee's plaques and framed degrees. She noticed awards from women's groups, the Civil Liberties Union. "It's going to be terrible, isn't it?"

"I just need as much information as possible," Lee said. "We don't want any surprises."

"I'm not sure I want to fight this. I did it. Can't we just get it over with? What's the point?"

"Is that what you want?"

"I don't want my life put out in public. I've seen what the system does to women like me."

Lee found Alison's seeming calm unsettling. "A little late for that, isn't it?" she asked.

"What do you mean?"

"Have you seen today's paper?"

"No."

"They know about the abortion."

Lee watched her closely. Alison's knees buckled and she struggled to grab the arm of the chair. Lee stood up to assist her.

"How did they find out?" Alison asked. "I'm sorry I didn't tell you at first. I wanted to keep it a secret. I can't believe this is happening. My God, the whole city knows about it."

"I understand. Listen, Alison. I'm your lawyer. You're going to have to confide in me. You have to tell me things you probably don't want to. That is, if you want me to be an effective advocate for you."

"God, I don't know what to do. I mean, I can't believe I actually shot him. It feels like it was another person, you know. How is he? Do we know?"

"I heard he's out of the hospital already. Just a scratch."

"Oh," Alison said, biting her lower lip. "I need time to think about this. What happens next? I haven't seen criminal procedure since the bar exam. I mean, I can't *believe* I'm a defendant."

"The grand jury will meet. Then you'll be arraigned."

"Then I need some time alone. I'm not making any decisions now."

Lee removed a business card from the dispenser on her desk, wrote down her home phone number, and handed it to Alison. "Call me day or night. There's no rush yet. We have time."

Alison stared at the card. Apparently, the meeting was at an end. For all her legal training, the rituals and roles of the attorney-client relationship were a mystery to her. "Thank you. I'll keep in touch."

In the lobby, Alison bought a newspaper. There was a box in the right-hand corner of the front page with a small headline: "ABORTION POSSIBLE MOTIVE IN PUBLIC GARDEN SHOOTING. Page 3."

Alison opened the paper and read about herself:

Boston police have discovered a possible motive for the Public Garden shooting. According to informed sources, Alison Moore, the suspect in the shooting of her boyfriend, Jack Donnelly, had an abortion on Wednesday. Soon after the abortion, Moore allegedly shot Donnelly in the Public Garden. The District Attorney's office would neither confirm nor deny the report. Lee Klein, Moore's lawyer, had no comment on the report.

Moore and Donnelly are attorneys at the law firm of Adelman and Kaplan. Donnelly has taken a leave of absence pending the outcome of the criminal investigation. The case will be presented to a grand jury. Moore is expected to be charged with attempted murder . . .

Alison stopped reading. She walked out to Washington Street. The air was thick with the acrid scents of stale food. Clouds of heat puffed out of grates from the subway below. The street was crowded. The denizens of the grimy cobblestones of Washington Street were unlike the shoppers strolling down Newbury Street or the tourists at Faneuil Hall.

She felt the eyes of these strangers peering at her with hostility; she was an unwelcome visitor in an alien culture. She knew these were the type of people who would soon be judging her, the lower-class readers of the *Herald*, people she usually had to confront only on subway trains, on uneasy walks through the Common. When she had bought the gun.

Alison made her way down the street with her head bowed, gripped with the thought that she would be recognized. Just two blocks ahead was the dead-end street where the pawn shop was located, between an Army surplus store and a store selling comic books. The pawn shop had a small sign in the window: WE NEVER

CLOSE. When she ventured there that early Saturday morning, there were no other customers. Most of the other stores had not yet opened, and the street's emptiness magnified the little activity taking place—the squeaky wheels of a homeless woman's shopping cart, the thud of bound newspapers thrown off trucks, the sidewalk shudder from the subway.

A bell rang from the top of the door as she entered. It was a dark, dingy place, the size of a walk-in closet, the air heavy with the smell of cigar butts. Behind a bolted wire-mesh cage, a few feet inside the entrance, just beyond the reach of the door, were displayed a variety of abandoned objects with prices attached—television sets, watches, rings, radios, stereo speakers, clocks. To the right, handguns inside a glass case were attached to metal clips on cork board.

Alison was surprised by the entrance of an overweight, middle-aged man she had seen leaning against the wall outside, lazily puffing on a cigar.

"New rules," he said, gesturing with the stub of his cigar. "No smoking inside businesses." He eyed her suspiciously. "What can I help you with?"

"I was looking for a gun," she said, her voice edgy and soft, and she thought of backing out.

"Uh-huh. Yeah. Nobody's safe these days. Some punks even broke in here once. What they wanted, I don't know. This isn't no Saks Fifth Avenue." He laughed. "You know guns?"

She shook her head.

"You gotta have a permit, you know, to carry one around."

He opened the wire cage and walked to the case.

Her hands trembled at the touch of the handguns he displayed. He extolled the individual virtues of each weapon, but she didn't hear him. She pointed at the smallest one, a .22-caliber pistol. It was sleek, silver, compact. He seemed pleased by the selection. She reached out for the gun, to stuff it quickly in her purse, but he stopped her, placing a clammy palm on her hand.

"Not so fast, miss. You're certainly an anxious one. Got someone in mind?" He chuckled. "You gotta fill out a form first. Just a formality. No big deal."

She stared at the sheet of yellow paper he placed before her. She thought quickly of using a false name, but such a ruse was unlikely to succeed. The form required the purchaser to produce identification. She handed the owner her driver's license. He stared at her picture with tight eyes. She feared he would ask her to remove her scarf, expose her eyes and face, to verify that she was the same pale, younger woman in the unfocused photograph.

"You look different."

"Yes, well, it's been a few years. I'm glad I don't look like my license picture. You know what I mean?"

"Yeah," he said, handing back the license. "Enjoy." He sold her the gun. She scampered out of the shop, the sound of the little bell echoing in her ears.


What had led her to such a drastic move? The world was a cold and lonely place. The series of men who had abused her emotionally seemed endless. Will. Jerry. Jack. She had placed her trust in them, given them herself, and they rewarded her with nothing but lies and deceit. Jack's utter indifference to her after wooing her and then getting her pregnant. The way he looked at her as if she were invisible. She had made so many mistakes. Her career, one that she had chosen when desperate, was wrapped up with this man she'd have to encounter every day. She couldn't face going back to the office. She had made a mess of her life.

She thought about how to relieve herself of the pressure. She hated Jack. She hated herself. In the newspapers, she had often read about women arming themselves against abuse from their spouses and boyfriends. It was the only way to stop them from hurting you again. Men think they have immunity. Her previous men had walked away unscathed, moved on as if she were a mere blip in their lives. Why weren't they made to hurt, to feel what she experienced?

She walked out of the shop with the pistol and didn't know if and when she'd use it, and if it would be on herself or Jack. She imagined him lying in a pool of blood, finally paying, but she told herself it was merely a fantasy, the gun a prop she'd keep to prevent herself from following through.


As she walked by the pawn shop now, she feared the owner would remember her, that the gun would be traced. How many women like her frequented these places? Who was this person who did these things—purchased a gun, had an abortion, shot at Jack? She wondered whom she could turn to. She thought about calling Carole, a partner in the firm. No, Carole was merely an acquaintance and her view would be compromised by her loyalty to the firm.

Her brother? Peter was either at work on a composition or on the Cape with his lover, manager of a bed and breakfast in Provincetown. He was rarely a source of emotional support anyway, lost in his music, unnecessarily estranged from the family by his sexual preference and need to break away.

Her parents? Their cloying expressions of support at this moment were not what she needed. Her father would suggest a high-priced lawyer. Her mother would make an appointment with her analyst and suggest the same for Alison.

She realized how friendless she was in this city. She admitted to herself that the bare facts of the shooting, outside the context of the event—the look on Jack's face when he saw the gun, the overpowering weight of the man falling on top of her, the gun tumbling off the bridge—were not explainable. Nobody would ever know how betrayed she was by Jack's withdrawal, his addictive, seductive lies.

As she walked into the lobby of her Back Bay apartment building, Alison realized hurting Jack had not freed her at all. She could no longer remember why she ever thought it would, how she had ever conceived her plan, a plan that seemed so pointless and counterproductive now.

Alison kicked her shoes off at the threshold of the door and walked across the living room. In the middle of a business day, all the building's sounds were audible—the hum of the elevator, the creaks and heaves of the walls and floors.

Alison's eighth-floor condominium was decorated in soft whites and blues. The sofa and love seat were an off-white. Next to them sat a pine rocking chair. The living-room walls were filled with crocheted hangings made by a friend of her mother's who ran a shop in Bloomington, a Kandinsky print purchased on her trip to New York with Jack, and a ballet poster, the dancer bent over in blue tights. The objects were all invested with memories. They seemed like pathetic attempts at building something; she had been a mother bird constructing a nest from gathered twigs.

She stood listlessly in the middle of the room, staring at the dining-room table, piled with documents from the Nelson case, unanswered mail, and a tablet of notes for a deposition. There was a sense of relief in knowing it was so irrelevant. Past the table, below a cupboard of china, silver candlesticks, and the wine rack, the red light of the answering machine blinked.

She rewound the tape and heard her father's voice. "Alison, this is your father. How are you? Your mother wants you to call her. I'll speak with you later. Good-bye." His voice was cheerful.

So, the news hadn't penetrated their secure world. Her mother would have to wait. Her father's surrogate pleas on his wife's behalf never involved an emergency. It was a tactic that was least effective when more often utilized. Constant reminders of her daughterly neglect did not produce the desired guilt but rather a petty obstinacy.

She entered the bedroom and switched on the bedside lamp. In the dim light, the figures on the bed appeared real. The dinosaur, bear, and rabbit sat dumbly on the comforter in a row. There were times she was self-conscious about this nursery holdover, especially with men, who usually teased her about them. Only Jack had been different. "I never had a stuffed animal or a pet when I was a kid." He said it in a neutral tone, a matter-of-fact self-pity about his childhood. He was always tossing out such remarks. She had been seduced by them.

She sat on the bed and rolled her nylons off her feet. It was strange undressing from her work clothes at this time of day. She stood up in her slip and shut the blinds, viewing herself in the vanity mirror attached to the closet. She had the figure of a girl, but she noted a slight heaviness in the hips. My thighs are getting thicker, she thought.

She went to the kitchen and uncorked a half-empty white zinfandel sitting in the refrigerator and poured herself a glass. Her free hand gripped the counter as she sipped, and she threw her hair and head back to swallow it fully. She closed her eyes briefly, picked up the bottle and glass, and went to the couch. In front of her, on the coffee table where she placed the glass, was a stack of magazines—*The New Yorker*, *The Atlantic*, *Architecture Digest*, and *Connoisseur*. The last was a subscription gift from Jack. He wanted her to teach him about wine. In South Boston, he said, an exotic drink was anything but a Budweiser. They went to the wine stores together, and she showed him her favorite whites, rosés, and reds from California and France. For weeks, he arrived at her apartment with fresh flowers and a new bottle, until she remarked that soon they'd be able to open their own store.

As with all her efforts at gentle teasing, he did not take it well, became somber, and never brought another bottle. Even at restaurants, he'd shun the wine list as a grim reminder of his folly. She learned to never criticize him; he was too thin-skinned. He said he wanted to learn things from her, become cultured, but he lacked the patience to be an able pupil.

She poured herself another glass, her head buzzing slightly and filling with cheap sentiment. He would arrive, ringing the bell, his arms full of roses, his face flushed with excitement, and kiss her sweetly, utter words of love, tell her how beautiful she appeared in the glow of the hallway light. He was what she had always dreamed of, a romantic, caring man.

She wanted to call him now, erase the last few days, the last six months, and return to the early moments, his sweet childish face before waking.

Was her life always to be so chaotic and disordered? Was it some genetic trait? She had watched Peter, her older brother, the putative genius of the family, go through such a period. He had prepared for the life of a concert pianist, but all those years of practice and training, through his adolescence, when Peter was disciplined and driven, failed to produce the desired result. He announced his homosexuality his senior year in high school, when Alison was a sophomore. Although she attached no moral judgment, his brazenness was alarming, unnecessary, and dangerous in Wallace, a small village in the middle of Indiana. She was ridiculed as the sister of the school's most notorious fag.

Peter took the verbal abuse in stride. He moved out of the house and in with Roger. Once the target had been removed, the schoolyard taunts disappeared. Her fellow adolescents turned their wrath on some other vulnerable creature. But the house was lonely and quiet without Peter's presence. She missed him. His kind frailty was a comfort from the harsh discipline of her father, who drove his children to succeed. Her father thought himself a failure, an ineffectual academic, who lacked the talent and genius he craved. He demanded the impossible from them.

Two months later, Peter had abandoned his plans to attend Juilliard, and moved to Boston. Alison feared being alone with her father; he would certainly turn his stifling attention to her. She stayed away from the house during the day, came home for dinner and was quickly out again, often to smoke pot with Sherie and Michael, two fellow faculty brats, on the Smithfield golf course. When she was high, she constructed a bright future for herself on the stage. She gazed at the dark blue, star-pocked sky and dreamed of New York, the glittering, ominous life force of Times Square.

Back in school, she played Juliet and Ophelia, those doomed, wounded, obsessive girls, to great acclaim. Her theater teacher praised her. Alison longed for an experience that would generate such emotions in real life, but her hermetic existence deprived her of anything but the most mundane concerns—clothes and childish boys groping at her blouse.

By the time she had graduated from Wellesley, she had twelve productions to her credit and was ready for fame. Not New York just yet, but Boston, a precursor, a testing ground. She lived with Sherie, who was doing graduate work at Tufts, and Margie, Sherie's roommate, in a working-class Irish and Italian neighborhood of double-decker bungalow houses and lawns filled with pale blue Virgin Mary statues.

The apartment was on the top floor of the house, up a winding staircase of fine faded oak. The living room was sparsely furnished with a couch and coffee table Alison recognized from Sherie's parents' basement, a black-and-white television set, and a floor lamp.

The only other room was hidden behind a closed door. "Margie's studio," Sherie whispered when Alison first arrived, as if it were a well-kept secret. "She's an artist. She's in New York for a couple of weeks."

"Are you sure this is okay with her?" Alison asked, glancing around the room, wondering where she was going to sleep.

"Sure. We got to break up this room anyway. We'll put a partition up or something. I'm *so* glad you're here." Alison was, too.

She settled into her new environment and auditioned for *The House of Blue Leaves* at the Brattle Theatre, securing a minor part as one of the nuns. She hid her disappointment from Sherie and consoled herself that this was only the beginning, that she couldn't expect to start at the top. She wandered through the Theater District, which bordered Chinatown and the Combat Zone, staring at the marquees, impatient for success. Her college theater teacher had recommended she send a portfolio. She dropped off black-and-white photos and a list of her prior credits at theater offices. The telephone did not ring.

On a hazy humid morning, she sat in her bathrobe, sipping a mug of coffee, reading the want ads in the *Globe* when Margie came home from New York.

"You must be Alison," she said, dragging her luggage into the room. "I always overpack."

"Margie?" Alison asked. She felt ridiculous in her bathrobe and toweled hair.

They shook hands. Margie's was soft and small. She had an open, welcoming smile. Short blond hair cut sharply around her oval face. Her eyes were a bright blue.

"Good timing, huh?" Margie said. "How long you been here?"

"A few days."

"Sherie said you're an actress."

"Alleged."

"Well, you act, don't you?"

"I have."

"Then you're an actress," Margie said decisively. "Don't get caught up in that credential crap. Believe in yourself. You free for breakfast?"

"Sure. I'm just reading the want ads."

"Let's go, then." She grinned and so, finally, did Alison.


On one of her many excursions with Margie and three of her friends, she saw Peter. They were at Swift's, a jazz bar in Harvard Square. She hadn't seen Peter since a cousin's Episcopal wedding in Columbia, Missouri, six months before.

Peter was playing piano in the jazz trio. The band was on a break when Alison entered, and he was standing by the bar, dressed in a black turtleneck sweater and pants. His brown hair was shaved thinly on the sides.

She squeezed her way through the crowd to the bar. "Howdy, stranger," she said.

"Baby sister," he said loudly, startled, hugging her. "What's a nice girl like you doing in a place like this?"

"I'm with a friend. It's so nice to see you."

"Me, too," he said, squeezing her hand. "You still living with Sherie?"

"Yes."

"Are you getting any good parts?"

"Not really. It's frustrating. I expected so much more."

"I know what you mean. This just pays the rent. Not exactly what I had in mind, but it'll do. I have no complaints."

She was sad for both of them. At one time, they had such big dreams. Now here they were. "Are we settling for less?"

"Do we have a choice?" He smiled weakly, then looked closely at her. "You're really upset?"

"I just don't know what to do. Nothing's working out. I'm wasting my life. I need an anchor, something. This all just seems like stupid pipe dreams."

"You're being too hard on yourself." He stroked her arm. "You were meant to be an actress."

"And I'm a waitress. I just don't know anymore."

They had been raised to believe that through art—painting, music, literature, theater—one could make a life, but they were unprepared for disappointment, setbacks. Peter couldn't resolve her problem because he shared it.

From the stage, the drummer gestured to Peter.

''I gotta go. Another set. Let's keep in touch.'' She watched him rejoin the band. An emptiness filled the pit of her stomach.

From her vantage point at the bar, Alison looked at Margie and her friends laughing at a table. Nothing was working out as planned. She had to change her life. In the year she'd been in Boston, she had little to show for all her efforts.

**8**

ate the next morning, Detective Hardy's gruff voice was on Jack's answering machine. Jack lay on his couch, still dressed in his suit, the shirt untucked and wrinkled, his tie askew, conscious of the odor of beer and cigarettes clinging to him. He couldn't make out Hardy's words.

He sat up, dropping his legs off the coffee table. After leaving the Purple Shamrock, he apparently had never made it to his bedroom. Rubbing his eyes with open palms, he felt the numbness in his arm and remembered what had happened. Today was a weekday, and he had no place to go.

Weak and woozy, his mouth dry, he stood up, walked to the bedroom, and began undressing. The sting in his arm produced tingles at the edge of his fingers. The doctor had said the wound would heal quickly. Removing his shirt, he touched the gauze and wrapping briefly and closed his eyes. He emptied his pockets of crumpled dollar bills and the change collected during the night, threw the clothes on his unmade bed, and went to the bathroom. In the mirror, he viewed his stubble of beard, the bloodshot eyes, the shallowness of his cheeks, the gray skin. He turned on the shower and watched the steam rise through the room until it surrounded him. Realizing he needed to protect the dressing on his shoulder, he washed gingerly, without satisfaction.

He dressed in his Harvard sweatsuit, a gift from Alison. The scent of her light lilac perfume was on it. After their lovemaking, she would often dress in it, and, alluring in that shapeless outfit, sit cross-legged on the end of his bed while they talked. He thought at those moments that he was in love or something like it because there was a warmth, an ease, in being together. These were feelings that didn't occur to him now, only the suspicion that she had bought the suit for him in mockery, reminding him of his lack of Ivy League credentials.

He decided to retrieve the *Globe* from the front step. Yet he hesitated at the door and listened for stirrings in the building, then smiled wryly. Everyone—Janet and Bill Wilder, the couple across the hall, the others downstairs he'd never formally met—was out, at work, except you, you idiot, he thought, closing the door behind him.

Back inside, he scanned the pages of the front section for any item about the shooting. Nothing there, nor in the metro section. He felt a combination of relief and disappointment. The whole episode seemed like something he'd imagined. The newspaper appeared to confirm that it was just that. He tossed the pages on the floor and walked to the answering machine.

"It's me." Alison's voice! His heart raced. He stopped the machine, then realized it was her last message, informing him of the time of the appointment. He forwarded the tape and heard his mother, calling to see how he was. She said she had seen the paper. There *was* coverage. Probably the *Herald* had picked it up. He thought of confiding to his mother, then realized the hopelessness of it. Her Catholic boy had made his girlfriend pregnant; she had gotten an abortion. He wondered what sugar-coated version he could offer her. Maybe Alison would plead guilty, he thought, temporary insanity, and avoid the whole mess. Then a semblance of his life could be saved. The notoriety would pass. Kaplan would welcome him back.

His hopes were dashed by the next message. "Donnelly. Hardy here. Boston P.D. We spoke . . . uh . . . the other night. We need to talk. Iron out some facts. The D.A. needs to see ya about your . . . uh, testimony. Give me a call."

Jack lit a cigarette. His throat was raw and constricted. Testimony? What would he say? She just shot me. I had no warning. He couldn't believe she was putting him through this. After everything, she was bringing him down with her. This confirmed his suspicions. She was manipulative, crazy, out to get him.

He shut his eyes, and his vision focused on her shaking hand

and the gun pointed at him. What had he been thinking at that moment? She was going to kill him. He would soon be dead. Only that sudden flinch had saved him.

He opened his eyes when the tip of the cigarette singed his fingers. He tried to remember how he had persevered through an earlier crisis, after his father's death, and wondered whether he could summon the strength again.

Freshly shaven, dressed in a blue-striped oxford shirt, corduroy pants, and a windbreaker, Jack headed across Beacon Hill and over to the Common, his loafers clicking steadily against the sidewalk.

He was full of nervous trembling. Despite the brisk air, he felt a warmth at his temples, the beginnings of sweat on his forehead. On the other side of the fence, a man lay sprawled facedown on a patch of faded brown grass. Across from the figure, three young men huddled, exchanging furtive glances, engaged in a drug deal. Otherwise, the area was empty. The only people out and about, Jack thought, are the idle, the criminal, and me.

etective Bill Hardy, thirteen-year veteran of the Boston Police Department, sat in a chair across from Hurley's desk, listening to him talk on the phone. Half this job, he thought, is listening to lawyers. They loved the sound of their own voices, the modulations, cadences, and rhythms of their language. Hurley was one of the worst. He always had his hidden agendas. His ill-timed press conferences screwed up investigations, and he berated cops involved in his cases. To Hardy, who had handled some of the most notorious murder investigations in recent Boston history, the Public Garden shooting was nothing to get excited about. Sure, it had some intriguing elements, what with the two white yuppies instead of the punks and dopers in Dorchester and Roxbury. But the victim was barely wounded.

Hurley spun his chair around to face Hardy and placed his feet on the desk. He was wearing light gray socks; sprouts of black hair were visible against pale skin on his calves. He rolled his eyes in exasperation. "No comment," he intoned. "The investigation is continuing. . . . Yeah." He slammed down the phone. "The vultures," he said. "Can't live with 'em or without 'em."

"Yeah."

"So, what we got?" Hurley shoved errant slips of paper and plastic coffee cups aside, revealing a legal pad beneath.

"We traced the gun. The pawn shop guy can't ID her from the photo, but the name's right. We'll do handwriting."

"Uh-huh, uh-huh," Hurley grunted, scribbling on the page. "When did she get it?"

"Two weeks ago."

"Excellent. What about that video guy? Any luck on finding him?"

"We're still looking. It's a needle in the haystack. Could be anybody."

Hurley got up from the chair. "Listen, Hardy. You're an experienced cop. You know your stuff, but this is the thing. She did it, okay? It's clear. Everybody knows it. The jury will know it. Hell, she'll probably admit it. That's not the problem. That's what we know. It's what we don't know and what we may find out later that's the problem. Like, what the boyfriend's deal is. From your report, some namby-pamby type, or maybe he whacked her a few times. Abuse. It's the latest defense. Last refuge of scoundrels. And it's the video age. People have to see it to believe it. Picture's worth a thousand words. Juries are people. They get bored with words. I need that video."

"We'll keep on it. Donnelly's out in the hall. You ready for him?"

While Hardy retrieved Jack, Hurley stood at the window, full of the inner agitation he always experienced with the prospect of a big trial. Although he derided Lee Klein's abilities as a lawyer generally—her high-strung presentations, her flamboyant clothes, the cloying emotionality she used to garner juror sympathy—it was these very qualities that might be effective in a case with the potential explosiveness of this one. He could envision her playing on the awfulness of the abortion experience, her client's lack of a criminal record, Donnelly's possible betrayal of her. The abortion question could play either way depending on the composition of the jury, but to Hurley it was a simple equation: Abortion was a means of birth control for the career woman.

When Lee called to explore plea bargaining, she was brimming with a confidence that gnawed at him, even though he thought it misguided. Hurley hadn't betrayed any doubts, either. He threw out offers he knew she wouldn't accept, especially at this early stage in the proceedings.


"Mr. Donnelly." Hurley greeted Jack with a firm grip and offered him a seat. "Coffee?"

Jack shook his head.

"How you feeling?" Hurley asked.

"Fine." Jack shrugged. "She just nicked me."

"Thank God for that, huh? Luck of the Irish, I guess."

"Something like that."

"Relax. We're just going to ask a few questions. We got to take the case to the grand jury early next week."

"What's going on?" Jack asked, his voice high.

"Nothing yet." Hurley resented Donnelly's type. Preppie outfit. Finely cut hair. They thought they ran the world.

"You plea-bargaining?"

"We're in preliminary stages. I don't hold out much hope, though. We're probably going to the mat on this one."

"Uh-huh," Jack said.

"It's a slam-dunk case. We just need some more facts, that's all. About you and the defendant . . . uh . . . Miss Moore. Well." Hurley shuffled the notes. "I got Detective Hardy's report here of his interview with you. You had no idea this was coming, I take it?"

"No."

"She never seemed . . . uh . . . crazy to you before."

"No. Not crazy."

"Well, what exactly?"

"We were kind of breaking up, you know, when this happened."

"This. You mean the shooting?"

"No. No. When she got pregnant."

"I see. And she wasn't happy about it?"

"Uh, no. Do we have to get into this?"

"Pick your poison, Mr. Donnelly. My questions are going to be a hell of a lot easier than her lawyer's. Cross-examination's going to be a bitch, unless we know what went on. She's going to try to make you look like the bad guy. That's the usual line with these type of cases. They'll put *you* on trial; focus on your relationship, how you treated her, how you reacted to the pregnancy. I'd guess the whole line's going to be that you dumped her when the going got tough. No great sin in the big scheme of things, but it won't look good to a jury."

The words struck Jack harshly. The enormity of the task ahead was devastating. His reputation would be destroyed. Then he thought of the irony: After years of practicing corporate litigation, he and Alison were finally going to trial.

"I just wish it would go away," Jack said.

"A little late for that. Some things you can't just flush down the toilet because you want to." Hurley could see by Hardy's startled eyes and Jack's obvious anger that he'd gone too far.

"It was the only option," Jack said. If anything, Alison's reaction only confirmed the correctness of their decision. What Jack could have prevented started way before the pregnancy. He should never have gotten involved with her. His anger subsided. Hurley was right. He was only uttering what the jurors would be thinking, what Alison's lawyer would want them to think.

"Okay. We've got to stay away from that anyway. It's not relevant," Hurley said. "We just want the facts. The truth. That's true. But it's emphasis that's all that's important. Still, I gotta know the straight poop. Your relationship. How you met. That kind of thing."

"I'm not ready for this now," Jack said.

"Well, when you think you'll be ready?"

"You don't need me to indict this case. All the damage has been done, don't you think?"

"Hey—" Hurley began, but Hardy interrupted.

"We'll talk later. You can go now. We'll give you a buzz."

"Jesus Christ. Great witness he'll be," Hurley said after Jack had left.

"He'll come around," Hardy said. "It hasn't sunk in yet. When he realizes that she's going to blame it all on him, he'll come around. No use beating up on the guy."

"You're probably right," Hurley said. "Slam dunk, my ass." He laughed ruefully. "This case is gonna be a ball-buster."

**10**

**A** crowd gathered around the seal pool outside the New England Aquarium. On the boardwalk, a hot-dog vendor, his blue overhead umbrella tilting in the wind, scrambled to hold down the fluttering napkins.

The inland water was choppy. A fishing boat, tethered to the dock connected to the Aquarium's side, creaked against the wooden planks. As she walked, Alison watched the boat being loaded with passengers. The destination was Plymouth, then Provincetown, the tip of the Cape, where her brother lived now, oblivious to her condition. Why she had come down to the wharf escaped her. She had walked through the tunnel into the North End and proceeded down the shore, past Pelican's, with its oyster bar and glass bowls of cold beer, scene of her final real conversation with Jack, only a few weeks before.

She had arrived at Pelican's first, and sucked nervously on the lemon rind among the melting cubes of her mineral water. Even then, she realized, she had a premonition that meeting him was a waste of time. She smiled to herself, thinking that she wasn't smoking or drinking because of the baby inside her.

He arrived breathless, preoccupied, as if suddenly awakened by an emergency. In his blue pinstripe suit, yellow tight-knotted tie, and polished black wingtips he appeared to her as a lawyer playing hooky, feeling guilty for leaving work before five.

"I came as soon as I could," he said, sitting down next to her and ordering a beer. He smiled weakly. "Well?"

She sipped from her glass. When she didn't respond, Jack looked around the near-empty room. "I've never been here before," he said. "Are you okay? Why are we meeting *here*? Your message was so . . ." He fumbled for the word.

"Cryptic. The word is *cryptic*, Jack."

He seemed confused at the ferocity of her tone.

"I've been to the gynecologist," she said.

He swallowed hard and licked his lips.

"Bad news?"

"You could say that."

"What are you going to do?"

She glared briefly at him, then moved her eyes down in disapproval. It all seemed so pathetic and sad to her then, his nervous energy, the tremor of his cigarette, as if he expected her to make him do something he wouldn't do. She would not make it any easier. She wouldn't indulge his disgusting self-absorption.

"I don't know. Any suggestions?"

"Well, you're not going to have it."

"Is that all you can say?"

"I don't know what to say. How did this happen?"

"The old-fashioned way."

"I didn't mean that. Didn't you use something?"

"The something didn't work."

"Jesus," he said. "I'm sorry."

"About which part?"

"This, damn it. I never meant to hurt you."

"That's what's so precious about you, Jack. You utter every cliché with the force of a new line."

The slight flicker in his eyes indicated that she had had an effect.

"I don't even know if it's mine."

"You son of a bitch. How dare you? You sleep with me, you romance me, and now you do this. What kind of person are you?"

She had spoken too loud, and he tried to calm her down.

"I'm just saying we can't have a baby. Are you crazy? We don't even like each other."

"Since when?"

"For a long time. I don't know exactly."

"So, that's it. That's your attitude. You're just going to end it."

"I'll go with you, you know, when you go," he said.

"I don't want you to."

"It's the least I can do."

"Well, you're certainly good at that. Remember how you said you'd stick with me no matter what?"

"That was before."

"Before what? Before you got what you wanted from me? You're full of shit, you know that?"

He shrugged his shoulders, refusing to respond. All was settled then. He asked the waitress for the check. She stood there while he scrambled through his pocket for money. Then he rose, straightening the lapels of his jacket and tugging on the knot of his tie.

Alison watched him walk away. She started crying then, and thought she would never stop.

t eight-fifteen A.M., in the thirty-third-floor conference room of Adelman and Kaplan, the complex litigation group was about to begin its weekly meeting. A tray of Danish pastry and a carafe of coffee sat in the middle of the rectangular table. Andy Gottlieb, in his purple paisley tie and matching suspenders, stood in the doorway drinking coffee, watching Mary Kelly—Virgin Mary, Alison had called her—writing notes on a legal pad.

"Ought to be quite an agenda today," Andy said.

"Pardon me?" Mary looked at him.

"You know, the Donnelly and Moore thing."

"Oh." She blushed. "It's just awful, isn't it?"

"She just nicked him. I saw him at the hospital." He set his mug down on the table, pointing to the spot on his sleeve where Jack had been hit.

The rest of the group entered and took their places at the table: Toni Williams, a black woman from Northeastern; Janice Horowitz, a former federal prosecutor a year away from partnership; Carole Miller, junior partner; Larry Kelm, and Drew Blake. There were two empty chairs. The room was quiet.

Hal Liebowitz came in, carrying the day's edition of *The Wall Street Journal*. He took a seat at the head of the table.

"Morning, people," he began. "Let's cut right to the nub. We all can read the papers. I don't have to tell you this is not good news for the firm. If anybody asks, there's to be no comment. But I'm sure there'll be questions from the police. Martin wants another lawyer present during these interviews."

"I have a friend in the D.A.'s office who says they have a solid case," Toni said. "Hurley's handling it."

"Who's representing Alison?" asked Larry.

"Lee Klein. A former p.d. Former president of the Women's Bar Association."

"Oh, boy," Andy muttered. "A feminist."

"Okay," Hal said impatiently. "Enough of that. We don't know what happened. We don't want any speculation. As far as the public is concerned, it's business as usual. Okay?"

He inhaled deeply. "Now, as you probably realize, this leaves us in kind of a lurch on the Microtech case. Losing two associates will require extra hours from all of us. Toni, I want you and Andy to pick up the slack. Get up to speed on the file. I think most of the documents are in ... uh, Jack's office. If not, check Alison's. Here's a copy of the deposition schedule." He pushed the paper down to Andy. "Split it up any way you want."

"Are they both gone?" Andy asked, looking at the schedule with chagrin.

"Yes. Indefinite leaves of absence. But I caution you, we're not presuming anything. Just trying to be fair-minded. Any questions?"

No one spoke.

"Good. That's all." He got up and left the room.

"Shit," Andy said, realizing he'd have to cover for Jack, an almost impossible schedule to maintain.

"They were always a mystery to me," Janice said. "So different. I mean, he's so outgoing. She was always so quiet. You could never get her to talk about anything."

"It's awful," Mary said. "I mean, what they both are going through."

"Donnelly always was an ass-kisser," Drew said. "He probably brown-nosed her because she was supposed to be some up-and-comer."

"Can we stop this?" Toni said. "You guys act like they're dead or something."

"For all practical purposes," Andy said, "they are."

At daybreak, the sky was dusty orange, and dew shimmered on the grass. The strains of rush hour not yet apparent, Lee jogged along Tremont Street outside the fence surrounding the Public Garden.

She began her working days in this way, to clear her mind and focus on her cases. Entering the Garden at the Washington statue, she jogged to the bridge and stopped. A hint of frost was evident on the railing. This is where it happened, she thought. There were no traces of the crime visible. It was difficult to think of this place as a crime site. In her mind, it had always been an oasis in the city. The Public Garden represented everything good about Boston.

Lee held the railing and stretched her legs. In the distance she saw pedestrians approaching and it struck her how irrational Alison's decision had been. She could not imagine a more public place. In broad daylight, Alison had pulled out the gun and shot her lover, the father of her aborted— She hesitated before uttering the next word to herself. Her instinct said "child" but, of course, it was not really a child. Fetus, potential life, fetal life, not a child. For Lee, the whole subject of abortion had always been significant. She had friends who devoted considerable energy to the pro-choice cause. Lee remembered those strident days celebrating the Supreme Court's decision in *Roe v. Wade*. She had attended consciousness-raising sessions in dim, cluttered rooms off Harvard Square, women telling their awful tales of illegal, back-alley abortions; botched procedures, self-induced abortions with coat hangers. The cause—freedom of choice—was right and just, Lee thought. If a woman could not have control over her own body, she had nothing.

What Alison's views were on this issue, Lee did not know. She had few real details. As of yet, Alison was unwilling to talk even abstractly about the events surrounding the shooting. Lee needed specifics, motivations, intentions. It was apparent from her conversation with Hurley that a favorable disposition was not possible. Hurley saw the potential publicity in the case, as did Lee, she had to admit. This could be a groundbreaker of sorts, a boon to her practice. Neither side was giving in. It was time to tell Alison the pitfalls of trial, and find out what she wanted to do.

With most clients, Lee offered only the illusion of choice. She chose her emphasis depending on what she perceived to be in the best interests of the client. Most people in the criminal justice system fell into one of two categories—the resigned and the defiant. The former always pled guilty, viewing their situation as hopeless and inevitable. They believed that they deserved their fate, if only because they had been caught.

The latter, the defiant, did not recognize wrongdoing or guilt. It was always somebody else's fault—the cops were hounding them, their girlfriends berated them, their bosses fired them, whatever. No matter what the odds, they persisted in holding out. They went to trial and got hammered at sentencing.

Alison seemed to be in a third category, the bewildered. Unable to grasp the significance of what she had done, she seemed shocked to find herself accused. Alison was educated, articulate, and had a lot to lose. Lee wondered whether she had been abused in some way by her boyfriend. This was a thread she must pursue. Was the abortion the final straw?

She hoped to answer some of these questions at lunch. She had arranged to meet Alison at Harvard Square. The indictment was certain to come down soon. The potential publicity must be dealt with, and they had to develop a viable defense to the charges.


When Lee arrived back at her apartment, sweaty and invigorated, Brian was propped up in bed underneath the sheets, drinking an espresso. The newspaper lay in sections before him.

"The newsprint!" she exclaimed.

"Sorry. Forgot." He smiled and threw the paper on the floor.

She found him easy to forgive. He meant well. His faults were purely inadvertent.

They had met five years ago. Brian had been working on a profile of her for *Bay State Magazine.* He had seen her give a speech before the Massachusetts Women's Political Caucus on the decline of civil liberties during the Reagan era. The article portrayed her as a 1960s idealist who had not sold out, a criminal defense lawyer with a (perhaps too) open heart.

Brian was thirty-two, ten years younger than Lee. They had been friends and part-time lovers for several years now, and neither seemed to want a stronger commitment than that. Lee found his brand of cynicism refreshing, for it was tempered by idealism, a sense of innocence lost.

"Good jog?"

With her back to him, she nodded. "It's going to be a long day."

Brian pushed his toes against her spine. "Meeting with the psycho killer today?"

"The alleged *attempted* psycho killer. What am I going to do with this case?" She turned to him for an answer. He shrugged. "You think it was a mistake taking it?"

"I don't know. It's got potential."

"Yeah. All bad. The facts suck. She's uncommunicative. The D.A.'s a pig. And there's the abortion. The Puritans and Catholics stacked on the jury will love that one. They'll think she's some slut. The old double standard."

"I did an article on right-to-lifers once. What a bunch they are. Anyway, that's when I heard about this thing, post-abortion syndrome. You know about it?"

"What are you talking about?"

"You've heard about the Vietnam vets who relive the trauma of war and turn violent later. The same thing happens to women who have abortions. It's a theory. There've been studies. The stress—"

"Oh, that's just bullshit. It's just propaganda. You know, along the lines of more people died at Chappaquiddick than in nuclear power plants."

"Still, maybe that's what happened to her."

"Give me a break."

"No, really. Listen, you know I'm pro-choice. I have to be." He laughed. "But you've got to admit it's possible."

"Not by itself. You'd have to be fucked up to begin with."

"And how do you know she wasn't?"

"She's a lawyer," Lee said, walking away and toward the bathroom.

"Which way does that cut?" The bathroom door closed. "Are we done talking?"

"I have to get ready. I work for a living."

"That's *your* problem."

lison and Lee sat at a corner table at Grendel's Den in Harvard Square. Bright sunlight bathed their table. They had both ordered house salads, but Alison's remained uneaten. Lee noticed traces of red in Alison's eyes. She had apparently slept fitfully.

"Do I have a chance in this case?" Alison asked.

"There are always possible defenses," Lee said. "You could have been traumatized by the abortion. The shooting might not have been premeditated. He might have provoked it. But I need to know facts before I can determine what's in your best interest, what will work. And so far you've told me nothing. Are you ready now?"

Alison lowered her head. "Yes. It's hard to know where to start."

"I know." Lee thought of extending her hand, but rejected the idea.

"Not childhood, I hope."

"Not just yet. Let's tackle the easy stuff first."

"Like what happened? That's not the easy part. I really don't know. I remember the clinic, that bald spot on the doctor's head, and the pulp of the orange juice afterward. What an awful place."

"Why did you go to that clinic?"

"You're not going to believe this. We—I mostly—he didn't care—wanted to keep it private. I didn't want to ask my gynecologist for a referral."

"Didn't care?"

"Oh, Jack. Yes. By that point we barely spoke."

"Did he suggest you have an abortion?"

"It wasn't really a choice. What were we going to do? He just assumed I'd take care of it, I guess. He hated complications, messy situations."

"But he went with you?"

"Of course he did. Residual Catholic guilt. He wanted to suffer."

Alison lit a cigarette. "I think you should know about Jerry if you're going to understand any of this."

Alison began recounting meeting Jerry and her decision to go to law school. There she was at twenty-four, waiting tables at the Pewter Pot, serving coffee to an endless stream of ambitious, steadily younger groups of students, moving on to bigger and better things. She was just another "wannabe," just another woman who thought that becoming an actress was a matter of adopting a bohemian style and chattering idly about upcoming tryouts and an impending move to New York. She tired of self-delusions. What did she have to show for her life? A few minor roles. A crummy little job.

Then, in the midst of her crisis of faith, there was Jerry. She was waitressing the graveyard shift when she met him. He was a first-year at Harvard Law, studying for his Contracts exam. He was all polish, sophistication, confidence, with his curly brown hair and dark, thick eyebrows, his perfect posture, his air of utter belief in himself and his limitless possibilities.

During that evening, they struck up a conversation, and when the crowd thinned out, she joined him at his table. The way he described the law and his ambitions, it seemed like something real, solid, practical. With his encouragement, she decided to apply for law school.

Only a few months after their first meeting, she'd moved out of Sherie's apartment and into Jerry's place in the Back Bay, an apartment on the first floor of a brownstone, with hardwood floors, oak bookcases, simple, functional-design furniture. Classical music echoed and resounded from a Bang and Olufsen stereo system with tiny square black speakers distributed throughout the apartment. From the street sometimes, on summer or spring days, Verdi dripped from tree leaves and down to the pavement.

Alison studied for the Law School Admissions Test, scored well on the exam, and was accepted into Harvard. They appeared to be the perfect, successful couple, moving on a smooth career path and deeply in love.

She had often wondered where Jerry's money came from. He vaguely spoke of a trust fund. His parents lived outside Portland, Maine, he told her, his father in early retirement from prudent investing. She imagined some great house with white pillars over-looking the ocean, but he rarely spoke of his family, and she never did get to meet them. He would often make plans to attend some charitable function they were having on the great lawn of her imagination, but somehow the date would fly by and he wouldn't mention it.

She surely had warning signs, but thought it was some Yankee stoicism that she had to endure or placate. In reality, it was simple selfishness. He simply had no use for anyone but himself or only for others who could be meaningful to him in some career way. How did she ever suit him for even five minutes? "Don't you know? You're everything I'm not. You're not a threat," he had said one night, a rare night when he was too tipsy after a party in George-town. She'd felt isolated, left out of the party conversations. "A bohemian. An actress. Can you imagine? For Jerry Prescott." So there it was.

Upon graduation, Jerry joined a lobbying firm in Washington and she landed a job at Perkins and Gray. Jerry spent most of his long days and nights working on the Hill. She thought she was finally living a focused life. Then Jerry confessed to an affair with a Congressman's administrative assistant.

"I couldn't believe it," she said to Lee. "I was so blind. I had these romantic notions. I still do. I could've killed myself then."

Alison's cheeks flushed. Lee was startled by the depth of her emotion. Lee saw accumulated hurt in her eyes and her pouty ex-pression. Her forehead was creased with anger.

"Then Jack," Alison continued. "I thought, this is it. I've gone to therapy. Got my shit together. Have a good job at this firm, making good money, and I'm independent. And there he is. I don't want a relationship. I just want to live my life. He was nice at first. Good-looking. Sweet, charming. I thought he was different. I wanted a friend, being so new to the firm. He seemed to need somebody. He was, I thought, lonely, vulnerable. I became infatuated, full of all the romance again. But he was the same as the rest of them. They say they won't hurt you, but that's all he did. It was all an act to sleep with me. Then he turned off on me. Shunned me. I couldn't take it anymore."

"So, you've had a string of bad luck with men," Lee said.

"Yeah, I'm one of *those* women. Always picking the wrong man."

"I'm not here to judge. Did he ever hit you?"

"No."

"Did you want to have the baby?"

"No. Yes. I don't know. Career women, we want it all. We do. You know, the supportive husband, the happy, healthy children, the great job, so there's this little part inside that can't help hoping. Still, Jack could never be a husband or a parent."

They walked across Massachusetts Avenue and through the ivied redbrick walkway into Harvard Yard. When they exited the yard, they crossed the street to the Harvard Book Store. Alison peered at the books displayed in the front window.

"When did you buy the gun?"

"Huh?" Alison said. "Oh, a couple weeks ago. I don't know why. I don't know what I planned to do with it."

She turned and faced Lee, folded her arms across her chest.

"You really don't know? I have to tell you that it's an important point. Your answer can't be you don't know. When you're asked in court, what's your answer? Were you scared or what?"

"Well, I guess I planned on using it in some way. I mean, yes, I was scared. Why else would I have bought it? I was so filled with hate and anger. I was so helpless, felt so used, and, my God, pregnant from this man."

"Uh-huh," Lee said. "That doesn't really explain it. I want you to think about it, really think, and come up with an explanation. We'll talk about it further. I know you're probably still a little shocked and want to forget the whole thing, but give yourself time to recall what you were feeling and thinking when you got the gun."

"Okay. I will. Well, what can we do? I want to fight this. People have to know why I did it. I had reasons. It's not like it seems."

"If you're ready, I am. That's what you hired me for."

They parted at the Harvard Square station. As Alison watched Lee walk down the steps to the subway, she wondered if she had been fooling herself, or Lee or both. What was she thinking when she pulled the trigger? She was full of accumulated rage. It was her entire situation—perhaps magnified by the abortion, perhaps not—that propelled her actions. But the result was unforeseen. She had not imagined what she would do at that moment when it came, but she had the gun for no other reason. She wanted to hurt Jack in some way, see him in pain. She supposed that obvious fact crippled any case she had.

She certainly hadn't thought of the consequences. If she was a criminal, she was an inept one. Why hadn't she devised some maneuver, some plot so that she wouldn't be caught? God, why dwell on that now?

14

ay leaned against a kiosk in Harvard Square, reading notices on the board. A macrobiotic lecture. A Revolutionary Student Youth Brigade meeting on American imperialism in Central America. Apartments for rent. Textbooks for sale. Concerts.

Ray eyed the magazine rack. He realized he lacked the true disposition of an artist. He had no patience. Ray believed he had to force the moment. So he'd done it. He'd called the station and talked to Wendy Thomas.

He had arranged to meet her at the Fill-A-Buster downtown, one of his favorite spots. He sat at a corner table facing Bowden Street. The place was nearly empty now, as Ray had figured. Across from him, a man read a folded *Globe*. She was late, of course. The bitch. You can never depend on chicks to be where they're supposed to be.

When she arrived, she appeared fresher, less plastic than on TV. It was true, he thought, the camera did add ten pounds. Behind her stood a tall lanky man with a scraggly beard, a camera bag slung over his shoulders. They came toward him.

"You Ray?" Her voice lacked that clipped quality he had come to love.

"Yeah," Ray said. "Who's this geek? We meet alone or it's no deal."

She seemed to consider this a moment. "It's okay, Jimmy," she said. "Wait outside."

"If you say so."

"Wendy Thomas," she said after Jimmy had left, stretching out a hand. Her palm was cold. She took a seat across from him.

"You want anything?" Ray asked, his heart racing. He could smell her perfume. "Coffee? The apple pie here's pretty good."

"No," she said.

"I understand. You on-air types gotta watch your figures. But Wendy—I can call you Wendy—not to say you need to worry. You look fantastic. You work out?"

"You said you had a tape," she said.

"Yeah. We'll get to it. I gotta tell you, Wendy, I've been watching you for years. A big fan. I got videotapes of you. A whole library of tapes I view late at night. Maybe you can come over and see them sometime. I could fix some pasta or whatever you like. Pick up a bottle of red wine."

"What about this tape? I'm on deadline, you know."

"You're so fucking important, you can't spend a few minutes with an admirer?"

"I'm sorry," she said, offering him a weak smile. "We get a lot of crank calls."

"Well, this isn't one of them. What I got, Wendy, you'll love. I got a tape of the Public Garden shooting. Not grainy at all. Got a great picture of the woman shooting the guy. A clear picture. Him falling down. The whole bit."

"What you want for it?"

"You don't sound too excited."

"All I have is your word. I haven't seen it."

"Well, I'm not going to charge you for it. Jesus. What kinda guy you think I am?" He was disappointed in her. She was like all chicks, better in your fantasies. "All I want is you to play it and mention my name. You'll like it. I promise you. You can't lose. What you say?"

"Deal," she said.

"I keep distribution rights, too."

"I don't know. I'll have to talk to our legal department."

"Don't let me down," Ray said. "I'm doing this for us."

He picked up the backpack and removed the tape, then hesitated, wondering if his faith in her was misplaced. "You promise to run it?"

"I don't make those decisions," she said evenly, but he could see the greed in her eyes. "But, you know, if it's what you say, I'm sure it'll play. There's nothing like a great visual. And no one else in town has this, right?"

"Of course not."

He placed the tape on the table and slid it across to her. She took it and stood up quickly.

"Hey, Wendy," Ray said as she headed for the door. "Let's do lunch sometime."

n Mount Vernon Street, across from Jack's apartment, a white truck with a Channel 7 logo was parked on the cobblestone walk, a satellite linkup protruding from its roof, surrounded by a crowd of reporters and photographers.

Jack noticed them as he climbed up the hill. It was dusk, and only embers of sunlight filtered down the street. A half block from his apartment, a gray-haired lady stood watching the activity.

"What's going on down there?" Jack asked as he came alongside her.

"Oh, it's where that poor young man lives," she said. "You know, the one who was shot in the Public Garden. Did you see that videotape on the news?"

"No." Jack subdued his alarm at the prospect.

"Some person taped the whole thing. When she pulls the gun out and shoots him. It's so awful. Violence is everywhere today, don't you think?"

Jack nodded. He was beginning to perceive the whole episode as something that had happened to a stranger.

"I mean, what's with people these days?" the woman asked, but Jack had already turned and retreated down the street. He would come back later when the hounds had given up.

On Charles Street, traffic was at a standstill. The workday was over, and he didn't have to hide from the world. He tried to remember what day it was. The Boys' Club would be at Sevens. Every Thursday, midlevel associates met for a few drinks and gossip. He hesitated briefly, but he had nowhere else to go. And something propelled him there—a curiosity about what was being said and where he stood.

He was glad the bar was dimly lit; he knew he looked awful. The boys were sitting in the back, the usual spot, a cove in the corner past the men's room. A half-empty pitcher of beer stood in the middle of the table. Jack waved to Mickey, the bartender, who answered back with a nod. The cast was assembled: Drew, Larry, Jay, and Andy.

"Speak of the devil. There's our hero now, boys," Drew said. "Bloodied but unbowed."

"Don't be a prick," Larry said, retrieving a chair from the next table.

"Occupational hazard, I'm afraid," Drew said. Jack figured Drew had drunk his limit, and was pontificating as usual. "A cautionary tale to us all, fellows. Wear a bulletproof vest when you're around the young professional woman today."

"Words of the wise," Andy said, placing an arm around Jack. "How you doing, guy?"

"Great. Enjoying my sabbatical. Listen, who do you have to screw to get a drink around here?"

"Mickey," Larry yelled, lifting the pitcher. "For your buddy."

"Have you seen the video?" Larry asked.

"Heard about it." Jack lit a cigarette.

"Maggie's taping it for me on the late news. Is this a nightmare or what?"

"It's a nightmare," Jack said flatly. He took a gulp of the beer. He hadn't been at the Boys' Club meetings for a while. Between the work on the Microtech case and his relationship with Alison, who was demanding and possessive, he now thought, and who ridiculed the ritual as primitive male bonding, he had avoided them. Now they were his mainstay, the people he could count on for support. But he still felt terribly alone.

"Bloodhounds are at my door, Larry," he said. "The media's staked outside my apartment. I need a place to stay, you know, until this thing blows over. Just a day or two at the most."

"Sure. No problem," Larry said. "I'm sure Maggie'll understand."

"Thanks." Jack said. "What's the scoop at the firm?"

The men exchanged glances.

"Come on, you guys. I can take it."

Larry spoke. "Well, Jack, you know, this kind of thing's not exactly going to help the client base."

"It's not doing wonders for me either," Jack said, slamming down his empty mug. He despised the pity in their eyes. "Who's taking over Microtech?"

"Yours truly," Andy said. "What an albatross that piece of shit is. Oh," he continued quickly, "not because of you two. We don't make the facts. We just twist them to our advantage."

It was the Microtech case that had brought Jack and Alison together and would outlive them. A chemical plant in East Boston had spewed out toxic waste into the Mystic River. Contamination had seeped into the soil of the surrounding neighborhood. Cancer rates there were four times the national average. East Boston was a working-class neighborhood of small, peeling clapboard houses around Logan Airport, a filthy, scarred, dark area without hope, until some plaintiffs' lawyer descended with promises of reparation for miseries. The case had been certified as a class-action in federal court. A hectic deposition schedule was set to begin. In the conference room boxes were stuffed with medical histories of the plaintiffs. Jack and Alison pored through the mass of data.

They were at it late one night, about a month after she had arrived. They hadn't spoken at any length except about the case. They sat together at a large conference table, eating pizza. It was her idea to order it. She had gone home to change clothes and picked it up on the way back to the office. Jack tried to concentrate on the work before him, but all he really thought about was how attractive she was.

"Some of this stuff is pretty awful," she said, after what seemed like hours of silence.

"Yeah, I know."

"I mean, these people." She put her pen down and folded her hands together. "Emphysema, heart attacks, cancer. It goes on and on."

"What can you expect living near the airport?" Jack said. "It's not exactly Phoenix."

"Phoenix isn't healthy. It's like L.A. Smog alerts all the time. I read an article about it in the *Times*."

"You know what I mean. You live in industrial areas like that, you're going to get sick."

"Some people don't have a choice."

"Right. Whatever you say."

"You disagree?"

"There are three types of people in this world: those who get it handed to them, those who go out and grab it, and those who sit around blaming other people for their problems. The last category are called plaintiffs."

"Thank you for your analysis, Mr. Reagan. Can we get back to the real world now?"

"Let's cut the politics and get this done, huh?"

"You're not upset, are you?"

"No, just tired. I need a break or a caffeine buzz or something."

"Would you like to take a walk? Stretch the legs? I guess we could call it a night." She stood up and walked to the window. The sky was thick with clouds.

"There's a coffee shop down the block," he said. "We can go there."

"I guess we better," she said.


The Parthenon was an Art Deco diner in the middle of Boylston Street, which had made no accommodation to the latest fashions. Somehow, among the trendy boutiques and specialty shops in the Back Bay, it had survived the gentrificator's wrecking ball. There was never more than a handful of patrons, and the night Jack and Alison went in there were only two. A man in a fedora and raincoat hunched over the counter, flicking his cigarette ashes on a yolk-stained plate. He stared absently at the glass display of pies.

The other customer sat at the far end of the curved Formica counter, close to the street window. She had spiked orange hair and wore green eye shadow, a khaki T-shirt, and a black bomber jacket. She was reading a tattered paperback edition of August Strindberg plays.

"It's like 'Nighthawks,'" Alison said as they approached the counter. "You know, the Hopper painting?"

"I don't know that one."

"No. Do you like art?"

"We barely know each other," Jack muttered and Alison laughed.

Jack bought two coffees and carried them to a booth. "I got it regular," Jack said, sliding the coffee across the table to her. "Hope that's all right."

"Fine."

"God, I'm tired. My eyes are burned out," Jack said.

"Yes, me too. What a way to spend your life. I should've continued my acting."

"Why'd you stop?"

"Reality intruded. I was afraid, I guess. Of failure. Or something. I don't know."

"So, you went to law school?"

"Yes. The last refuge of liberal arts majors. Actually, I fell in love and went to law school."

"Really," Jack said, intrigued and mildly jealous.

"What about you?"

"I haven't been in love, I don't think. Unless sixth grade counts."

"You know what I mean."

"I grew up in South Boston. I went to UMass-Boston. I was a commuter student." Jack recited the basic facts with pride. "Then I went to law school. I didn't aspire to anything else. I don't have other talents. I'm basically a nuts-and-bolts guy."

"You seem to have conceived a great plan for yourself and achieved it," she said. "I've never had a great plan. I've been careening from place to place. Like most people, I don't know what I want. You seem directed. I envy you."

He laughed.

"What's so funny?"

"I envy *you*. Your education. Your . . . something. Freedom."

"It's overrated. You're not trapped. Do you feel trapped?"

"No. I'm content. Really." He ran his hand over the coffee-stained Formica table.

"Good for you," Alison said. "*I* feel trapped. I don't know why I do this."

"I don't want you to get the idea that it's been easy. My father died a couple years back." Jack stopped, wondering why he suddenly blurted the information out. He feared a spoiling of the mood.

"I'm sorry," she said, but he waved her off. "Your family must be proud of you."

"Why, because I'm not a cop or garbage man? We Irish have branched out."

"I didn't mean it like that."

"I know you didn't," he said, reaching over to touch her hand.

"Let's call it a night, okay? I'm beat," she said.

Jack thought he had overstepped some undisclosed boundary. "Can I walk you home?"

"I've always depended on the kindness of strangers," she said in a Southern drawl. "Yes. I'd like that."

They walked to her apartment building on Exeter Street. He waited on the sidewalk in front, watching her climb the steps to the lobby door, where she turned and said, quietly, as if someone were listening in, "Good night." He gave her a wave, his hand cupped like a child's.

Soon they settled into a routine. Late-night coffees and drinks at the Parthenon or at cafés on Newbury Street. During the day, he would sit at his desk, hoping to see her walk by his office. He loved to watch her figure retreat down the hallway, the sway of her hips, the suppleness of her calves and ankles. His fantasies of her were relatively innocent—fervent kisses on the mouth and neck, a gentle caressing of her nyloned thighs while she sat on his desk; vague dreams without possible consummation. He couldn't explain that intense attraction. Why she, of all people, stirred his ardor was a mystery to him.

"So, what you gonna do, Jack?" Drew asked.

"What do you mean?"

"You know, job-wise." Drew was obviously attempting to provoke him. "Have you thought about where you want to work? The market's tight all over."

"That's a little premature, I think. Jack'll be back soon," Larry said.

"Come on, can we be honest? I know, it's not in our blood. I mean, we're all friends here, right? Let's be frank. He's through. We know it. He knows it. Don't you, Jack?"

"Drew, calm down, will you?" Larry said. "This isn't the time."

Drew grunted and walked away.

"Asshole," Andy said to his back.

"What was that all about?" Jack asked. "I never did anything to him."

"There's an impression—I'm not saying it's correct—that you're just getting your comeuppance. That you were arrogant, you know."

"What you talking about? I've never been arrogant in my life. I got shot. How come *I'm* feeling like I did something?"

They ignored his question and began talking about possible firm partnership offers for the coming year. They felt no obligation to include him in the conversation. He was old news.

The next morning Jack awoke on Larry's couch. Maggie Daly, Larry's girlfriend, was doing knee-bends in a purple leotard and matching headband on the living-room rug. She was wearing earphones, a portable radio clasped to her waist. Beads of sweat were in the cleavage of her small, tight breasts. A slight flush of exertion was on her cheeks. Jack had met her a few times before at office functions, but her figure was always hidden beneath an unrevealing dress.

"Did I wake you?" she asked. He sat up tentatively, dizzy from the night's intake. He vaguely remembered dipping into whiskey shots late in the evening.

Maggie removed the earphones, draped them around her neck, and placed her hands on her hips. "Long night, huh? There's some coffee made in the kitchen." She had the discordant cheerfulness of an elementary-school teacher.

"Thanks," Jack said.

"So, Larry told me Drew was a piece of work last night."

Jack caught a hint of her perfume and thought of his own stinking self. He felt as if he were a vagrant who'd been taken in off the street.

"Well, I think it's just awful what happened," she continued. "How's your wound?"

"Oh, it's nothing. Barely a scratch."

"God, watching that tape, I'm amazed you're alive. Oh, I'm sorry. I probably sound like such a jerk. Let me get you some coffee. You take it regular?" The way her hair curled around her chin, the dance in her green eyes, filled him with the dread of desire. He steadied himself and nodded.

On the television screen, the local news began with Wendy Thomas delivering her report. He saw the Public Garden. There he was, with Alison on the bridge. Then the burst of the gun, and he was down. And then she was down, her body enveloped in the jogger's. He could see a close-up of his face, pale with fear, and then the gun falling into the water. Maggie was right. For the first time since the whole episode he thought of how lucky he had been. Until now, he thought he would be better off dead.

"See what I mean?" Maggie said from behind the couch. In her hands she held a cup of coffee and a plate of bagels and cream cheese. She came around and set the display before him on the table. "I thought you'd like something to eat."

"Thanks." Jack smiled. The idea of eating was slightly repugnant, but he knew he should. Where did Larry find such a sweet woman? She went to the television and shut it off.

"Thanks again." Jack spread cream cheese on the bagel. "I'm getting sick of that woman's face."

"Who? Wendy Thomas?"

"Yeah. She's everywhere I turn. She was even at the clinic that day." The bagel tasted wonderfully warm and fresh. He realized he hadn't eaten much in the last few days.

"The clinic where they had that demonstration? You're kidding?"

Jack shook his head.

"She got the video from a man in the Garden," she explained. "The guy who shot it. Her big scoop. You're probably tired of talking about this."

Jack shrugged. "Kind of hard to avoid it."

"I guess. Larry says that's all they talk about at work."

"What else does Larry say?"

"He probably told you. That she was crazy. Stuff like that. How's the bagel?"

"Terrific." He feared she was intentionally avoiding the subject and it filled him with suspicion. Was there something going on that nobody wanted to tell him? Or worse, had the firm ordered them to remain silent?

"Well, I have to get ready for class." He watched her ascend the stairs. "If you need a ride, I'll be heading to B.U."

Jack walked to the picture window at the front of the house. Outside, a light rain fell, placing a thin layer of mist on the sidewalk and the browned grass. He heard the shower upstairs and tried to suppress the image that was forming of Maggie's naked body. The thought made him feel lonely.

He wondered how long he would have to live like this, how long the process would take before his life could return to normal. Or was that impossible now? No. Not if he cooperated. He would head back down to the District Attorney's office and give them his story.

Maggie came bounding down the stairs. Her hair was still wet at the ends. She was wearing an oversized Boston University sweatshirt and faded blue jeans. As she came closer, Jack took in the fresh strawberry scent of her shampoo, a smell that reminded him of Alison.

**16**

They had gone to New York to take a deposition of the plaintiff's expert witness in the Microtech case. "We want her to handle it," Hal had said, in a meeting that infuriated Jack. Her evident prestige and growing reputation in the firm gnawed at him. Still, Alison did have considerable experience in the area, and Jack had yet to conduct a deposition. But he'd drafted all the discovery motions and interrogatories, and he reminded Hal of it. "Exactly the point," Hal said. "You'll both go." Suddenly, Jack's disappointment evaporated. They could develop the further intimacy he sought.

Their weekend in New York began early with a knock at his hotel room door. They had retired to their separate rooms almost immediately after the deposition the night before. Alison was dressed in a peach sweater, blue jeans, and crisp white tennis shoes. This is a woman I could love, he thought.

"Ready to go?" she smiled, impish dimples forming on her cheeks, and walked into his room. He was self-conscious about the unmade bed, his clothes draped on the dresser, his socks a ball on the floor. She parted the drapes to let in the morning light.

Alison planned to see everything—the Museum of Modern Art, Broadway, the Statue of Liberty. She wanted to walk through Central Park, lunch at Tavern on the Green, shop in Greenwich Village. They accomplished it all through a flurry of cab rides and miles of walking. His feet were sore by the end of the day, but they had to get dressed for dinner and the theater. They were to see *Six Degrees of Separation* at Lincoln Center, for she had been in one of John Guare's plays years ago. Jack didn't understand the play, but Alison said it was about alienation and how we all crave connections in an urban world.

After the play, they went to a bar on the Upper East Side, a famous hangout for theater people, according to Alison. Baskets of popcorn, checked tablecloths, candles burning in smoked red glasses. They touched glasses—her vodka and vermouth, his beer—to the successful weekend.

"You never said why you didn't just move here when you got out of college," he said.

"Fear. I was familiar with people in Boston. Thought I could get started, you know, big fish in small pond, get noticed, move on with productions that made it to NYC. But things didn't work out that way, and then I met Jerry.

"He swept me off my feet, like the saying goes. I was stupid. The law sounded good. It would give us something in common. But let's not talk about that. Don't you think it's rude when people talk about their past affairs?"

"It'd be a short conversation with me."

"Yeah, right. A good-looking guy like you."

"Really. I went out with a girl for a while in college, but that's about it."

"I don't believe you. Men are funny. They'll talk to each other about the pussy they've had, then shut up when a woman asks."

"I'm not lying," he said, too forcefully, a bit surprised by her use of the word. "Her name was Roberta. She was the only one." Why am I saying all this? Jack asked himself. He felt foolish.

"I'm sorry. I didn't mean anything by it." She reached across the table and touched his hand. "I guess I'm jaded. Most guys I've dated have been major-league assholes."

"Maybe you've just picked the wrong guys. We're not all bad. I can't imagine anyone being mean to you."

He leaned over and kissed her. She blushed, then ran a finger around the rim of her martini glass. She was quiet for a moment, and he thought he'd upset her.

"I don't understand why you didn't leave Boston," she then said.

"Why would I do that?"

"Most people with the opportunity run away from home, don't you think? I did. I wasn't going to spend my life in Indiana."

"Boston's a big city. I did run away, to a different part of it, a different world. I like Boston."

"Oh, I do, too. It's not New York, but it's not Fort Wayne either. It's obvious I'm there for life."

"I wouldn't want you to leave."

"That's sweet. You know, you've never really told me about your father."

"No, I didn't. There's not much to tell. He's just a guy who didn't know what he wanted. Or he knew, but it's like he had no idea how to get there. Too much of the sauce."

"That's sad."

"It was good he died."

"I didn't mean to get us morose."

"Does that sound bad? I just mean it was good for Mom and me. I never would've made anything of myself, I think, if he was around."

"Parents can fuck you up, can't they?"

"Only if you let them. People are always blaming others for their problems. People are responsible for what they make of themselves. I hate all that crap we hear these days about abuse and alcoholism."

"You don't have much compassion."

He shrugged. "I just don't waste my time feeling sorry for myself. We all have things we could blame people for."

"Even you?" she asked mischievously, but he wouldn't bite at her suggestion.


They went back to her room. She stretched out on the bed, her dress wrapped around her. He sat on a chair with his tie askew. He called room service and ordered a bottle of champagne, and he wondered if he could bill this extravagance to the firm. They toasted their evening together, and he kissed her wet lips.

She slowed him down. "You know, that was a great play. God, I wished I'd become an actress. You can't imagine what it's like to dream about something for so long and know, finally, that you'll never have it."

Her somber tone was unexpected; she had been full of such gaiety only moments before. He was sure he could think of plenty of things he wanted, like her at that moment, and feared he'd never have.

"You look so sad," she said.

"I'm not."

He joined her on the bed, kissing her softly at first, and then smoothing her hair.

"Wait," she said, pushing him lightly on the chest. "I'm not sure I want to do this."

"It's okay," he said. "It'll be all right."

"I don't want to be hurt, that's all."

"Don't worry."

She seemed satisfied with his soothing words. She walked to the bathroom, and shut the door behind her.

He was temporarily stunned by the pace of events, overwhelmed with desire. He felt dizzy and he looked around the room for guidance. Undressing to his underwear, he folded his slacks, tie, and shirt neatly on a chair and crawled underneath the comforter on the bed. She came out of the bathroom wearing only her off-white slip, her nylons a ball in her hand. She smiled with a tight grin that somehow looked sad and pulled the comforter down. While she lay on top of him, he removed the straps of her slip, ran his hand over her shoulder blades and down her arms to the elbows. The skin was soft, smooth, cool. His fingers touched the hint of sweat between her breasts.

"I love you," he said into her matted, wet hair, a grunt barely audible as he entered her. He climaxed quickly. She fell off him and to the side.

Despite the considerable warmth in the room, he felt a chill. He leaned over and kissed her on the forehead and she smiled, gesturing with an extended arm for more champagne. He filled a glass for each of them and sat cross-legged on the bed, while she slid under the bedcovers, covering her breasts. She held the lip of the glass with two hands and took tiny sips. There was an awkward silence. He thought how clumsy and fumbling he must have seemed to her.

"Don't be so hard on yourself," she said, as though reading his thoughts. "You knew this was going to happen, didn't you?"

"What?"

"This."

"I didn't plan it. Really."

It felt sordid and desperate to him, not the magic he expected, not the pleasant intrigue. Maybe it was the alcohol, or that he was disappointed in himself, but he also thought that it was only a beginning, and they could recover.

———

When they got back to the office the following week, he felt he had won a great victory. He had a secret, but it wasn't really a secret. Everyone in their litigation group seemed aware that something had happened on their trip. How did they know? he wondered. Did his features betray him?

In meetings, there was a palpable sense that everybody was talking behind their backs, but Jack was only indirectly approached on the issue. Andy and Drew would linger a few extra minutes in his office, as if expecting him to offer comments. They even prompted him to discuss Alison by mentioning her work on a case or how good she looked in an outfit. Jack was nonresponsive at first, but still he knew they knew.

The official "coming out" party, as Alison termed it, was the Barristers' Ball, an annual charity event sponsored by the Boston Bar Association. The chosen charity of the season was the Coalition for the Homeless.

This was Jack's third appearance at the ball. On previous occasions, he had made small talk with fellow single attorneys, sucking down plenty of scotch and regretting his loose tongue by the next morning. Even though he had reached a measure of success with Adelman and Kaplan, he still felt inadequate. He didn't share an eating club experience at Princeton, the rugby games at Yale, the great law professors at Harvard. Alison was part of that elite. She told him he overestimated the differences. One little SAT score was all it really was, she said. But he knew differently. You were set for life with a degree from those places.

The Barristers' Ball was held in the Copley Plaza Hotel. The firm had booked several tables at fifty dollars a head, all for charity, and thus deductible. How different the female attorneys looked, made up, with more jewelry, carefully tended hair. To Jack the air was rife with the sexuality of the well-off.

As Andy said to Jack, when he came to the cash bar, the usual suspects had arrived: Drew's wife, Mona, a pale blonde with muscular legs; Mary, in a simple but expensive blue dress; her fiancé, Bob, an accountant from Worcester; and Maggie and Larry, the perfect couple, playfully affectionate.

"Where's your date, Romeo?" Jack asked, ordering a Heineken for himself and a white wine spritzer for Alison. Andy had been lately seen in the presence of Cathy Yates, a word processor in the firm.

"I'm here stag. You think I'm going to bring *her* here? You think I'm a sadist? You might get away with your little fling, but my reputation'd be dog meat."

"Everybody knows anyway."

"Everybody doesn't know shit. I'm discreet."

Alison was wearing a black velvet dress with silver buttons. She sat next to Bob, her hand on her jaw, index finger on her cheek. Bob spoke about the new house in Worcester that he and Mary planned to purchase. He described the square footage, the expansive backyard with tall shade trees.

"Thanks," Alison said when Jack brought the drink. She swiftly downed half of it. "I'm parched," she said to Bob, a nondrinker.

A pall hung over the table. The unthinkable was occurring: Lawyers were being laid off at firms throughout the city. There were rumors of potential mergers between firms, Chapter 11 bankruptcies, young attorneys taking work at paltry salaries. Jack thought it a bit melodramatic. He didn't feel threatened.

"It's just deadwood they're getting out," he said. "Overexpansion in the early eighties. These salaries are ridiculous. A family in Southie could live like kings on the dough first-years are getting."

"Jack's just pissed they gave him the B.C. salary range."

"Just be happy they don't pay *you* what you're worth, Drew," Alison said.

"Ouch!"

"I understand you transferred from Washington," Mona said to Alison. "I have friends who live in Alexandria. They have a fabulous place."

"I bet they do."

"How's business, Mona?" Jack asked quickly. Mona was an interior designer.

"Overwhelming. Too much on my plate these days."

"Maybe she should put some of it on her bones," Alison whispered in Jack's ear.

"Look, guys," Drew said. "It's Carole with her latest hubby. Number three or four, I believe, but who's counting."

"*She's* not," Andy said. "Some partner at Davis and Snow. I hear he's heir to a fortune from a clothing store in Chicago."

"How'd it go in New York?" Drew asked Jack. "We haven't heard."

"Alison was awesome. At the deposition, I mean. We kicked some serious ass. They'll fold. Right?"

"We did okay."

"Oh, she's being modest. You should've seen her slicing up that guy. I thought opposing counsel was going to burst a vein in there."

"He exaggerates," Alison said. "I think he was just constipated."

"Don't you guys ever talk about anything but work?" Mona asked.

"All *she* wants to talk about is shopping," Drew said. "Furnishings. Swaths. Wallpaper."

"Let's get another drink," Jack said, standing up and pulling out Alison's chair. They headed for the bar.

"He says such awful things about his wife," Alison said.

"I tune him out."

"He's too obnoxious to tune out. Even Andy's better. The way he talks to her."

"She's a big girl. I'm not gonna feel sorry for some rich bitch who marries him. And I don't like arguing in public."

"It's not my favorite indoor sport either."

"Then let's not argue. Did I tell you how great you look in black?"

"Yes, but you can tell me again," she said. "You should see my underwear."


After dinner was served, they danced. A jazz band on a raised stage played the standards.

"I haven't danced since the prom," Jack said as Alison led him to the floor.

"I thought you told me there was only that Roberta girl?"

"I said relationship. Prom was high school. I barely touched *her.*"

"I wasn't accusing you of anything," Alison said. "Come on, I love this song."

They danced slowly in short circles around the crowded floor. One of Jack's hands was on her back, the other around her waist. During the dance she locked her arms behind his neck. She was light in his arms, and he was reminded how delicate and lithe her figure was. He liked the way she had to tip her face up to talk to him. As the dance concluded, he kissed her lightly.

"We can do better than that," she said, holding the sides of his face and giving him a full kiss on the lips.

They held hands while they headed back to the table, which was now half-empty, topped with wrinkled napkins, water glasses, wineglasses, coffee cups, and bottles of beer. Drew and Andy were talking seriously behind the table. Mona came up to them, apparently from the bathroom. She looked unnaturally pale, grim-faced. She touched Drew on the shoulders, and they quickly said their good-byes.

"Morning sickness," Andy said to Jack and Alison as they left the room.

"He's propagating the species?" Alison said.

"Yes," Andy said. "Sick thought, isn't it?"

"How far's she along?"

"I don't know. She's not showing, that's for sure. She's still anorexic."

The band was breaking up, and the crowd milled around in various degrees of departure. Jack, Andy, and Alison walked out to the lobby, and waited while Alison made a final stop in the bathroom.

"She looks great," Andy said. "What's she like in the sack?"

"I take the Fifth."

"C'mon, Jack."

"You're out of line."

"Must be serious."

He realized that it was.

n the third floor of the Suffolk County District Attorney's office, Hurley and three of his assistants were in his office. These meetings were a weekly ritual, and the assistants enjoyed Hurley's florid language, the wild gesticulations of his arms, his bulging eyes, the way he pulled on his thinning hair and shook his hands in a rage. According to his office mates, there was no better free entertainment in town.

"Sometimes it's just a matter of breaks," Hurley said. "Defendants are stupid people generally. The anonymous tip. The observant bystander. Like the Walden case. This crazy Thoreau-reading defendant, Guy Borby, who kills his girlfriend and decides to dump her in Walden Pond in homage to his hero. Well, he gets choked up with emotion. He's got this girl in the trunk, and he goes up to where the cottage is. You know, where Thoreau built his cabin?

"On the site now are only stones. So, Borby leaves the victim in the car and goes to pray at the shrine. He claims Thoreau told him to confess. He finds some park ranger who's giving a little tour and pours his guts out to him. So, what you think happens? Slam dunk. Piece of cake, right? No way. Not in the great US of A. Not in this haven for wackos, deviants, and murderers. I'll tell you what happens. At trial, Borby claims insanity. He gets the nuthouse, but then he offs himself with his bedsheets. That's justice." He paused. "You gotta have a morbid sense of humor in this business."

"Jack Donnelly's here to see you," Hurley's secretary said from the doorway as his assistants left the office.

"Well, well, the victim's had a change of heart. Bring him in."

"Mr. Donnelly," Hurley said when Jack entered. "How can we help you?"

"I wasn't sure who I should see about my testimony. You're the lawyer. You'll be trying it, right?" Hurley gave a perfunctory nod. "Sorry about my attitude before. I guess I was still in shock or something."

"Understandable. We were all a little on edge."

"It's just that I'm not that comfortable talking about my private life in public. But I guess it's inevitable with this press coverage and the video. I want to tell the truth, my side of the story. Where do I begin?"

"Wherever. What's on your mind? We'll get into the details later. In your own words."

On the way over, Jack thought of what he could comfortably say. With each step, his anger built. That conniving bitch. Someone had to know how it really was.

"I felt a sick, warm emptiness when the shot hit me. Blood. I could feel it on my hands. My own blood. It was all very fuzzy, and I could see Alison underneath some guy, and I didn't know what was going on. We were just standing talking at the bridge, and she said something like 'Remember the swan boats,' and then I saw the shiny metal, and I thought it was a joke. You see, I always told her we'd ride the swan boats, and we never did for some reason. Every time we thought of it the weather was bad or something else came up. So I just was going to give her a hug because I knew how sad things were. After all, she had an abortion. It was over between us, but it didn't mean I couldn't feel for her. I didn't hate her. I just wanted her to go away. Maybe that's why she did it. Shot me."

"Is that what you really think?" Hurley said, assessing Jack's credibility. He certainly didn't look like a liar. He could be a good witness.

"I don't know. She *was* kind of screwed up in the head. I knew that, everyone told me. But at first I thought that she was no crazier than most people. Then, as time went on, she acted like she was abused or something. She was paranoid. She thought everyone hated her. She was probably right, but she gave them no reason to like her. She was not friendly or anything. Everyone thought she was a cold bitch.

"I don't think there's anything I could've done to prevent it.

I went to the clinic with her. I offered to pay. I didn't want to go, but I felt like I should. It's the least I could do. She said that once. That I always did the least. We weren't in love or anything, so what was the big deal? We're grown-ups. Or I thought so. I took responsibility for the pregnancy, but I'm not responsible for things I'm not to blame for. It's not my fault what guys came before me or her bad childhood."

Jack stopped, out of breath.

"Then you're saying she gave you no warning?"

"No. Well, I knew she was upset about being pregnant. She had these violent mood swings. One minute she wants to be close, wants to have sex, the next she's angry, cussing about some guy in the past who burned her. She wasn't generally a happy person."

"She always like that?"

"No, of course not. Not in the beginning. I mean, I wouldn't have been interested in her if she was like that then."

"How long did you two go out?"

"I guess it depends when you start counting. Let's see, I met her in March, so about six months. I can't remember now *why*, but it seemed like a good idea at the time. It was kind of an accident. We were working on a case together and spent a lot of hours working late."

Jack shifted in the chair. He couldn't tell Hurley that sometimes you want something so badly you can't remember why you wanted it. Then when you get it, you don't want it anymore.

"I know these are personal matters," Hurley said. "I just have to know ahead of time. I have to anticipate any possible defenses."

"What kind of defense can there be?"

"We don't know. You'd be surprised what they come up with. Battered woman's syndrome—"

"I *never* hit her!"

"Okay. Okay. I'm not accusing you of anything." This guy's never going to survive cross-examination, Hurley thought. "You're a Southie boy, Donnelly. I'm Dorchester, born and raised. Let's be honest. The world's not like the way we grew up. Whether that's a good or bad thing, I'm not here to argue. It's just different. We got two things here that we got to contend with. One, the law favors criminals. Two, criminals are people who can't take personal responsibility. We're not talking a Catholic conscience here. It's not what Father Whoever told you. Everybody's got a defense. Everybody's got an excuse. See what I mean? Know what I'm getting at?"

"You think there's something I know I'm not telling you. And I'm telling you I didn't do *anything* to deserve this."

"I believe you. I just don't want to be back-doored. Sometimes witnesses don't realize what's important. Things get magnified in court. You're under a microscope. Things *appear* different. That's all."

"Maybe she just snapped," Jack said.

"Snapped, huh?" Jack noticed the hint of skepticism in Hurley's voice. "Did she ever exhibit any behavior that made you think she might be unbalanced?"

"Yes. There were times when she'd become strange. Not insane or really physically violent or anything. Just—well, you know how women are—overly sensitive to things. We'd have fights because she thought I was ignoring her. Which I guess I was, but you know, there's no easy way to end these things. You always look bad in the end."

"Why'd you want to break up with her?"

"I don't know. I just did. It's like I said before, she was annoying. I wasn't getting any pleasure out of it."

Jack stopped briefly, fearful that he was treading into dangerous territory. He was unwilling to articulate the real reason, that he saw his whole life disintegrating when Alison said she was pregnant. He looked at Hurley and thought he would have as much understanding as a celibate priest in the confessional. Some things, he said to himself, you just can't explain.

His face was apparently betraying his thoughts.

"No one wants to talk about this stuff," Hurley said. "All witnesses, especially victims, hate having to reveal intimate details. You're resentful. You think, 'I'm the one who got shot and my life's on the line.' Well, that's just the way it is.

"Anyway, all this might be moot. The video might make her plead guilty. But first things first." Hurley stood and walked to the window. "We're taking the case to the grand jury next week. I'll need you to testify. It's no big deal. I'll just ask you questions. Sometimes the grand jurors will ask you something, but not often. We'll talk again before you go in."

Jack stood up, realizing the meeting was over. "I want to thank you for coming by," Hurley said, leading him out of the office. "I know it wasn't easy. We'll make it as painless as possible."

18

At the intersection of Newbury and Exeter Streets, the apartment facades were refurbished Victorian with wrought-iron railings, bowed fronts, bay windows, and mansard roofs. Below the apartments were assorted shops: a beauty salon, an ice cream parlor, small galleries displaying the work of local artists, ethnic restaurants of great variety—Chinese, Indian, Moroccan. From his vantage point on the stoop in front of his sister's building, Peter felt nostalgic for his days in Boston. Then he remembered the pain of living here.

An urgent phone call from his mother came while the guests at his bed and breakfast were sipping coffee in the main anteroom. Her clear, unaffected voice was an instant signal to him that a matter of grave importance was about to be revealed. Mother was always charged with the difficult duties. Peter could see his father sitting in his armchair in the background.

The first question that Peter asked when his mother mentioned the videotape was "Since when do you watch television?" It was at someone else's house, he learned. They were at a faculty party. "Can you imagine, Peter? Hearing our daughter's name. A criminal." His mother's ability to contain her emotions could sometimes seem an admirable quality, but at moments like these, she appeared brutal. "Your father's mortified. Alison won't answer her phone. What's going on?"

Peter was sent to find out. He drove down to Boston, but when he arrived around eleven-thirty, Alison was out. So he sat on the porch steps of her building, sipping coffee until an hour and a half later, when she returned.

"Alison," he said, standing as she approached. She was startled, and folded her hands to her chest. He hugged her softly. She clung to him, clumping parts of his shirt in balled fists.

"What are you doing here?" she said, taking her keys from her purse as they climbed the steps.

"Mom called."

"Is everything all right?"

"I'm here about you. The shooting."

"You read it in the papers?"

"No. Mom saw it on TV."

"Shit. It was picked up nationally?"

He shrugged. "You got to admit it's dramatic. How often do you have a video of a shooting?"

"What the hell are you talking about?"

"You haven't seen it?"

"Seen what?" she asked, her voice pitched.

"Some guy recorded it. You on the bridge and everything."

"Hah," Alison said, and began to laugh. They entered the lobby and climbed the stairs to her third-floor apartment.

"Oh, God, Peter," she sighed. "I've really fucked up this time." She poured them each a glass of wine and gulped hers down. "I thought I really had things together. What are you going to tell them?"

"Who?"

"Mom and Dad. They must be freaked out."

"What do you want me to tell them? You have a lawyer?"

"Oh, yes. I'm not so crazy I didn't remember that. She's got a good reputation, although I don't know how she's going to defend me."

"I'll say—to them—that you're taking care of things. They'd probably come here if you wanted."

"I don't want them here. You tell them that. Tell them it won't help things."

"Okay," he said. "Why don't *you* come to the Cape for a while? Get away from this. Escape from the media."

"Yeah. Their latest femme fatale. They love stories like this. Women are shot, beaten, abused every day, it's barely a blip on the screen. What they like is a Lizzie Borden."

"You'll love the place. We'll give you scrumptious meals. A great view of the water."

"I must admit it sounds inviting. Clear my head, for God's sake."

"You'll do it, then?"

"I got to check with Lee, my lawyer."

"You need permission from your lawyer?"

"I'm out on bail. Maybe I can leave her a voice mail."

They finished their glasses of wine. For the first time since the ordeal began, she had a sense of calm. With Peter she didn't feel strained or the burdens of masquerading.

"I think I'd better stay. There's probably going to be court appearances and meetings."

"I understand. I'm just worried about you."

"You think I'm going to do something rash? If men weren't such shits, none of this would've happened." She rose from the couch. "Straight men, I mean."

In the kitchen, she stood at the sink, convulsed with some nervous turmoil she couldn't pinpoint. She began to cry, the tears dripping into the drain. She turned the faucet on, hoping to keep Peter from hearing. The effort of restraining the tears constricted her throat, and she gagged.

"Are you all right?" Peter asked from the alcove.

"I'm fine."

"You've been through a lot," Peter said. It occurred to him that they had yet to discuss any of the facts of the shooting. She had not even mentioned the abortion.

"You want to go out for a drink? How about My Apartment? Is it still around?"

"Far as I know. It's been months. Jack and I never went there. He liked his bars dark and dingy. Let me change. Don't give me that look. It'll only take a sec."


My Apartment was located on the ground floor of a grimy sandstone building on Commonwealth Avenue in Brighton. Peter and Alison picked up their drinks at the bar counter and found an open couch against the wall. They sat in silence for a while, Peter's legs crossed, a menthol cigarette resting in the tips of his fingers. He sipped his Heineken.

"You playing anymore?" Alison asked.

"Oh, piano." He waved a dismissive hand. "The family always

overestimated my ability. I play a little. Pick-ups in bars late at night. It doesn't occupy me."

"Whatever happened to us? What's with this family that we are compelled to piss away our talent?"

"You're being melodramatic."

From across the room, they both noticed a group of people huddled on a couch, staring at them. A woman stood up, teetering on three-inch black heels, smoothing her rumpled skirt. One of the men pushed her from behind. She walked toward Alison and Peter.

"What do you think this is about?" Alison asked.

"I don't think she's going to ask for a match. I'm afraid she's going to fall on her face."

The woman stopped in front of them. "Excuse me," she started haltingly. "Me and my friends were wondering. Are you the lady who shot her boyfriend? The one on the video?"

"Yes," Alison said without hesitation.

But the woman was already gone, walking back to her friends. "See, I told you. I knew it was her," Alison heard her say.

"I'm going to have to be thick-skinned about this," Alison said. "It's in the papers. What am I going to do, hide in a cave till it's over?"

"You sound like you actually enjoy it."

"I wouldn't go that far. I'm just not going to get rattled about it. You want to be my publicist? Oh, come on," she added, reacting to the alarm in his face. "I'm kidding."

**19**

Brian munched another bread stick from the wicker basket on his table and took a sip from his Sam Adams. He was in Michael's, a seafood place on the waterfront.

He'd always thought there was some unconscious motivation in people who were chronically late, perhaps an expression of power, but he sensed none of that in Lee. The explanation in her case was less sinister: She packed her days with events—court appearances, client meetings, and community activities. She was, he thought, a member of every conceivable group, from the symphony orchestra to the various legal causes she felt some affinity with—the Gay and Lesbian Alliance, the Women's Bar Association, National Abortion Rights, the Alliance for Criminal Justice. She had no time to organize her life or to realize it was impossible to maintain such a schedule.

Besides, Brian had no compelling reason to complain. He wasn't working on anything in particular. He had no deadline to pursue. In fact, he was searching for his next subject.

"Hi, stranger," Lee said, breathless, as she plopped on the chair across from him. "Did you order yet?" She opened her menu. "Don't give me that pout. I'm always late."

"I'm not pouting. I just hate when you get too involved in cases. I never see you."

"This is the noncommittal relationship, remember? No pressure on anybody. I spread myself too thin, that's all."

"I'm honored, really, that you could squeeze me in."

She ordered a scotch and soda and a salad. He asked for a refill on the beer and an order of calamari.

"Is that all you're having?" she asked.

"I'm watching my figure. I must've had a loaf of bread."

"That damn Hurley won't return my calls. Word of mouth is they're going to indict. The guy's a true pig. A cheap pol. Ego the size of a Mack truck."

"Tell me what you really think."

She took a sip of water.

"Lee," he said finally, unable to retain the information.

"What?"

"You haven't seen the tape, have you?"

"Tape of what?"

"Some guy taped the shooting."

"What?" She set down her glass. Her drink and salad were delivered by the waiter.

"Yeah, some guy had a camcorder in the garden and filmed the whole thing."

"Who's your source?" she asked quickly.

"Source? The damn TV. They showed it on the news."

"You're kidding me. It was on TV?"

"Yep. Even the networks picked it up."

"Holy shit. What was your reaction when you saw it?"

"A powerful piece. It's going to take lots of explaining."

"Well, the defense is not that she didn't do it."

"I'm not a legal expert, but Hurley's probably licking his chops. She doesn't look like a victim in that video, I'll tell you. He does."

"The sonuvabitch must've leaked it. I'm going to get this case moved."

"The reporter, that Wendy Thomas on Channel Four, said the guy who took it gave it to her."

"I'm sure. After some gentle prodding from the D.A.'s office."

She was clearly agitated by the news. It occurred to Brian that the only interruption they ever had from the barrage of law, all the interminable discussions on procedure, judges, D.A.s, was during sex. And, even then, after they were done, she'd be off on another riff. He sighed, exasperated by the torrent he'd unleashed.

She tossed her napkin on the table. "I better call my machine. Alison's probably panicked." Then she was quickly off, in search of a pay phone.

"No message. No answer," Lee said when she returned. "What the hell am I going to do for her?"

"Let's discuss it."

"You don't mind?"

"What are friends for?" He smiled. "I've been through this before. What's the major problem with the case?"

"Only the facts. You can't generate sympathy for someone who tries to kill somebody without any apparent reason. Looking at it from any angle, it's a loser. Now a videotape. I've got to work on an approach. She needs my help."

"You like her now?"

"You know how I get. I put myself in her shoes. She was a newcomer, an outsider, at the firm. The associates were jealous. Don't let anybody tell you it's still not difficult being a woman in the law. It's no different from when I was coming up. You won't understand. You're sensitive enough, but it's not something you'll experience."

"I'm offended."

"Don't be. Look, who was going to suffer in the firm if their relationship fell apart when she got pregnant? Jack? Give me a break. Not him. The man is never to blame. And another thing. Alison's a romantic. She believed in him. She *wanted* to believe in him. He used her. I can see how hurt she was. I've been burned a few times myself. I know that helpless feeling."

"But shooting him? That's quite a step."

"I know. It's a fine line between the ones who just stay angry and the ones who snap. She snapped. She obviously didn't mean to kill him. She easily could have on that bridge."

"Sounds like you're working up a defense."

"Maybe. I have to do something. I can't let her lose. If I had it in my power, I'd put *him* behind bars."

# 20

That night, Lee sat on her couch, dressed in a gray sweatsuit. Strewn beside her on the couch and on the coffee table were papers, note cards, transcripts of a trial. She was working on an appeal before the Supreme Judicial Court. Spencer Coleman, a black teenager from the Roxbury projects, had been convicted in the drive-by shooting of a four-year-old, and Lee had been appointed to represent him on appeal. It was a task with little promise of success. Coleman had confessed to the shooting after a five-hour interrogation by Boston police. Her only hope was to find some way to knock out the confession.

She sipped from a mug of tea. It had been a cold October day, and she was chilled now. Her feet were wrapped in thick wool socks. Old habits die hard. Although she had gained some measure of financial stability, she still maintained the routines of the poorly paid public defender. She turned the heat on in her apartment only during the coldest winter days.

Lee knew she was overextended with work. A handful of criminal appeals, pending employment discrimination suits that had lain dormant and were reaching the deposition stage, and the Moore case, for which, if it was going to trial, she needed to gear up—prepare witness interviews, map out a strategy.

She switched on the eleven o'clock news. Channel 4's original airing of the videotape meant it had a vested interest in follow-up stories. Nightly, the station reported on the case, even if there was nothing new to relate. They had sent an investigative team back to Indiana to do a profile of Alison's hometown. Alison was portrayed as a troubled outsider, a drifter. This contrasted with the stories on Jack—his working-class childhood in South Boston, his thirst for education, his climb up the ladder at the law firm. Lee was frustrated and angered by these stories. It was typical of the media to reduce complex cases into neat, explainable dichotomies. But she watched anyway. This was a battle of public perceptions. No word had come out of the D.A.'s office, but an indictment was imminent.

Wendy Thomas was on the screen standing outside the Middlesex County courthouse. She had turned the abortion rights controversy into her personal beat. Behind her a group of pro-lifers with cardboard signs were chanting slogans. Members of the Pro-Life League had been arrested for violating a restraining order by trespassing at a clinic. Those charged had appeared in court and refused to give their names to the judge. The judge had them locked up.

The camera panned to a small gathering of reporters around Karen Hill, the woman the press consulted for the pro-life reaction to the latest Supreme Court case or legislative enactment.

"There are many victims of this crime against the unborn and against nature," Karen said. "Not only the unborn children murdered every day in this state, but the women and girls who think they have no choice. Women like Alison Moore." Lee sat up on her couch and increased the volume. "She is just another victim of the anti-family, anti-children, anti-life forces on the rise in this state. She exhibited all the symptoms of post-abortion stress syndrome."

Wendy Thomas interrupted. "Massachusetts Women for Choice issued a brief statement in response to Ms. Hill's comments: 'Ms. Moore's case is an example of why safe abortion is necessary. She was in an unstable relationship. The baby was unwanted by its father. It is shameful how these anti-choice groups use their propaganda to exploit an individual human tragedy. Ms. Moore is merely a pawn in their cruel games.' Clearly, the debate over Alison Moore's motivation for the shooting has just begun. Wendy Thomas, News Four."

They all wanted Alison to be a victim, Lee thought. Alison herself wanted to be a victim. Lee realized it was the only way to save her. But a victim of what? She switched off the television and set Coleman's transcripts aside.

Tea mug in hand, she went to her study and flipped the light switch. She was looking for the article Brian had written on the pro-life movement. She decided to call him.

"Are you awake?"

"Howdy, stranger. Yeah. Just watching the news. You see the story on Four?"

"It's why I'm calling. That man you interviewed about post-abortion syndrome. What are his credentials?"

"You interested in that now?"

"I'm exploring it."

"You certainly got a hot one here. National press. Feeding frenzy."

"It's only going to get worse."

"Come on, you've never shunned the limelight."

"It's out of control," she said wearily.

"That's only because you haven't decided how to approach it. Face it, this case is really insignificant. A little nick in the arm. But it's got its own engine. People love it when women strike back. It's the fear of all American males: rampaging female hormones."

"Sounds like you're working up a thesis." Sometimes she tired of Brian's dissections of society. He tried too hard. "What's the guy's name?"

"Henry Sutherland. Ph.D. in psychology from B.U. Works out of this house in Somerville. You want me to set up a meeting?"

"No, I'll do it," she said. "I'm going to check him out further. I'll keep you informed, but I'll decide what and when."

"Understood. Let me ask you, do you really think you can turn this into a referendum on abortion?"

"I don't intend to. I'm just exploring my options."

In fact, Lee was uncertain in what direction she was heading. She couldn't see herself arguing plausibly that the stress of the abortion had caused the shooting. She wanted the focus to be on the accumulation of events in Alison's life, how her relationship with Jack caused her emotional trauma. The facts to support her defense were not in her hands; she didn't even know if they existed.

**21**

ay was ecstatic. Over the last several days, his video had been broadcast nationally by Brokaw, Rather, and Jennings. Always, there was a flicker of the date and time in the corner of the video captured by him, Ray Ballard. The only downside was Wendy. No calls. No thank-you note. Nothing. Typical ungrateful broad.

But why dwell on the negative? This was his big break. He could envision the day when dishwashing would not be a means for him to make money, but a fit subject for a documentary. Maybe he could revitalize the old WPA method—Walker Evans and James Agee among the Alabama sharecroppers. He would do the kitchens of Boston—the illegals from Mexico and Ireland scrubbing grimy plates in cafés and restaurants for the privileged and bohemian. But he was getting ahead of himself. Bask in the celebrity, Ray.

He was sitting alone at a table at the Blackstone House, listening to poetry readings. Over there was Natalie Goodman, with bleached white hair above her ears, wearing a black turtleneck. She was an artist of the neo-Expressionist mode—garish paintings of disease and plague, the ravages of AIDS. He'd seen some of Nat's work at a gallery on Newbury Street. Too derivative of Munch, he thought, but impressive nonetheless. She was a little too grim for his taste, with her long painted nails and pale face, which was now buried in a cup of cappuccino. He walked over to her table.

"Nat," he said.

"Ray," she said. Without asking, he took a seat; she frowned.

"You seen my piece on TV?"

"*Please*, Ray. TV?"

"Oh, I forgot. No pop culture for you."

"I *read* about it. You a crime-stopper now, agent for the fascist state?"

"You're just jealous," he said. He lit a Camel. "Video's the cutting edge. You still at the frame shop?"

"Better than dishpan hands." She glowered at him. "I know people who know that woman. The woman who shot the guy."

"Yeah, like who?"

"She used to live with this girl I went to art school with. Real butch chick. And see that guy over there? Garrett Walker. She was in a couple of his productions."

Garrett's table was busy. A mix of patrons came by to greet him, as they would a mafia don. A red beret was pushed back on his head. He had a thin mustache and closely cropped brown hair.

"I pegged her for the bohemian type," Ray said. "Real granola. What she'd be doing as a lawyer I don't understand."

Nat shrugged. "No balls."

"That's everybody's problem," he said. "I feel sorry for her."

The poet onstage was replaced by a wispy woman with stringy blond hair, a purple dress, and black patent-leather shoes. She began to sing "My Funny Valentine."

"Interesting talent here tonight," Ray said, but Nat was whispering to a young boy in a white T-shirt and khaki fatigue pants.

"You're Ray Ballard, right?" the boy said with an eager smile. "The video guy."

"Yeah," Ray said. "What of it?"

"Mr. Walker, Garrett, would like to have a word with you if he may."

"Why doesn't he come to me?"

"You have to kiss some ass sometimes, Ray," Nat said.

"Okay, I'll see him. But I only got a few minutes."

He walked with the boy over to Garrett's table. When he got there, the boy disappeared.

"Ray Ballard. I'm Garrett Walker."

"What can I do for you, Mr. Walker?"

"Sit down. Can I get you something to drink?"

Ray took a seat and ordered an espresso. Garrett was nursing a glass of red wine. "As you may or may not know, I'm a theater director."

"I'm familiar with your work." Ray was conscious of a caffeine buzz that was aggravated by his genuine thrill to be in such company. His public exposure was working! He could have languished for years without even a glance from the likes of Walker.

"I'm planning a multimedia production on the Public Garden shooting. Alison and I have worked together in the past. It's in the early-development stages. In fact, if you could keep this in the family, I'd appreciate it."

"Sure," Ray said. "Sure. I understand."

"Where you come in is on that video of yours. I saw it on the TV." He flicked a long ash in the tray. "What exactly is the status of your rights to the video at the present time?"

"Rights? It's mine."

"Yeah, but what's your arrangement with the TV station? They may have an interest."

"I'm not worried about that. Me and Wendy—you know, the reporter—we're tight. We're close. She's not going to screw me on the video. We have no formal agreement. I just gave it to her in exchange for the publicity or rather, you know, my public spiritedness. I felt I owed it to the justice system."

"Uh-huh," Garrett said. "How noble of you. But really, Ray, what do you say we discuss terms ourselves? I have to admit it's an intriguing little piece of work, for its documentary value alone. It's not often we have actual footage of a crime in action."

"You really think it's something? I got plenty of others that are better."

"I'm only interested in that one specifically for my production. It's usually not my sort of thing. Artistically, I find the video age a disturbing trend. To each his own, though. So, you think you'd be interested in helping us out on the production?"

"Yeah, sure. No problem."

"We'll keep in touch. A lot depends on how the legal process works itself out. Right now she looks cooked, wouldn't you say? Don't get me wrong. I feel for her. I'm sure she had her reasons. I'm only saying it would affect the production, how things turn out."

"Anything can happen," Ray said. "The system sucks. Anything can happen."

"Yeah, well. We'll see. Nice talking to you, Ray."

"You need a phone number or something? How will you reach me?"

"You're working at Von's, right?"

"Yeah, but it's not like I'm gonna be there *forever*."

"When I need to find you, I will."

ell, folks, they're baaack!" Barry Lindstrom's nasal voice, laced with sarcasm and unremitting anger, blared from Jack's bedstand clock radio. "Just when you thought it was safe to read your paper and watch your TV, the libbers and other assorted wackos are out again. They've come out of their cave to give us some more of their crap. And who is the victim of the week? The poor girl who killed her baby and shot her boyfriend, that's who. Some spoiled yuppie! Boo-hoo, I'm crying crocodile tears here. Can you believe this? Tell me what you think. Talk to me about the Public Garden shooting. What does it mean? Why do we care? Don't we have better things to think about? This is the Night Owl. Two-two-three-WNCU."

It was two-thirty in the morning and Jack was sitting up in bed, drinking a Budweiser.

"Kevin from Brockton, you got the Night Owl."

"Yeah, Barry, um, I just want to say right on, man. Girls think they can get away with murder these days. They should fry her."

Jack was more entangled with Alison than ever. She was there every day, everywhere he turned. Jack's mother had called earlier from the Stop & Shop. She told him reporters had been poking around in the neighborhood. You fuck them, they think they own a piece of you, Jack thought. What was it Alison said? "You can't get around the fact that it's essentially an act of violence, a penetration." It seemed as though a violent penetration was happening to him.

He would have to remember key moments in their relationship, testify to the facts, as Hurley said. Jack replayed them in his mind. The most vivid was when he saw her at her apartment for the last time. He continually went over that episode. It was his crucial mistake. Maybe she already knew she was pregnant, and he had sparked some hope in her that night. Still, how could he have foreseen what she would do?

"From a car phone in Brookline, Sid."

"What ever happened to the presumption of innocence, Lindstrom? Why don't you go to Russia, where you belong?"

"Oh, listen to this folks, Mr. BMW, cruising around. Innocence? She's not innocent, pal. Witnesses saw her shoot the poor guy. It's all on video. You blind?"

"But you don't know the truth. You don't know why she did it."

"No, friend, we don't. If she wants to kill people, maybe we should just send her to the Middle East."

That final night Jack had been sitting at an outside table at Salty Dog in Quincy Market with a few new associates. It was a muggy August night. Alison walked by. She was with Garrett, the theater director she'd introduced him to at that weird play they'd seen in Cambridge about two guys waiting for Godot. Jack wondered if there had once been something between Garrett and Alison. Now, here they were.

A feeling of possessiveness and jealousy flushed warmly to his cheeks, but he resisted the temptation to call out her name. He watched them for any signs of familiarity, an arm around her shoulders, an intimacy of conversation.

He had no grounds for this concern. In fact, he'd distanced himself emotionally from her, but he was not ready to see her with another man, as if it were her idea to end it.

He walked up to them while they were looking into a shop window. Alison turned when she saw his reflection. She was momentarily startled, blushed, then recovered her composure.

"Jack. You remember Garrett."

"What are you doing?" Jack asked.

Garrett walked away, giving them privacy.

"What do you mean?"

"Is this your new boyfriend?"

"You care?"

"Give me a break. What's going on with us?"

"You tell me." She bit her lip. "You've been ignoring me. When's the last time we even had lunch?"

"I've been busy."

"Don't give me that. People find time if they want to."

"You're sleeping with him, aren't you?"

"You asshole."

She tried to move away from him, but he grabbed her arm.

"Let go of me. You don't own me."

He glared at her, tightening his grip on her forearm. She winced. "You're hurting me." He released her. She went over to Garrett.

"Alison," Jack yelled. "Come back here." But she turned the corner at the end of the shopping area. He decided not to pursue her further.


He stopped on the way home for a nightcap. He was mildly drunk and restless with desire. He missed sex with her. He wanted that back. After two beers, he started home. On a street corner, a man stood in a gray T-shirt, selling single red roses out of a white plastic bucket. Jack bought one, then flagged down a cab and was dropped off in front of Alison's building.

He rang the buzzer a half dozen times before she answered. "It's me. I came to apologize." There was no response immediately, and he feared rejection, but she let him in.

When she opened the door, he thrust the rose across the threshold. She took it with a weak smile. She was dressed in a sheer silk robe that revealed the cleavage to her small breasts. She opened the door and he walked in.

"Your love is like a dying rose," she said. The couch was piled with work—a bound deposition transcript and legal pads. On the table was a half-empty glass of wine. She walked to the kitchen and returned with a vase of water with the rose inside. He walked up behind her and hugged her at the waist, nuzzling his face in her neck. "I'm sorry about tonight," he whispered in her ear.

She wriggled free. "You're drunk."

"Yeah, but I'm sincere." He smiled. In the pale light of the room, her face looked tired and drawn, but the sight of her bare skin excited him.

"What are you working on?"

"Crap for a trial." She cleared a spot for him on the couch. They were separated by a stack of papers. He cleared his throat, congested by too many cigarettes, and his breath felt rancid, scotch mixed with beer.

She picked at her toenails, the polish chipped, those delicate feet of hers, like a child's. He tried to avert his eyes from the smooth white skin of her chest.

"I've missed you so much," he said.

"I miss you. I miss the way you used to be."

"Nothing's changed. I still want you." He leaned across the sheaf of papers and kissed her full on the mouth. "I love you. I want to show you."

She smiled, but there was no joy in it. He took her by the hand and led her to the bedroom. His brain was swirling as he took off his clothes. He removed the robe from her shoulders, but he had no patience for foreplay. She grabbed his head roughly as he licked her breasts, and they fell to the bed. He was inside her quickly, she guiding him, and it didn't feel like pleasure at all, but something he was compelled to do. She made barely a sound. Without warning, he came. The urgency was gone, and he felt lightheaded, dizzy.

Her eyes were glassy, hopeless, plaintive. He had nothing but contempt for her. He couldn't imagine whatever had caused him to pursue her so ardently. She appeared pathetic to him. He pushed himself off her, kissed her on the forehead, then once lightly on the lips. He wanted to be out of her room, away from her at that moment, but he had no graceful exit in mind.

She sat up in the bed, propping her pillows behind her, and reached for the ashtray and her cigarettes on the nightstand.

"Do you have any aspirin?"

He walked to the bathroom and took two aspirin, avoiding his face in the mirror. The bedroom filled with the smell of her cigarette. He picked up his wrinkled clothes and began putting them on.

"You're not going," she said. "You're not going to just come in here and fuck and run."

"It's not like that."

"What do you mean? You waltz in here with your sad face, saying you love me." She snuffed out the cigarette. "If you go now, don't ever come back."

He left without another word. She screamed at him. "I hate you. I hate you, you son of a bitch."


"Stay tuned for my next guest," Barry said. "Ray Ballard, the man who made the video of the shooting. Peeping Toms. They're everywhere, folks."

Jack switched off the radio, and finished the remains of the beer. He had enough of her for one night.

**23**

The quarterly meeting of the Massachusetts Women's Bar Association was held in the grand ballroom of the Marriott Hotel on the wharf.

Prior to her speech, Lee sat at the dais, next to the podium. The fifty or so tables were filled with the browns, grays, and blacks of the attenders' outfits. Lee felt somewhat dubious about this bourgeois feminism. They were too much part of the establishment to effect much progress. She had attended this function for many years; she was MWBA's former president.

Susan Pressman, current president, sat beside her. "Well," she said. "You've become quite the celeb."

"I guess so."

"It's a troubling case. I'm afraid it won't look good for us."

"Us?"

"Women. You know, I'm afraid it'll be a setback. She's really not that sympathetic."

"What do you mean?" Over the last few days, Lee found she couldn't countenance any criticism of Alison.

"You know," Susan said with a wave of her hand. "If she can't make it with all her advantages, it makes all of us look bad."

Lee felt herself blushing, but before she could respond, Susan was up off her chair and at the podium.

"Welcome, members of the bar. Thank you for coming today. This is the eighteenth year of our organization, and I'm old enough to remember when there was only a handful of us out there. As the slogan says, 'You've come a long way, baby!' "

Polite laughter from the crowd.

"Our main speaker this morning is someone I'm sure you all know. She was a past president of this association. She's been a criminal defense lawyer for fifteen years, first as a public defender, now in private practice. She's successfully argued the battered women's syndrome defense and been an active member of numerous civic and political groups for many years. She's currently involved in the well-publicized Public Garden shooting case. Please welcome Lee Klein."

Lee stood up. There was tentative applause from the audience, as if they were waiting to listen before they committed themselves to a show of real enthusiasm. Lee placed her notes in front of her, then stuffed her hands in her skirt pockets, and stared out at the sea of faces.

Her main theme was the backlash against women's rights. Women still suffered the same indignities in the workplace—the absence of upward mobility, the lack of child care, the double standards—as they had for years. "The media is the engine of all this," Lee explained. "The media continues to perpetuate ancient stereotypes. To give only a recent example, one I'm intimately concerned with: the Public Garden shooting. Look how the press portrays the parties. The woman is a vixen, a femme fatale, mentally unstable. The man is an innocent victim. The media assumes she's guilty, that he is blameless. They ignore the pervasiveness of domestic violence. Our society fears a woman like Alison Moore. A striving woman with a good career. She's seen as dangerous, unnatural. As fellow lawyers, you understand what I'm talking about. Who's to blame? Always the woman. But Alison is the victim here. She's suffering the pain, while Mr. Donnelly is lionized as the Great American Male, besieged by an aggressive woman. Isn't this the way they always state it? Think about it. And think about Alison's pain. We must see through the media's distorted lens to the real person."

After lunch, Lee stood in the hallway as women scrambled to individual workshops. She was approached by a petite redhead who clutched a binder to her chest. "Ms. Klein," she said. "Jenny Armstrong. I just wanted you to know that there are women who are pulling for Alison Moore. He must've been an asshole. Aren't they all, really?"

Lee nodded.

"I have friends at A and K who say she was treated like shit. It's still a men's club over there. And her boyfriend, he was just a typical ass-kisser."

"That's interesting."

"They had some knock-down-drag-out fights in the office."

"Really?"

"Yeah. That's what my sources say. Anyway, I gotta go." She touched Lee's arm. "Nice meeting you."

Amy Cohen, counsel for the Reproductive Rights League, was at a table outside one of the rooms, distributing leaflets. Lee went up to say hello. She had known Amy since their law school days at B.U. when they were in the Women's Law Caucus.

"Quite a case you got there," Amy said.

"Sure is," Lee said cautiously. It seemed as if every conversation these days had a hidden agenda.

"I want you to know we didn't plan on getting involved. It's kind of a messy case, but we can't let the anti-choicers get the upper hand. Did you see the demonstration where they claimed her as a victim of abortion? They're turning her into their latest poster child. We can't just sit back and watch. That poor woman. We're all behind you."

Lee was weary of the subject. "I don't see this as an abortion rights case. This is a criminal case. Anyway, I think you know where I stand." Lee checked her watch.

"You got to go? Okay. Well, remember what we always say— and it's invariably true—the personal is the political."


Lee couldn't tell Amy about her next appointment; she didn't even want to think about it herself. From her years of experience as a defense lawyer, she knew you could find yourself in unlikely positions—defending child abusers, rapists—and it rarely troubled her. Her role was to protect the guilty and possibly innocent from the excesses of the state. But this visit was more nearly a betrayal of personal beliefs. She didn't want to face the implications of her pro-choice views, the fact that an abortion was a traumatic experience capable of unhinging a woman. As Brian often said, scruples are a luxury a successful criminal lawyer could not afford.

A block from the Sullivan Square station Lee found the office of Dr. Henry Sutherland in a white clapboard house with black shutters.

Dr. Sutherland was considered an expert on post-traumatic

stress disorder and had advanced a thesis (controversial, decried) in an issue of *The Journal of Contemporary Psychology* on how the malady was often found in women who had undergone abortions. Post-abortion syndrome, as it was called, had never been applied in the criminal context, but Lee thought it might apply here.

Lee had called a former colleague at the public defender's office who said Sutherland had been used in the past as a defense witness for his client, a Vietnam vet who had discharged his rifle into the windows at City Hall. According to Lee's friend, Sutherland's practice had diminished into semiretirement. But if Lee was to raise a trauma defense, she needed a reputable expert, someone the courts had found qualified to render an opinion in the past.

Lee was prepared for the figure who answered the door. He was a tall, rangy man who stooped to shake her hand. He had shocks of white hair. Round wire-rim glasses covered heavy pouches under his eyes. He wore a lime-green cardigan sweater buttoned tightly over an ample waist, and bolo tie. Birkenstock sandals covered gray wool socks.

"You must be Ms. Klein," he said, escorting her in. The living room was tastefully, if simply, decorated, with a leather recliner and sofa, shelves lined neatly with books, predominantly fiction and psychology. On the walls were a Turner landscape print and framed diplomas and recognitions from colleges and societies.

"I just made tea. Would you like some?" She accepted and sat down on the sofa. He poured a cup for each of them.

"You said on the phone you're representing the woman who did the shooting in the Public Garden. Interesting case. Where did you get my name?"

"A friend of mine interviewed you for an article once. And lawyers in the p.d.'s office recommended you. I used to work there."

"Ah. I used to do a fair amount of work for them. I was kind of the hired gun, so to speak."

"You come well-regarded, Doctor."

"Henry. Call me Henry, if you will." He sipped his tea. "Yes, you had a great combination of psychotics and sociopaths over there. A regular laboratory. A gold mine for a man like me."

"You know why I'm here."

"Oh, yes. Certainly. PAS. Not many takers for that one." He stood up and shuffled over to the fire. "Keep talking."

"Well, I have to admit to a little skepticism myself."

"Ah. Every theory has its doubters, Ms. Klein. It's what science has always to endure. Think of Freud, the scandal of Vienna.

Not that I'm comparing myself to the great man, or making any pretense to prophecy; merely expressing the general point. Just remember, people resist what they fear to imagine. For example, why are you skeptical?"

"I'm not sure. It sounds like pop psychology, too simplistic."

"Do you doubt that veterans of war can experience trauma that may affect them in later life? Do you believe battered women suffer experiences that distort them and lead to eventual violence?"

"I'm not willing to concede the situations are comparable."

"Ah. And why *is* that?"

"Abortion's merely a surgical procedure."

"*Merely* hardly describes it. Not only is there the procedure itself—being strapped in the stirrups—"

"You've obviously never been to a gynecologist. I hardly think—"

"As I was saying, the procedure is at best discomforting. And the consequence. Sex. Motherhood. A child. All those societal forces. It's crushing to destroy something dependent on you, something inside you."

"But those feelings are not endemic to the experience; it's imposed from without. From others who make you feel you killed something."

"Are you merely playing devil's advocate or preparing me for cross-examination?"

"Both."

"Let's be open-minded, shall we? Post-abortion syndrome has all the diagnostic criteria to fit within recognized psychological diseases that may affect criminal intent. First, there is a stressful event, one beyond the range of normal human experience. You must admit this applies. Then, reexperience of the abortion through recollections of the procedure. Avoidance is another symptom. A woman will exhibit estrangement from others, a numbness of emotional capacity, depression. She may appear hyper-alert, have recurring sleep disorders. Then there's guilt. This is all well-documented through clinical experiments. The Moser study in 1989 examined a variety of women from differing backgrounds and experiences—single, poor, middle class, married, all religions. It can be verified."

"Then how come it's not well-recognized?"

"Politics. The prevailing opinion in this country, what the majority wants is to make the abortion experience commonplace, innocuous. Pro-choice groups don't want to admit there are any side effects. Medical organizations can't admit it—abortion has been an acceptable procedure for hundreds of years and a quite lucrative one, for some. Pro-life groups also seem to be split. Some can't reconcile their belief that a woman having an abortion is a murderer *and* a victim. They think PAS lets her off the hook, so to speak. PAS suggests an evasion of personal responsibility to them. Which, by the way, is the reason most people are generally unwilling to accept the PAS defense. Juries, however, the people who count, are comfortable with looking for an excuse.''

''We don't even know if she—my client—fits the profile,'' Lee said.

''That's certainly true. I'd have to meet with her.''

''There could be other things in a person's life that might contribute. Things apart from the abortion, I mean.''

''Certainly. Some people are well-adjusted. Some vets came back unscathed. Some battered women leave their husbands and re-marry successfully. Your client's past experiences are relevant in any diagnosis. Family background. Other experiences with men. And this man in particular.

''I've testified in about fifty trials, I'd say, and since my prac-tice has slackened, I've become an inveterate courtroom watcher. Trials are narratives. Tell a story. In this case, the press has already provided a kind of narrative between the innocent hometown boy who pulled himself up by his bootstraps and the sophisticate. She's the temptress as it stands now. The germ is there for another angle. What you want to do with it is, of course, your business. You want to know what I think?''

''Please.''

''They're both sick. With their personalities, there was bound to be an explosion. Here's a man who's driven by one thing: ambi-tion. He probably runs away from all emotional entanglements. And her. A classic. Overshadowed by her genius brother, her father, raised in a family expecting her to be important, everything's failed. This is not the life she imagined. Sure, she seems healthy on the surface—with her fine education and good job—but she feels slighted somehow, ignored. She's dying for an emotional commit-ment from someone. I'm not trying to be sexist here, but she obvi-ously needed a man for approval.''

''You know all this from news reports?'' Lee asked.

''And my training. Essentially, we are all types, predictable profiles.''

Initially, Lee was surprised that Sutherland was making snap psychological judgments on individuals he knew only through press reports. But, she thought, we all do that. We reach conclusions based on cultural stereotypes, try to pigeonhole people into familiar, recognizable categories. The "hysterical woman" angle could be used precisely because it conformed to preconceived notions about aggressive women that the media and the public at large could accept. How to synthesize that idea and the idea of women as victims could be the way to successfully defend this case. Would she be exploiting Alison? Not really. It was the only way to win.

Lee's job was to assign a motive, a reason for aberrant behavior. What event is the catalyst that crystallizes all the parts into one moment of violent reaction? With the poor it was easy—greed, drug addiction, anomie, hopelessness. Alison was obviously a troubled person before Jack Donnelly had come along. What had he done, though, to make her snap?

"I see you read the tabloids," she said.

"Ms. Klein, stereotypes exist and are perpetuated because they have a kernel of truth."

"Doctor, we're individuals."

"I sense hostility. Tell you what. Why don't you read my article on the subject and think about it? I'd like to help you. And compensation's not an issue. I don't need the money. I enjoy the give-and-take of the courtroom. You don't know how frustrating it is to sit in there and not be part of it. Trials can be a real adrenaline booster. There's probably something sick in that, but we all walk around with neuroses. Hell, trial lawyers themselves are a great study in neurosis. Isn't it peculiar that even the most seasoned D.A. can get sick with nervousness the day of a trial? Isn't there something odd about human beings who voluntarily put themselves through such agony?"

"It's called masochism."

"That it is."

**24**

wo days later, the following story appeared in the *Globe*:

Alison Moore, the 28-year-old woman accused of shooting her boyfriend, was raised in a small town in Indiana, earned degrees from Wellesley College and Harvard Law School, and was an associate at one of Boston's most prestigious law firms. Beneath this professional success, Ms. Moore, who is expected to plead not guilty to charges of attempted murder, assault, and possession of a weapon, had a history of troubled romantic relationships, a failed career as an actress, and a reputation as an unfriendly, difficult person, according to investigators and persons familiar with her.

The police say Ms. Moore's loss of her relationship with Jack Donnelly, a fellow associate at Adelman and Kaplan, led her to fire a bullet at him at close range in the Public Garden on October 3, 1990. Ms. Moore was arrested after being tackled and disarmed by a bystander walking by the Garden bridge.

Ms. Moore met Mr. Donnelly in March of this year at Adelman and Kaplan, a Boston institution since 1917. She transferred to Boston from a law firm in Washington, D.C. They are both on administrative leave pending the outcome of the trial, according to a spokesperson for the firm.

Ms. Moore's lawyer, Lee Klein, a former public defender, contends her client is the real victim in the case, but will not elaborate. As for Ms. Moore's relationships with men in the past, her attorney had no comment.

Ms. Moore's parents, Harold and Louise, live in Wallace, Indiana, a small town outside Indianapolis. Her father is a tenured professor in the history department at Wallace College.

According to interviews with acquaintances and former classmates, Ms. Moore was academically successful and spent much of her time with fellow children of faculty members at Wallace College. During high school, she began appearing in theater productions. It is said she dreamed of moving to New York City and starring on Broadway.

Ms. Moore's brother, Peter, was a promising concert pianist. Peter Moore attended Berklee School of Music briefly, then performed in jazz bands in Cambridge and Boston. According to a former high-school classmate, Ms. Moore resented what she saw as the preferential treatment of her brother by her father.

Ms. Moore also had a rebellious streak. In senior year of high school, she moved in briefly with a man ten years her senior. According to court records in Indiana, she filed a number of assault charges against the man, which were eventually dismissed. She moved back home after one of these alleged assaults.

After graduation from high school, Ms. Moore attended Wellesley College, graduating summa cum laude in 1984, with a bachelor of arts degree in drama. She settled in Boston and appeared in a number of productions in small theaters.

Ms. Moore was frustrated with her acting career and eventually decided to attend law school after meeting Jerry Prescott, now a lawyer in Washington. Ms. Moore moved to Washington with Mr. Prescott upon her graduation from Harvard Law School. Attempts to reach Mr. Prescott were unsuccessful. His office said he was on vacation. According to Ms. Moore's attorney, her client left Washington to pursue a job opportunity. Sources say Mr.

Prescott left Ms. Moore for another woman and that Ms. Moore sought psychiatric help afterward.

Ms. Moore arrived at Adelman and Kaplan in March. According to sources at that firm, she was highly regarded, but others resented her. "She had an imperious manner," one said. "She thought she was better than everyone else." While at the firm, Ms. Moore worked closely with Mr. Donnelly on a number of cases, and they began a personal relationship. Colleagues expressed puzzlement at their relationship. "They were nothing alike," one said.

**25**

xiled in gay Siberia. That's how Alison described her condition. Provincetown wearing a dormant mask. It was normally a lively place, the Eastern counterpart to San Francisco, a town full of exiles from suburban repression, various closets of identity. They came there to express themselves, to be free of fear, like Jews who go to Israel and finally feel safe from anti-Semites.

Lee had convinced her to accept Peter's offer to stay with him. The media had staked outside Alison's apartment building every day since the shooting. Lee thought it was a good idea to escape the publicity.

Alison was in the main sitting room of the bed and breakfast Peter and David owned, going through newspapers for articles about herself. She was curled up on the couch, her feet tucked underneath, dressed in an oversize Scottish wool sweater and black leotards, white socks on her feet. Alison was fascinated by the publicity. Every morning since arriving, she went down to the local newsstand and bought newspapers, tabloids, magazines—the *Globe*, the *Herald*, *Them* magazine, the *Aurora*. The papers and magazines were in a heap at her feet.

David arrived with breakfast on a tray, a poached egg, wheat toast, orange juice, and coffee.

"Thank you," she said. "I feel like the queen in exile."

David bowed and took a seat in the rocking chair across from her.

"My talents go to waste in the off-season," he said. "I've tried to convince your brother to go to Key West or something for the winters, but he won't. He says he loves the change of seasons. Me, I could handle some hot sun beach right now. The heating system's abominable in this old house. How's the egg?"

"Terrific," she said. "You guys are spoiling me."

"We aim to please." David gestured to the papers. "You probably shouldn't be reading that junk. Against doctor's orders."

"I know. I feel like some housewife in the supermarket line. You know, my hair in curlers and hair net, reading about Liz's latest hubby or Diana's problems with Charles. Some of the stories are exactly that real."

Who were the sources for these statements about her? She thought about theater people—Garrett, Debbie, Sarah Ann—and she wondered who was giving the interviews. How did they find out about Will Grimes? An awful man. A fling, until he began to hit her.

What Jack wanted out of her was still a mystery.

Unconscious, unspoken expectations. She'd seen women ruined by this trap. Hell, she'd done it with Jerry, assuming this was it, the big one, the real one, the forever one. Forever was not a concept Jerry imbided. But she didn't expect permanence from Jack. Just honesty, respect, companionship. It wasn't too much to ask.

She walked to the window and watched white-capped waves rolling to the surf.

"Sis, we got to get a move on," Peter said, entering the room. "You have to be in court by two."

he corridor outside Courtroom 14 was crowded with cameramen waiting for the defendant-of-the-day to exit the courtroom after entering her plea.

Inside, Alison and Lee sat behind the defense table; her case was yet to be called. While Lee had a whispered conversation with a former colleague from the public defender's office, Alison concentrated on the activity in front of her. A young man with droopy eyes and quivering lips came up to the podium, his hands shackled, dressed in a khaki smock.

"Who's his lawyer?" the judge asked brusquely, peeking above bifocals on the edge of his nose. "Does this man have a lawyer?"

"This is bullshit, judge," the man said.

"Mr. Jones, foul language is not allowed in this courtroom. You understand me? We're going to appoint a public defender to represent you. You're charged with murder in the second degree. You want the charges read to you?"

"No, Judge. I know what they are. I know what you want to know. Not guilty, Judge. Not fucking guilty." The bailiff grabbed Mr. Jones's arm and took him out the back door of the courtroom.

"Next case," the judge said wearily. "Commonwealth versus Moore." Lee took Alison's elbow and guided her to the podium. "Your Honor, Lee Klein for Ms. Moore." Lee saw a woman standing at the other counsel table.

"Julie Bellamy for the Commonwealth, Judge." Hurley sat behind her, his legs crossed.

"We'll waive reading of the indictment, Judge," Lee said.

"How do you plead?"

As instructed, Alison bent into the microphone and heard her voice emerge, unnaturally loud. "Not guilty."

"On all counts, Your Honor," Lee added.

Lee knew Hurley was going to have Julie at the trial to counteract the female sympathy problem he faced. Sometimes the dynamics of a trial depressed her, that one had to go to such lengths. She wondered if Julie knew or even cared that Hurley was using her, the Commonwealth's token of the moment.

After Alison's arraignment, the judge recessed court and left the bench. In the hallway outside the courtroom, reporters and photographers followed Alison and Lee, forming two rows shuffling along behind them. Alison reached into her purse and pulled out a pair of black sunglasses, standard equipment for her role, Lee thought, watching her client. The femme fatale, caught in a scandal with the whiff of sex. She would have to talk to Alison about her dress and demeanor.

At the bottom of the staircase outside the courthouse, a crowd was gathered, some chanting, others displaying homemade posters. FREE ALISON, one read. WE ARE ALL ALISONS. "Way to go, Alison!" a woman's voice shouted, and clapping began, rising to a crescendo like cheers at a sporting event. Then Alison noticed the other signs. ABORTION IS MURDER, one read.

Microphones were shoved in Alison's face, but Lee pulled her along. The reporters continued to converge. This is why they call them the "press," Alison thought.

"No questions, please," Lee told them. "We'll do all our talking in court. My client intends to fight the charges against her."

Voices overlapped from the press corps, while the crowd chanted, "Alison! Alison! Alison!" Through the din, a booming male voice recited passages from the Bible. Lee led Alison to Peter's waiting car, and they drove off.

Hurley viewed the scene from the top of the courthouse steps. "It's gonna be a circus. No doubt," he said aloud, and waited for the media to turn its attention to him.

ergen's Restaurant was located in the Financial District, near the federal courthouse. Lawyers didn't come to it for the food; it was part of a world where they all congregated like a segregated community. When he first came to Adelman and Kaplan, Jack had been a frequent denizen, but now he felt a bit out of place sitting with Andy, a little exposed. Andy was doing nothing to alleviate his anxiety. He had been wary when Jack phoned to arrange a lunch. "It's my running day, Jack, don't you remember?"

"Can't you run tomorrow?" Jack noticed the pleading in his own voice and wished he could swallow it. He didn't want to tell Andy too much, how desperate he was feeling, the sleepless nights he'd been having.

Andy agreed to meet with him, but now that he was here, Jack realized what a bad idea it was. Andy seemed distracted. He frequently glanced at the clock above the bar.

"I hear they're going to make at least three partnership offers from our group," Andy said. "So, let's say the shoo-ins are Janice and Larry. I got a fifty-fifty shot, right?" Jack felt a flash of resentment. I'm ten times the lawyer Andy is, he thought. This is pathetic.

A waiter brought a fresh beer for Jack.

"Did you always drink at lunch?" Andy said. "I don't remember."

"It's one of the perks of being unemployed."

"Don't sweat it. You'll get another job. You got good creds."

"I already have a job!"

"Yeah, well . . ."

"They can't fire me because of this, you know. *I* didn't do anything."

"That's where you're wrong," Andy said, lowering his voice. "You think they give a shit. They don't. We're all expendable. And you gave them a reason to ding you."

The finality of Andy's words hit him with astonishing force. "I did good fucking work for them. I worked my ass off. I billed twenty-two hundred hours last year."

Andy rubbed his fingers together. "Dollars, Jack. It's a business. Where's your business development? And I wouldn't talk like that too loudly around here."

"Oh, fuck, Andy. I'm pissed off. I got a right to be."

"I don't blame you, but you got to think like them. Put yourself in their shoes. The whole firm's involved now."

"What do you mean?"

"Her lawyer's been poking around. Talking to everybody."

"What's she asking?"

"You know, about you and her."

"Like what? What are people saying?"

"How the hell do I know? Christ, I feel like I'm talking out of school."

"Don't I have a right to know this? We're friends, for Christ's sake."

"Kaplan's pissed. All this prying."

"That's not my fucking fault."

"Well, I didn't say it was. Don't beat up on me about it."

Jack ran fingers through his hair. "I'm sorry. I just want to know what's going on."

"She's just asking questions, all right? About how you two acted and stuff like that."

"So, what did *you* say?"

"Nothing. Nothing."

"You one of the witnesses for the defense?"

Andy signaled for the check. "I'm going to tell the truth if I'm asked."

"What's that mean? What truth?"

The waiter produced the bill. "I got this one," Andy said.

Jack slumped back in the booth. "What was I supposed to do,

have a kid with her? Is that what everybody thinks? I'm sure Kaplan would've loved the unwed expectant mother walking around the halls."

"Nobody's judging *that*," Andy said. "It's not a moral issue. It's just bad luck, that's all. Some guys skate forever without their dick ruining their lives."

"*My* life's not ruined."

"Yeah, well, whatever. How's your arm doing?"

"It only hurts when I laugh," Jack said.


He had an appointment at Massachusetts General to check on the progress of his arm. It had been healing nicely, he thought, although in the middle of the night sometimes it still hurt. The doctor said it would be some months before he was perfectly healthy. "Your body has taken a great shock," he explained. "You have to expect healing time." The doctor had neglected to mention the psychological effects of suddenly looking at the barrel of a gun.

"Jack Donnelly." A nurse in a blue smock, a matching mask strung around her neck, read his name from a manila file. She escorted him to a small room with an examining table covered with a stiff white sheet of paper.

"Roll up your sleeve, on the good arm," she said crisply. "I never had a famous patient before." She took his blood pressure.

"I'm hardly famous."

"You're in all the papers. TV."

"Great."

"How does it feel, you know, to be on TV?"

"I didn't exactly choose it."

"I know. It's awful, isn't it? Normal." She ripped the velcro off his arm.

"Well, the jury's still out on that." He smiled, but she offered only a quizzical expression, a mild grin.

"Remove your shirt. The doctor will be with you shortly." He loved that ambiguous time frame they gave you. It was so vague it couldn't be challenged.

The doctor walked in with his file in her hand. She was a pale blonde in her mid-thirties, dressed in a white smock and white stockings, a stethoscope slung around her neck. She stopped in the center of the room, closed the file, set it on the sink, and washed her hands.

"Hello, Mr. Donnelly. I'm Dr. Weston. Let's see what we

have." She walked over and kneaded the muscles up and down his arm.

"Can you feel that? Does it hurt?" She moved from his shoulder, bypassing the wound, to his elbow, down to his wrist. She smelled of soap.

"You're progressing nicely," she said. "No pain besides that ache?"

"More like a tingle, you know. Like when you hit your funny bone."

She tore off the Band-Aid and lifted the gauze pad. The spot on his arm was a dull bruise, purple and black. He thought he should mention the insomnia, the recurring flashbacks, his jitteriness, but he decided against it. How could he tell this woman he didn't even know that he was an emotional wreck?

"You're a lucky man, Mr. Donnelly," she said. "It's a miracle that you avoided most of the impact of the bullet."

"Quick reflexes," he said. He was tired of being told how fortunate he had been. "Did you treat me that night?"

"Yes, I was in the ER. It was a hectic night, but your situation was memorable."

"Yeah, for me, too," he said, laughing.

Dr. Weston told him to come back in for a checkup in a few weeks. She wrote some notes in the file, clasped it to her chest, and was gone. When he put his shirt back on, the sleeves were wrinkled.

he phase between arraignment and trial was the time for the full court press, as Hurley termed it. Digging for the dirt, searching for the precious nugget of information. His investigators busily scurried through Wallace, Indiana, South Boston, Wellesley, Harvard, Boston College, UMass-Boston, through school corridors and local papers. They found reviews of Alison's high-school performances and Jack's Saint Christopher medal for perfect attendance in first grade. In the newspapers, stories continued to proliferate despite the absence of motion. Boston was fascinated with the quotidian aspects of Jack's and Alison's lives, or at least the media fed this impression.

It was all dizzying for Alison. Along with the many letters of support from women across the country were the lecture requests from battered women's support groups, rape crisis centers, feminist consciousness-raising groups. Both the pro-choice and pro-life forces wanted her services. Then there were the networks vying for her story, editors offering advances. Tabloid television shows wanted to do a reenactment of the crime. Some of the proposals were contingent on the outcome of the trial—an acquittal would elicit more cash than a conviction.

Jack was besieged as well. Newspaper reporters and magazine editors telephoned him without success. Letters were written soliciting his input. Didn't he want to tell his side of the story? No. It's nobody's business. He told the reporters that he was concerned for Alison's right to a fair trial. They snorted with displeasure, apparently believing he was holding out for better financial offers.

His only source of comfort and solace was Maggie, Larry's girlfriend. One afternoon she had come by his apartment as a diversion from her jogging. "I was in the neighborhood," she said. "Thought I'd stop by. Is this a bad time?"

She was in baggy gray sweatsuit, and a blue headband held down sweaty bangs.

"You came from Arlington?" he asked.

"No, school. I'm between classes. I thought you might like someone to talk to."

They went for a walk along the Charles River.

"Did you ever see the Pops on the Fourth?" she asked, gesturing toward the bandshell. "We went there like every year when I was a kid."

"You from Boston?"

"Woburn. You want to talk? I find emoting is important. Repression's not good for the soul."

"I don't want to burden anybody."

"It's no burden. I'd like to help."

"Why would you want to help *me*? You barely know me."

"Why not?"

"What do you get out of it?"

"God, you're cynical. I've just been keeping up on the story and thought this must be a terrible time for you."

"I don't like to talk about myself," he said.

"You know, by their very nature, there are two sides to every relationship. It's amazing people ever connect. I'm sure if you asked Larry, he'd say something different from me. I mean, for example, why we live together and we're not married. Stuff like that."

"Uh-huh," he said.

"You're not much of a talker, are you?"

"I've got nothing to say."

"I doubt *that*. You're just afraid to."

"It's so pointless," he said, but under her penetrating gaze, her obvious warmth, he opened up. It was all so confusing, he said. He got interested in Alison. He was infatuated, that's all. She seemed to want something he wasn't prepared to give.

"That always happens. People have different expectations."

"Yeah, well, it was all new to me."

"That's just it. It *was* new to you. She, on the other hand, had all these past relationships where she'd been hurt. She was very, unnaturally needy and obviously screwed-up emotionally. Why *did* you like her?"

"I thought she was pretty. She was smart."

"And you really didn't know her or understand her, right?"

"I don't know what that means. I can never figure out women."

"Some people are just mismatched. You can't beat yourself up about it."

They had walked down to the edge of campus.

"Listen, I hate to stop, but I have a class."

"Well, thanks. You've made me feel better."

"No charge." She smiled, then jogged away.

Maggie was good for his self-esteem, he thought. The cruel, impassive man that was emerging in press accounts was a caricature. He came away from his talk with her with renewed confidence that he would prevail, once the real story came out.

ith the trial set for the first week of December, Lee compiled a list of people to interview at Adelman and Kaplan: Sally, Andy, Mary, Drew, Larry, Toni, Janice, and Carole. The firm wanted all interviews recorded by a court reporter and requested copies of transcripts. Lee reluctantly complied. Still, she resented the interference.

The interviews began awkwardly at first; the firm's counsel frequently interrupted with objections. Exasperated, Lee pointed out that these weren't depositions, that the attorneys were not compelled to speak with her at all. Eventually, she was able to learn that Alison was disliked, not part of the team. Jack and Alison were an odd couple, their attraction to each other a mystery to their fellow associates.

With the exception of Mary Kelly, who offered nothing, they were disdainful. Lee found them arrogant, self-absorbed, in short, corporate lawyers. She perceived tremors of anxiety beneath this facade. The wary glances they threw toward the firm's counsel at a delicate point in Lee's questioning were signs that they didn't feel free to speak their minds, as if saying, Am I doing all right? Is this going to hurt me? Nobody had anything of a personal nature to offer regarding Alison. Depending on the perspective, she was either reserved or haughty. She had come to the firm with an excellent reputation as a strong litigator, and she was seen as smart, hard-working, and aloof.

Lee came away from the interviews not knowing whether they were helpful or not. They confirmed what Alison had already told her. How any of this would assist in her defense, Lee was at a loss to say.

There was also the question of whether to use Dr. Sutherland and post-abortion syndrome as a defense. When Lee proposed the idea to Alison, her only response was pragmatic: "Do you think it would work?" She was willing to meet with Sutherland if Lee thought it necessary.

The first session was held in Lee's office. Sutherland arrived almost a half-hour early, wearing a faded green suit and brown dress shoes. In Lee's foyer, he sat on a chair, a straw fedora in his lap, staring absently at the walls. Lee's heart dropped briefly at the sight of him. Alison came in nervously, dressed in blue jeans and a sweatshirt.

The three walked into Lee's office. Alison and Dr. Sutherland sat in chairs across from the desk.

Dr. Sutherland began by asking Alison about her background, her upbringing, then her relationship with Jack. Alison loosened up in his presence.

"What led you to have a relationship with him?"

"I didn't want to at first, but he worked on me. He pressed all the right buttons."

"Like what?"

"A lot of things. Lee will understand. We all want men who will show us something. Attention. Jack paid attention. He had a romantic streak in him—the flowers, the wine, the comments on my appearance. He noticed the clothes I wore, my perfume. He said I was beautiful. He made me feel beautiful."

"And then you got pregnant."

"Yes."

"How did you feel about that?"

"Scared. Angry. I wouldn't have necessarily felt that way if things were different between us, but we were over with. The last time I saw him he came to the apartment and used me badly. He didn't want me anymore. What was I going to do? I was depressed."

"Was your first reaction to have an abortion?"

"No. Yes. I'm not sure. I wasn't thinking straight. I met with him to tell him I was pregnant."

"That's when you decided to have the abortion?"

"I didn't decide, he did. He wanted to end our relationship. He wasn't interested in me. He just wanted me to go away. He wouldn't take responsibility. He was dumping me. What was I supposed to do?"

"What did you *want* to do?"

"Well, it would've been whatever he was *willing* to do. I didn't ask him for anything. I don't know what I expected him to do. He had control over the situation, not me."

"You thought it was his decision?" Lee interjected. It occurred to her that Alison had wanted Jack to choose. He rejected her when she depended on him to comfort her, provide her a solution. Despite Jack's nasty behavior, there was a part of Alison that still wanted him, that still wished that everything would work out.

There was a notable contrast between how Alison was perceived by her peers—talented, self-confident, even haughty—and the frightened woman she appeared to be in Lee's office. Lee saw that she had no self-esteem, depended on a man for her self-worth. Her failed relationship with Jack had wiped away the veneer she presented to the outside world.

"Yes, it was his decision, wasn't it?"

Sutherland paused a moment, then continued. "How were you feeling the day you went to the clinic?"

"God, so miserable. I hated myself for being there. But I hated him, too. When I met him at the station, I guess I thought there was still a chance he'd change his mind, but no. He was indifferent. I don't know why he even bothered coming with me."

"But you wanted him to?"

"Yes, I did. Because I thought he'd make it all better. Then when I knew he wouldn't, I wanted him to suffer like I was suffering. I wanted him to see what he'd done to me."

"What had he done to you? Did he hurt you by *making* you have the abortion?"

"By everything he did and didn't do. By giving up on me when I needed him most."

Alison recounted the scene inside and outside the clinic, the abortion procedure.

"How did that make you feel, once you had the abortion?"

Alison hesitated, put her lips together. "Like it was finally over. He had killed something between us and there was no going back."

"What did you think you were killing?"

"The whole thing."

"What do you mean?"

"Us. Anything between us."

"Did you think you were killing your baby?"

"No, no, it's not a baby." Alison began to cry.

Lee ached for her. She wondered if it was time to break off the session.

"Well, if you didn't think you were killing your baby, why were you so upset?"

"I was upset with *him*. Don't you understand? He had done this to me, gotten me pregnant, and it didn't matter to him at all."

"But it's the abortion that was causing all these feelings?"

"No, not totally. I began to feel that way earlier. When he met with me and acted the way he did."

"So, you didn't feel bad about the abortion procedure. You didn't feel bad about the fetus. You knew you and Jack were over with. What did you think you were going to accomplish by hurting him?"

Alison stood up and walked to the window. She began to cry harder. "I don't know. I really don't."

# 30

On Thanksgiving morning, Jack went home to South Boston. His mother had insisted he come for the holidays. Initially, he said he was too busy preparing for the trial, but he relented. She sounded lonely, desperate to see him.

His mother answered the door, wiping her hands on an apron. She was out of breath, her hair in sweaty curls. "Thanks for coming," she said in a whisper. "It means a lot to me."

The house smelled of the cooked turkey. The furniture and shelves were covered with doilies. Figurines of animals and statues of children dotted the tables, along with dog-eared copies of *Maryknoll* magazine. On the wall was a picture of the Nativity scene Jack drew in first grade. On the other wall was a photo of JFK and an etching of Pope John XXIII.

Once inside, Jack saw Father Walsh sitting in an armchair. The parish pastor was in his mid-forties, Jack guessed, with speckled gray and black hair, a cherubic face and eager grin. He had a firm handshake and stared intently into Jack's eyes as if trying to read something. That gaze was supposed to communicate sincerity, that you were the most important person in the world, that he was deeply concerned about your well-being. He wore a red-and-green-checkered shirt underneath a blue Boston College crewneck sweater, dark blue slacks, and brown tasseled loafers.

I've been set up, Jack thought. Father Walsh had been summoned to redeem or console him. He was angry, but tried to maintain control.

"I asked Father Walsh to drop by," his mother said.

"What for?"

"Nice to see you again," Father Walsh said. "It's a blessing this time of year to have friends from the parish to visit."

"I have to check the turkey," his mother said. She exited to the kitchen.

"She's a sweetheart, your mother. She thought we should talk."

"Did she?"

Walsh leaned forward on the edge of the chair, his hands cupped around his knees. "It's a difficult time for you, Jack. I know it must be."

"I really don't want to talk about it."

"If you'll pardon me, it's been my experience that it's better to talk about these things."

"What things? I've got nothing to say. I didn't ask for your counseling, and I'm not offering penance. Accidents will happen. I've got nothing to feel sorry for. I have nothing to confess to you or anyone."

Father Walsh cleared his throat. "I'm not talking about blame. I'm just interested in your well-being. It must be a trauma to be shot by someone, especially someone close to you."

"We weren't close. I don't think we even liked each other."

"That's sad."

"That's the way life is, Father. The church doesn't understand that. You can't understand what I'm going through. To tell you the truth, Father, I stopped listening to your message ages ago."

"Jack!" his mother said, entering the room. Father Walsh stood up.

"It's all right, Mary. He's a little on edge."

"Who wouldn't be?" Jack said.

"You shouldn't talk to Father Walsh that way."

Jack walked to the front door. "I'm going for a beer." He walked outside.


He decided to have a few drinks at Billy Malone's Tavern. On Thanksgiving, there was always a pretty good crowd gathered to watch the football game.

Why did everybody dwell on what happened? he wondered.

It was over. There was nothing Walsh could do about him and Alison. His mother wanted him to confess, receive understanding through faith. None of that would change the facts. He had done something wrong in the eyes of the Church. He didn't need reminding; he needed forgetting. True consolation, he thought, was available at Billy Malone's.

# 31

lison stood before the bathroom mirror, wiping makeup from her face. Her hand trembled. This was the most nervous she had been in months. The trial was only twelve days away.

It was Thanksgiving Day, late evening. For hours she had been ridding her apartment of every trace of Jack—his past issues of *Connoisseur*, his deodorant stick in the medicine cabinet, his wrinkled white dress shirt in her laundry basket, his green and white coffee mug.

The day before, Garrett had called and they met for dinner at Legal Sea Food. He greeted her with a light peck on the cheek and a consoling touch at her elbow. It seemed ages since she had seen him, and it was a comfort to relive anecdotes, catch up on the latest projects, the progress of the careers of former colleagues.

"You miss the stage, don't you?" he asked.

"Yes, of course I do. I shouldn't have left. Look what happened."

"I know, but we have to think about your future, when this is all behind you." Alison welcomed such a change. She had been overwhelmed with the present ordeal. "In that vein, I've been working on a new idea for a piece. Tell me what you think. Keep an open mind."

He dipped an oyster in the butter dish. She was mildly drunk from the beers.

"What's it about?"

"You."

"Me? What about me?"

He put up his palms. "Hear me out. I've been thinking about your story."

"Yes."

"It has everything. The abortion issue. How women are perceived and portrayed in the media. That sort of thing. A sociopolitical piece about the current condition."

She laughed uneasily. "You're kidding, right? Your legendary black humor."

"No, I'm totally serious. And here's the best part. I was thinking you could play the lead, yourself."

"I'm listening."

"I haven't worked out the details. We could examine the whole role of women in contemporary America. You could be an example to others. Am I offending you?"

"It sounds ghastly. This is not some fictional thing. My life's on the line."

"I know that. I'm not insensitive to that. I thought some good could come out of all this. We could do a multimedia collaborative project. You could get back on the stage again, where you belong."

She imagined a biography in *Playbill*: "Alison Moore returns to the stage after a brief hiatus. She is a native of Wallace, Indiana, and a graduate of Wellesley College. Her credits include *A Doll's House, Hurlyburly, Hamlet, The Glass Menagerie,* and *Talley's Folly*. Most recently, she has been charged with attempted murder."

Garrett's idea intrigued her. After the trial was over—the results of which she didn't want to imagine—she would have to start again. Garrett was filling her head with old dreams and ambitions.

"I can't think about this now," she said. "You're spinning my head."

"Just say you *will* think about it."

"I will. Anything to keep from thinking about the trial."

# 32

O n the morning of the day Commonwealth versus Alison Moore was set to begin, the police arrived early, setting up wooden barricades to keep back the anticipated crowds.

The mayor had ordered maximum security to prevent potentially violent clashes. Pro-choice, the mayor had been getting bad press for his treatment of anti-abortion protesters in front of clinics throughout the city. The Sunday before, during his sermon at the Holy Ghost Church, Cardinal Quinn, head of the Archdiocese of Boston, had tied abortion to the Moore trial. "Violence against the fetus begets further violence. You let the genie out of the bottle, this will happen." Outside church, he was asked by a reporter what he thought about a Catholic boy participating in such an act. "I don't believe the Vatican considers Mr. Donnelly a Catholic, practicing or otherwise," he said.

When asked to respond to the cardinal's remarks, the mayor stated that he believed the cardinal had the absolute right to comment on public affairs, but religion should be kept out of the judicial process. This led the cardinal to respond that the mayor, with his stand on abortion, was risking excommunication. The mayor and the cardinal eventually held a reconciliation meeting in full view of cameras in the middle of City Hall.

At seven A.M., Hurley was already in his office. He could never sleep the night before a trial. Since before dawn, he had been reading over his notes. He had played out the trial for days in his mind. His usual nervousness and caution were heightened by the stakes involved. He knew the press interest surrounding the case was disproportionate to its importance. Where were the onslaught of stories when his bureau was doing the gritty, important work of truly violent crimes, rapes, armed robberies, murders, drug cases? But he did not create the opportunity, and he would not shy from it merely because others in his office thought it was trivial.

All trials have pitfalls, unexpected events, surprise testimony, but he was reasonably confident of this one. What worried him was the defense. It was clear that Lee was going to raise duress as an issue, but Hurley thought it was ludicrous. Although Hurley himself regarded Jack with disdain, the jury would see him as a victim, a basically honest, forthright man who'd been caught in a bad situation. He couldn't imagine there would be some unanticipated bombshell. Lee's notorious inability to separate her emotions from the law, some feminist cause she couldn't resist, were the only reasons the case was going to trial. That was always her failing, Hurley thought. She was a good lawyer, but she had a soft heart for the truly despicable, whether the petty career criminal or the one-time would-be killer like Moore.

Hurley had confidence in his themes, but he went through them aloud to see how they sounded. Rarely, if ever, did he take anyone else's advice. Still, he listened to what Julie said about how most people favored abortion as a matter of choice in the abstract but couldn't reconcile themselves to it in practice; it was still a dirty secret.

He didn't regret his decision to have Julie second-chair the case. She had the meek appearance, unobtrusive attractiveness, that would avoid the inevitable appearance that this was a case where the state (male) was beating up on the defendant (female). Hurley knew that the dynamics of a trial often had little to do with the merits of each side's argument. Lee could sway sentiment by presenting Moore as a victim. Gently, ploddingly, Hurley would counter that tendency by focusing on the facts. His motto for effective trial technique was make it quick and clean. His case would take just a couple of days, buttressing his plea to the jury that this was a simple, straightforward crime. And there was the videotape. Ray Ballard, that slimy little punk, was a savior.

No matter how liberated you may be as a woman, Lee thought, no matter how much progress has been made for women in the workplace, the essential question remains: What do I wear? To be feminine without being provocative, to look serious but not grim and stiff. On her bed, three outfits were displayed on hangers. She finally settled on a blue suit with white blouse, a string of pearls with simple matching earrings.

Her hands always had a slight tremor on trial days. It didn't interfere with her effectiveness and, in fact, the shakes disappeared once the battle had begun. Sure, she realized all this disorganization, this thrashing around in her bedroom and bathroom were signs of stress, but in that it was no different from any other day. She was naturally harried, rushing from meeting to meeting with no time to spare. It had been easier at twenty-five than it was at forty-two, but not dramatically different.

She was nervous about the trial. Alison had placed great faith in her. Lee was responsible for her fate. The case would be extremely difficult to win, but she would give it her best.

Lee had arranged for a car to pick her up and meet Alison and Peter outside Alison's apartment. She had instructed them to wait in the building's vestibule and to dash toward the car when they heard the horn sound. Lee feared some of the media would be stalking the premises for yet another shot of the famous defendant.


"I'm nervous, I don't mind telling you," Alison said to Peter. "Is it too late for a plea? To anything? I can't go through with this."

Peter had been a valued friend through the ordeal. His attention was uncorrupted whereas everybody else seemed to have an agenda, shaping and fitting her into a mold of their making. Peter was a steadying influence.

The car drove up to the door. When they heard two short beeps, they exited the building. Lee slid over to the far side of the backseat. She checked her watch. They were on schedule.


Jack sat with Maggie at Madeliene's in Cambridge. He was desperate for companionship, and she had agreed to meet him. By eight A.M., he was on his third Bloody Mary, and his omelet was barely eaten.

"They told me I probably won't be called for a couple of days," he said, "but I have to sit in the witness room at the courthouse anyway."

As the trial approached, Jack increasingly believed he would be vindicated. Once the trial was over, the air would clear and he would return to the firm. He'd be knocked down a peg or two, but he'd still make partner. Today, though, he was filled with anxiety. What would it be like sitting on the witness stand with Alison in the room? What would he see? Those cruel, angry eyes or the flirtatious, mischievous ones that had dazzled him into calamity? He did not want to confront her again.

"You didn't have to come with me, you know. I'll be fine."

Maggie grinned. "It's my nature." He picked up her hand and gave it a light kiss. She blushed.

"I couldn't resist," he said. She looked down at her lap. "Sorry. I didn't mean anything by it." She began to cry.

"What's the matter?"

"I just feel so bad for you."

"Oh, don't," he said. "Really, don't. I don't need your pity." He'd made his choices, he thought, his resolve strengthened by alcohol; he had to live with them. Outrage and anger was one thing, pity was a meaningless emotion.

"I'm sorry," she said. "I'm okay." He found it remarkable she felt such compassion for him.

"Why don't we get out of here?" he suggested. "Take a walk. Get some fresh air."

He paid the check and rushed her out the door.


The courthouse doors opened at eight-thirty A.M. An orderly line formed outside the courtroom behind a metal rope and the watchful eyes of the police. Many of the prospective spectators wore buttons indicating their stance on the abortion issue; equal numbers on both sides. The hallway hummed with the murmurs of the impatient.

When Judge Kaufman entered to begin the day's proceedings, the courtroom was packed. He began by admonishing those present that he would not tolerate disruptions, that this was a criminal trial, a solemn event. "Both the defendant and the Commonwealth deserve a fair trial. I know emotions run high on this issue, but this is not a place for political posturing. The First Amendment does not apply inside these doors. Keep your political battles outside on the street. We don't want this erupting into a sideshow or a circus. I would appreciate, nay demand, restraint from the visitors, including members of the press. I would also appreciate it, Mr. Hurley, Ms. Klein—although I'm not issuing an order at this time—if you two would keep the rhetoric during the course of these proceedings to a minimum. Let's try this case based on evidence from the witness stand, and not from the front pages of our city's great newspapers. Shall we? We shall.''

After the jury was selected, Hurley stood to offer the opening statement on behalf of the Commonwealth. He walked over to the television set placed before the jury box and inserted the videotape into the VCR. It had the desired impact. The jurors started when they saw the flash of light from the gun, and Jack fall to the ground.

"That's the essence of the Commonwealth's case, ladies and gentlemen," Hurley said, his arm on top of the television, indicating the frozen image of Jack prone. "Plain as day. All the evidence you need to find the defendant guilty of the crimes charged.

"You will also hear from the victim, the man lying helplessly on the ground there. Jack Donnelly is his name. You will hear how Mr. Donnelly grew up right here in South Boston, pulled himself up by his bootstraps, and landed a job at one of the city's most prestigious law firms. He had a good job. He was going places. Then he met the defendant." He paused. "She was a lawyer at the same firm, well-educated, smart. They dated. They had a relationship."

Hurley held his hands before his mouth, in the shape of a steeple. "But things didn't work out. The defendant became pregnant. She decided not to have the child.

"On the day the defendant shot Mr. Donnelly, she had an abortion. Freely, voluntarily, without coercion. It was her choice; she did not consult him about it. He had no warning, ladies and gentlemen. Walking through the Public Garden, trying to comfort her after her ordeal, their ordeal, she, in cold blood, tried to kill him.

"This wasn't an unplanned act. Oh, no. You will hear testimony that the defendant purchased her weapon, a .22-caliber pistol, some weeks before she shot her boyfriend. This was no accident. This shooting was premeditated, deliberate, carefully planned.

"This is a simple case. The evidence will be clear. As clear as the images on that television screen."

Hurley resumed his seat. Lee stood and faced the jury. "Keep an open mind," she said. "Pictures don't tell the whole story. That video isn't all the evidence that will be presented in this case. This case is not about a videotape. This case is about people. Two people. You will hear from these two people. I expect that you will see that the facts, like real life, like real people, are complex, that there are reasons for the actions framed in that short piece on the TV screen. After you have heard *all* the evidence, a different picture will be painted.

"You will hear from Alison Moore," Lee continued. "You will hear about her suffering. You will hear about the abuse she suffered at the hands of Mr. Donnelly, the man the Commonwealth claims is a victim. Yet here's your real victim, ladies and gentlemen." She pointed at Alison. "She's the one who was abandoned. She is the one who was carrying Mr. Donnelly's child. She is the one who was traumatized, frantic, desperate, scared.

"Dr. Henry Sutherland will testify. He is an expert on what's called post-abortion syndrome, or PAS for short. He will testify that some women who have abortions suffer severe aftereffects, of guilt, fear, and anger. Those aftereffects were present in Alison that day. Mr. Donnelly had used her, then abandoned her when she was pregnant. She was under tremendous stress the day of the abortion.

"Now, these things, these facts, are not in the videotape. This is not a simple case. It's ambiguous, fraught with conflicting feelings that occur when two people get together. So, the case is not a one-minute video that your kids would see on MTV. This is life. Please remember that when you hear all the evidence, when you judge the credibility of the witnesses. I know you will be fair. That's all Alison asks."

Detective Hardy was the first witness to take the stand. He testified about the scene in the Public Garden, and then how the police found the gun in the pond and traced it to the pawn shop where Alison bought it.

Lee had only a few questions. "When Ms. Moore was found on the scene, what was her condition?"

"She seemed calm."

"Detective Hardy, she was bleeding, wasn't she? There was blood all over the sidewalk and on her clothes."

"Yes."

"And she was taken to the hospital from the scene because of her injuries?"

"It's my understanding that it was spotting from the abortion."

"You said she was calm when she was arrested. That's not true, is it? She appeared quite shaken up, didn't she?"

"Her face was calm. She wasn't crying or anything."

146

"She was pale-faced, bleeding from her vagina, but she was calm. Is that your testimony?"

"Yes, it is."

Lee decided to let it go. He wouldn't budge from that position.


Joe Bruno, the manager of G.I. Joe's pawn shop, took the stand. He described the nature of his business. Hurley asked him to describe his usual clientele.

"Kind of a riffraff crowd, you know. People who need a few bucks quick-like. You don't get many pretty lawyers like her comin' in, put it that way. You know, guys who need a couple bucks to tide them over for a bottle or something. I don't knowingly sell to drug addicts or criminals."

"Do you remember the defendant coming into your shop on September twenty-second, nineteen ninety?"

"Yeah, sure I do. Like I said, I don't get many ladies in there. I was having a smoke outside, I think, when she came by. She was real nervous-like. Shaking like a leaf. She bought a twenty-two. It's recommended for the ladies. It's lightweight."

"What did she do after selecting the gun?"

"Oh, she just picked it up, like she could walk out right away. She was in a real hurry. I told her she had to fill out a form first. You know, show me an ID."

"And did she?"

"Yeah. I mean, she was nervous about that. She was, what's the word, flustered. Her hand was shaking real bad. Real bad. She showed me her driver's license. We were joking about it because it didn't look like her. You know, those pictures make you look bad."

"Why did you think the driver's license didn't look like her?"

"Well, she had these sunglasses on, in the store, so I couldn't really see her face good."

"She was disguised, then."

"Objection, leading," Lee interrupted.

"Sustained," the judge replied.

"Is the person who bought the gun you've described in court today?"

"Yeah." He pointed at Alison. "She's sitting over there."

"Your witness," Hurley said to Lee, who then stood up to question Bruno.

"She used her real name on the form?" Lee asked him. "She did show you a form of identification."

"Yes, ma'am. I wouldn't have sold it to her if she didn't."

"She wasn't hiding her identity."

"No."

"She didn't say what the gun was for?"

"Personal protection, I think. I'm not sure. It's not my business to ask. It's like I said, she didn't seem to know nothing about guns."

"She was uncomfortable, ill at ease."

"Oh, yeah. Most people, they come in for a gun, it's no big deal. With her, it was like life or death or something."

"Thank you, Mr. Bruno."


Hurley next called to the stand the nurse from the Beacon Street clinic. He wanted to establish that Alison was not suffering from duress prior to the shooting.

"You've been a nurse at the clinic for six years. You've observed numerous abortion patients. How did the defendant appear that day?"

"No different from most patients. She was quiet, passive."

"Were there any complications from the abortion procedure?"

"No."

"The procedure went smoothly."

"Yes. Alison is a healthy woman. There were no signs of any adverse effects."

On cross-examination, Lee asked, "In your experience, Ms. Seymour, aren't a lot of the patients who come to your clinic passive, as you term it?"

"Oh, sure."

"And this procedure, you admit, can be traumatic for some patients."

"Objection," Hurley said. "There's no foundation for this witness's opinion."

"Your Honor, she's testified she's been a nurse at that clinic and observed many abortion procedures. I believe she's qualified to answer the question."

The judge agreed.

"Sure. You have to understand there are a variety of circumstances that lead a woman to choose this option," she answered.

"In fact, your clinic makes a prospective patient fill out a personality profile?"

"Yes, we do."

"And you do that so you know beforehand whether the person is stable."

"Partly for that reason, yes."

"And you provide counseling services."

"If necessary."

"And you do that because for some women this is a traumatic experience."

"Potentially, yes. Like all procedures."

"Abortions can have complications, physical and emotional."

"Yes, but it's a very safe surgical procedure. Safer than actual childbirth really."

"You're not saying the *psychological* effects are the same, are you, between an abortion and having a baby full-term?"

"I'm not qualified to answer that question."

"Do you have an *opinion* based on your experience?"

"I haven't done obstetrics in many years."

"Well, would you admit there's a different attitude exhibited between a mother who's just given birth and a woman who's terminated her pregnancy?"

Hurley's objection to this question was sustained, but Lee felt she had made her point.

It only occurred to her later that she was stating a pro-life position.

**33**

n the afternoon of the second day of the trial, Jack was called to testify. He took his seat in the witness chair and adjusted the microphone to mouth level. Hurley was standing at the podium with a legal pad. Behind him, blurred faces. Jack couldn't recognize anyone. They would hear his story. The day he'd dreaded for months had arrived. He didn't look at the defense table. He might fall apart by the mere sight of Alison, or erupt into some rage he couldn't control.

After establishing Jack's background and where he was employed, Hurley moved to the day of the shooting.

"Do you know the defendant in this case, Alison Moore?"

"Yes."

"How do you know her?"

"We used to work together. We dated for a while."

"You dated?"

"Yes, we dated. For about six months."

"On October third, nineteen ninety, did you see the defendant?"

"Uh, yes."

"Where did you see her?"

"In the Common. At Park Street station. We met there."

"What was the purpose of your meeting?"

"Um, well, we—she—had an appointment at the family-planning clinic on Beacon Street."

"What was the appointment for?"

"An abortion. She was going to have an abortion."

"Did anything unusual happen there?"

"Well, you know it was kind of crazy outside there. There was a demonstration."

"Uh-huh. Did the defendant say anything to you at that time?"

"No, not much. Just that she wanted to get it over with. Something like that."

"The abortion?"

"Yes. I guess so. She said something like 'There is no good time.' "

"So, did she have the abortion?"

"Well, yes. I mean, I presume so. I wasn't there when it happened."

Hurley didn't relish asking where Jack was when Alison was in the clinic—it would make Jack look cold and insensitive—but it was going to come up anyway on cross-examination, and maybe he could put an effective spin on it.

"Where were you?"

"At the Red Lion Lounge."

"Why did you decide to go there?"

"I was nervous."

"What do you mean? Why were you nervous?"

"Well, you know," Jack said, feeling his face blanch with shame. He tried to think back to that day, and what he was thinking and feeling. He just wanted it to be over, that's all, but he couldn't very well say that. By the time that day came around he had no charitable feelings for Alison, and the idea that they were killing *their* child didn't occur to him. He remembered Hurley prepared him for such a question, but now he didn't know how to respond. Should he say he felt guilty?

"Will the witness answer the question," the judge said.

"Could you repeat it, please?" he said to Hurley, who did.

"I felt bad," he said. It was the only explanation he could give.

Hurley had to contain the damage of this statement; it would open the door wide open for Lee to explore the source of those feelings. At least, Hurley thought, he didn't say the word *guilty*.

"You were raised Catholic, weren't you?" Hurley asked, and Lee was out of her seat, objecting, "Irrelevant."

"Sustained," the judge said, but it was out there. Hurley was sure the jury would understand the inference.

"Okay, after you left the clinic, what did you do? By the way, Mr. Donnelly, who paid for the abortion?"

"I volunteered to pay for it, but she insisted we split the cost."

"Okay. Please continue."

"We got back on the train. I didn't get up from my seat until she did. We got off at the Arlington Street stop."

"Near the entrance of the Public Garden?"

"Yes."

"What happened next?"

"She asked me to walk with her. We went down the path and over to the bridge. You know, the bridge where the swan boats are."

"What, if anything, happened on the bridge?"

"Well, we stopped on the bridge."

"Did she seem angry or upset?"

"No." Jack shrugged. "I mean, she wasn't smiling or anything, but it wasn't unusual. She was just quiet. It made me nervous because she was so quiet. So, we stood on the bridge and she stopped. We were looking down at the water. And then she said, 'Remember the swan boats, Jack,' just like that, and she turned to me. I thought we were going to hug or something. Then I saw the gun."

"What did you do then?"

"I don't know really. Reflexively, I moved to the side. I realized, I guess, that she was going to shoot me. I was scared to death. And then she shot. Into my arm. I remember falling back on the ground, but everything was pretty fuzzy. There was blood everywhere, all over my suit. I thought I was going to die. Then I saw some guy tackle her to the ground. The next thing I remember I was in the emergency room."

Hurley paused, let the facts settle in the jury's mind.

"When you saw the gun, where was it pointed?"

"At my chest."

"Did she move the gun to hit your arm?"

"No. When I flinched, my arm must've got in the way."

"Did you think she was trying to kill you?"

"Objection. The witness's state of mind is irrelevant," Lee said.

"Yes, absolutely. I thought I was a dead man," Jack said before the judge sustained the objection.

"No further questions, Your Honor," Hurley said, and resumed his seat at counsel table.

During his direct examination, he never looked at Alison. When Lee stood up to begin cross-examination, though, he threw her a quick glance. Her hair was shorter and she wore little, if any, makeup. She had on a sweater with a floral design, a white-collared shirt, a gold-heart necklace, and glasses with big round frames. She never wore them, Jack thought. She hated them. They had sat unused on her bedside table. Why was she wearing them now?

"Mr. Donnelly, my name is Lee Klein. I represent Alison in this case." Jack sat back on the chair, breathing heavily.

"You were a third-year associate prior to the incident you described, isn't that correct?"

"Yes."

Lee asked Jack a series of questions about his background. His upbringing in South Boston. Attending UMass-Boston. Boston College Law School.

"Hometown boy, am I correct?"

"Yes."

"Lived at home until law school?"

"Yes."

"Never been married or engaged, right?"

"No."

"In fact, you've never had a serious relationship with a woman, have you?"

"Objection, Your Honor," Hurley barked.

"This is cross-examination," the judge said. "I believe a little latitude is called for. Proceed, Ms. Klein."

"Mr. Donnelly?"

"Uh, I guess not. What do you mean by serious?"

"Well, before you met Ms. Moore, how many women were you sexually involved with?"

"Your Honor," Hurley said plaintively.

"Judge," Lee said.

The judge held up his hand. "I'll allow it. Answer the question."

"Before Alison, I only slept with one other person."

"One person. That would be a woman named Roberta, correct?"

"Yes," Jack said. Alison would have been the only one to know that name. Everything he ever said to her, every confidence, every intimate detail, had surely been betrayed and communicated to her counsel.

"You went out with her a short time during college?"

"Yes, briefly."

"Other than that, the only woman you were ever serious with was my client."

"What do you mean by serious?"

"Well, how would you describe your relationship?" Lee knew better than to ask open-ended questions, but she believed in this instance it would work to her advantage. Jack was easily roused to fits of temper, Alison told her. He would have to be baited.

"Serious," he said contemptuously.

"Thank you, Mr. Donnelly. You met Alison in March of this year?"

"Yes. At Sevens."

"A bar on Charles Street?"

"Yes. The litigation group often went there after work. I was introduced to her or I introduced myself."

"Which was it?"

"I believe I introduced myself."

"You were attracted to her, weren't you?"

"Yeah, sure. So what?"

"We're just trying to get the facts straight."

"Your Honor, can Ms. Klein be instructed to confine her editorializing?" Hurley objected.

"Sit down, Mr. Hurley," the judge said. "Ms. Klein, please."

Jack knew he should not be fighting the minor points. Of course he was attracted to her. There was no sin in that. Why not simply admit it rather than go through these pointless games with the attorney? Because it was a setup. Each concession, however seemingly minor or innocuous, could doom him.

"You were interested in her romantically."

"Yes."

"Right away, weren't you?"

"I suppose so."

"And she didn't seem interested in you."

"No, not really. I think she was shy."

"In fact, Alison told you she had just gotten over a difficult relationship, didn't she?"

"Something like that."

"Something like what?"

"She said she'd broke up with some man recently and she wasn't ready for a relationship."

"But that didn't stop you, did it?"

"You make it sound like I calculated the whole thing."

"Well, you did, didn't you?"

"No!"

"You didn't care what she was going through, did you?"

"Going through what? What are you talking about?"

"I'm talking about you, Mr. Donnelly."

She pointed her finger at him. He felt a tightness in his stomach. He craved a smoke, to escape these questions.

"Your Honor," he said to the judge, "would it be possible to take a brief break? I'm not feeling well."

"I object," Lee said. "I'm sorry I've made Mr. Donnelly uncomfortable, but I'm in the middle of cross."

"It's about time for the midafternoon break," Judge Kaufman said. "Ms. Klein, you can pick it up from here. Fifteen-minute recess. You may go back to the witness room, Mr. Donnelly."

The judge, counsel, bailiff, court reporter, and spectators rose as the jury filed out of the courtroom. Jack stepped off the witness stand. Hurley and Julie followed him through the side door.

The witness room was empty. As soon as he entered, Jack lit a cigarette. When he saw Hurley in the entryway, he exploded with rage.

"Why do I have to go through all this? Everybody I know will hear this shit. Who's on trial here, for Christ's sake?"

"Getting pissed isn't going to solve anything. This isn't kid-gloves stuff," Hurley said. "I told you she was going to do this."

"I wasn't ready for the real thing. How're we doing?" Jack asked.

"Fine." Hurley's voice was cold.

"I'm trying to control myself."

"Yeah. Lawyers always make the worst witnesses. I'm not coaching you, you understand. The truth is all you're obligated to say. No explaining. Don't sweat the details. Just answer the specific question asked. She's trying to goad you, make you look like some asshole—excuse the language. But come off as you are, the all-American boy. I'll take care of the damage on redirect."

Jack wanted to ask "What damage?" but Hurley said, "That's all. Don't worry about it." He left the room.

"It's hard," he said to Julie. "She's trying to trap me."

"They put a microscope on your life," Julie said.

"Yeah."

"Nobody can blame you for feeling angry. Now listen, I know

you've been told this before, but you have to avoid getting too defensive up there. You can be angry. In fact, it seems more natural if you are, but just answer the questions. Hurley'll give you a chance to provide details on redirect."

"I have to answer this stuff?"

"Afraid so. This judge is pretty liberal in allowing the defense to impeach. Okay?"

Jack nodded. He promised himself he would do better.


"I hope you're feeling better, Mr. Donnelly," Lee said when his testimony resumed. "I didn't mean to upset you."

"You didn't."

"Fine."

Lee asked Jack about the purpose of the trip to New York. She made him describe how they had booked separate rooms but had both ended up in hers.

"Whose idea was it to have sex?"

"What do you mean? It just happened is all."

"You weren't planning it?"

"No."

"Isn't it a fact, Mr. Donnelly, that you thought the New York trip was your big moment, your big chance?"

"No," he said, more vehemently this time. "What's this got to do with anything?"

"You planned everything, didn't you?"

"I didn't plan it. Things just happened."

"Just happened. You ordered the champagne."

"We both did. It was both our idea."

"You were the one who wanted sex. You pressured her."

"I didn't force her."

"Isn't it true that Alison said she didn't think it was such a good idea that you two have sex?"

"Something like that."

"But you pushed it, didn't you? You said, 'Don't worry, it's okay, I won't hurt you.' You remember saying that?"

"I might've, but not exactly like that."

"How did she react when you said that?"

"She said she wasn't ready to have a physical relationship, but I knew she didn't mean it."

"No means yes. You know that from your vast experience with women?"

"Objection," Hurley said.

"Withdrawn. You didn't bring a condom, did you?"

"No, I assumed she would protect herself. She did, you know."

"Did she?"

"Yes. She told me to wait a minute, and she went to the bathroom. She had a diaphragm."

"So, you had sex?"

"Yes."

"And that changed the relationship for you?"

"What do you mean?"

"You felt different after that?"

"I guess so. Who wouldn't?"

"How did she react?"

"She was the same."

"The same?"

"Well, she became more affectionate."

"How nice," Lee said. "Sex became a regular thing with you two, didn't it?"

"What's regular?"

"You had sex all the time, didn't you?"

"A lot, yes. It seemed a lot to me."

"You had sex in her office once, didn't you?"

"Uh . . . yes, after hours."

"I assume you didn't bill for *that* time."

"Objection."

"Withdrawn. Let's move on to another subject. You were confident about your future at Adelman and Kaplan?"

"Yes."

"You anticipated being made a partner?"

"Yes, at least I thought so. I had high billable hours. I should have been considered."

"You worked hard."

"You bet."

"And Alison was a lateral hire from another law firm."

"Yes. Perkins and Gray. A D.C. firm."

"She was competition for you, was she not?"

"No, not really. I wasn't threatened."

"But you were impressed by her credentials, weren't you?"

"Sure. Who wouldn't be?"

"That was important to you?"

"In what sense?"

"Is that why you were attracted to her?"

"No. I didn't think about it."

"You were impressed and didn't think about it? Which is it?"

"You're confusing two different things. I mean, if she was ugly, I wouldn't have been impressed." When the words came out, he realized instantly how they sounded and longed to take them back.

"So, she was good-looking?"

"Yes. Sure."

"You acted on that attraction, didn't you? To use the common expression, you chased her?"

"I didn't chase her. I already answered this. Even if I did, she was ready to be caught."

"She chased you, then?"

"Not exactly. That's not how things happen."

"Well, Mr. Donnelly, how do things happen?"

"We spent a lot of time together at work, and we became close. That's all."

"Yet you said earlier that Ms. Moore didn't want a relationship."

"That's what she *said*. I didn't believe her. Maybe subconsciously she did want one. She was obviously open to one."

"Are you testifying as a psychiatric expert or a clairvoyant, Mr. Donnelly?"

Hurley's objection was sustained.

"There came a point when you decided the relationship was over?"

"It's not that simple."

"Well, did you decide you wanted to end the relationship?"

"Yes."

"Long before you actually did?"

"About a month, I'd guess."

"And why did you want to end it?"

"I thought she was unstable. She'd act crazy sometimes. She'd fly off the handle at every little thing."

"Mr. Donnelly," Lee said, picking up a manila folder and removing a piece of paper. "You were interviewed by Detective Hardy the day after the events you've described, after the abortion?"

"Yes."

"During that interview, didn't you say you had no warning she would attack you, that Alison had never exhibited any signs of instability?"

"Yes, but . . ."

"And didn't you also say, 'It's all my fault'?"

"Yeah, but that was right after the shooting. I was totally confused."

"So, were you lying to the police or are you lying now?"

"Your Honor," Hurley said, "counsel's not allowing the witness to complete his answers."

"I'm sorry, Mr. Donnelly, were you about to say something?"

"Sure, I felt bad right after. I felt bad about the abortion. And she *was* crazy. I thought she was a nut. That's why I wanted to get away."

"When did you decide she was a nut, when you found out she was pregnant with your child?"

"No, way before that."

"When?"

"I don't remember exactly when."

"You don't remember because you're making it up."

"Objection!" Hurley yelled.

"Sustained."

"So, there came a point in time when you decided you wanted it to be over, isn't that correct?"

"Yes."

"And you didn't communicate that to Alison?"

"Not in so many words."

"In *any* words, Mr. Donnelly. You never told her the relationship was over?"

"No, I didn't, but—"

"Thank you."

"I want to finish," Jack said. "She *knew* I wanted to break up. She knew. She knew it. Just ask her."

The judge pounded his gavel. Jack was suddenly aware how strident he sounded.

"Mr. Donnelly, this was all a lot simpler than you're pretending, wasn't it?"

"I have no idea what you mean."

"You broke up with her for a simple reason: She was pregnant with your child and you thought it would ruin your career."

"That's a lie. You have no proof of that." He looked at Alison. She appeared pale and tired.

"I'm asking the question."

"No. That's not why."

"Well, what was the reason? You haven't told us yet."

"It just happened, that's all. It wasn't some bad thing on my part. People break up all the time."

Lee asked him when he found out Alison was pregnant. He

recounted their meeting at Pelican's, and she asked how he responded to the news.

"Well, I felt bad. For her. It was a bad situation."

"Why was it a bad situation?"

"Because both of us, well, we weren't married."

"Anything else? Any other reasons?"

"We weren't ready to have children."

"*You* weren't ready, isn't that correct?"

"No, both of us."

"Because of *your* career."

"Well, yes, but it's not like you're saying. I already said my career wasn't the reason."

"Did you discuss your options?"

"No, I mean, I didn't think it was anything I could decide."

"You were the father, weren't you?"

"I assumed so. She said I was."

"You don't have any doubt that you were the father, do you?"

"No," Jack said reluctantly.

"But you didn't care what happened?"

"I didn't say that. I cared. There wasn't any other viable option."

"But again, did you discuss options?"

"No. Like I said. Plus I think she'd made up her mind."

"Did you ask her whether she wanted to keep the baby?"

"No. We didn't talk about it."

"So, it wasn't your problem, is that it?"

"I didn't say that. I felt responsibility. I offered to go with her."

"How noble of you. Prior to the meeting at Pelican's you had last seen Alison at her apartment, isn't that correct?"

"Yes."

"Why did you go there?"

"I wanted to see her, that's all."

"And you bought flowers."

"Yes."

"And you had sex, isn't that right?"

"Yes."

"Then you left right afterward."

"Yes. Shortly thereafter. It was early in the morning."

"So, you went there to have sex?"

"No, no. I missed her."

"Why didn't you stay?"

"I just didn't want to."

"Why, because you got what you wanted? You wanted sex, but not her?"

"That's not what it was at all. She wanted me, too."

"She did? You knew that?"

"She was willing."

"She was willing, as you say, because she thought you still loved her."

"I don't know why she'd think that. We weren't in love."

"Did you ever say you loved her?"

"No, I don't think so."

"Never?"

"I don't remember. I didn't love her."

"So, you were lying? You lied to her when you said you loved her?"

"I said I don't remember if I ever said it. But if I did, it wasn't a lie. I felt it at the time."

"When you were having sex?"

He closed his eyes. "Yes."

"How was she to know you didn't mean it, Mr. Donnelly?"

"I—we—were having sex, you know, and I might have just blurted it out. Heat of passion, I guess."

"Oh, is that your defense?"

"I'm not on trial here."

Before Hurley could object, Judge Kaufman admonished the witness and counsel to avoid arguing with each other.

"Let's talk about the day of the abortion, Mr. Donnelly." Lee led him through the events leading up to their entrance into the clinic, the protests out in front, the violent confrontation. "You decided to go to that clinic because she didn't know anyone there, correct?"

"I don't know why *she* decided where to go. She just told me to meet her at Park Street station, so I did."

"Didn't Alison tell you she didn't want to go to her regular gynecologist?"

"She wanted to keep it private. I was respecting her wishes."

"She wasn't eager to have the abortion, was she?"

"I don't know how she felt about it."

"Well, did she say, 'I'm going to have an abortion' when she told you she was pregnant?"

"No."

"You didn't give her a choice, did you?"

"It wasn't my decision, it was her decision. It's her body."

"You didn't stay with her when she had the abortion, did you?"

"No."

"You left her alone there, didn't you?"

"It's not like I could be in there with her. I went down the block."

"For a couple of beers, right? You were enjoying a few drinks while she was having the abortion?"

"I wasn't enjoying anything. I . . . I was nervous. The place was crazy. It made me sick staying in there with all those people."

Looking into the fog of the crowd of faces, he thought of the horror of that day. Surely, if he could explain himself, he would not seem so awful, but he knew that this forum would not allow him to do it, that the questions and answers were outside his control.

"You felt that way, yet you left her all alone to face it by herself?"

"You act like it's my fault. I was shot for no good reason!"

"Move to strike, Your Honor," Lee said.

"Granted. Ladies and gentlemen of the jury, disregard the last comment by the witness. It's not evidence."

None of this is evidence, Jack thought. Evidence of what? What was this trial all about?

"Now, after Alison had the abortion, when you were getting off the subway at Arlington Street, you were just going to walk away, right? You said you had an appointment."

"I did. I did. I wasn't lying. I had to meet with a client. It was an important meeting."

"I'm sure it was. More important than consoling Alison?"

"She didn't look like she needed any consoling. She seemed fine. Normal."

"She has an abortion every day, a normal experience?"

"She didn't look to be in distress."

"You were only thinking about how you could get away from her, isn't that true?"

"Well, no . . . yes, I don't know what. I felt bad. I did."

"Not bad enough to want to stay with her. Not bad enough to not abandon her?"

"I didn't abandon her. I went with her to the clinic. That's more than most guys would've done."

"Really? What would most men do?"

"Objection, Your Honor," Hurley said. "Mr. Donnelly can't testify about what others would do."

"Overruled. He opened the door, Counsel. Answer the question."

"I guess most guys would've just let her go by herself and have nothing to do with her."

"And would that make it right?"

"No. I didn't say that."

"So, it's not right?"

"No, it wouldn't be."

"How were you any different?"

He couldn't answer the question. She had boxed him in a corner, but he had to say something.

"I went with her."

"And that's enough, as far as you're concerned?"

"Uh, yes."

"Thank you." Lee paused. "Now, on the bridge, Alison said, 'Remember the swan boats.' I believe you testified to that on direct examination. And you knew what she meant."

"Yes."

"And that was what?"

"We were supposed to go on the swan boats once."

"Didn't you in fact promise her a romantic picnic and a ride on the swan boats?"

"We were busy all the time at work. It was just an idea."

"Well, she certainly remembered it, didn't she?"

"Apparently."

Lee paused in her questioning. It was four-thirty. She wanted to end the day by giving the jurors something to think about during the evening, some dominant image that would stick in their minds.

"Now, Mr. Donnelly, you've testified that the abortion was the only option—"

"The only *feasible* option."

"From your point of view."

"From both our points of view."

"But you never discussed it, so you wouldn't know her point of view."

"We discussed the abortion."

"You didn't offer any suggestions, such as adoption, getting married, living together?"

Jack reluctantly answered in the negative. How could everything seem so different now? No, he hadn't considered such options; he wouldn't have thought of them under the best of circumstances.

"The fact is you abandoned Alison because she was pregnant and threatened your career."

"That's a lie!" Jack shouted. "You keep saying that. It's just not true. I wasn't going to have a baby with that crazy woman."

"When did you decide she was quote crazy?"

"I don't know. I always thought so."

"You went out with her even though you thought she was crazy?"

"I don't know when I realized she was acting strange."

"Isn't it true that Alison became crazy, to use your word, after she became pregnant?"

"I don't know. Ask anybody about her behavior then. They'll tell you. Nobody liked her. Nobody."

"And you liked her for the sex?"

"I liked her before we had sex."

"You wanted to have sex with her the day you first met her, isn't that correct?"

"Yes, but—"

"And you no longer wanted her when she became pregnant?"

"No, that's not the way it was."

"Well, that's the sequence, isn't it? You lose interest, you break up with her *after* she is pregnant."

"It was over by then."

"In your mind, not in hers."

"I don't have the foggiest idea what was in her messed-up mind."

"Yet you seem to know she didn't want to have the baby, that she wanted the abortion?"

"If she didn't want to, she could've said something."

"But it wouldn't have made any difference, would it? You had no intention of continuing your relationship with Alison."

It was a question he didn't want to answer, for he could see how damaging the truth would be. Lee stood at the podium, seeming to relish his agony. Everything he'd ever had was probably gone forever. With this performance, Kaplan would never let him back in the firm. How could he face those accusatory looks from every secretary, paralegal, associate, and partner?

"Mr. Donnelly," Lee said. "Do you want me to repeat the question?"

"No. The answer is no."

"No further questions at this time," Lee said.


At the end of the day's testimony, as there would be throughout the trial, standing microphones were set up outside the courthouse at the bottom of the steps. Demonstrators lined both sides of barricades separating them from the microphones.

"We want to hear from Alison. Alison, speak!" a voice in the crowd said, and a murmur of support arose, but Lee stilled the cries with a raised hand. Alison admired how Lee, supposedly eschewing the publicity, made sure the evening news would have pictures of them outside the courthouse, confident yet sober.

"We won't be making any statements of substance during the trial," Lee said. "But I think it went very well today. We heard Mr. Donnelly's version of events."

"Are you saying he's lying?" a reporter asked.

"That's for the jury to decide."

"What if it was *her* decision?"

"As a father, he had responsibilities too."

Jack viewed the scene from a barred window inside the court-house that overlooked the front steps, like a schoolboy yearning for recess. Why wasn't his pain mentioned? How he suffered with nervous exhaustion and insomnia since the shooting. How he was suffering without a job. He waited for the hubbub to die down before he ventured out.

he day after Jack's testimony a banner headline appeared in the *Herald*:

SOUTHIE KID
BAD BOY

■ Dumped Pregnant
Girlfriend

■ Catholic Admits "Abortion-Only Option"
■ Defense Scores Points In Cross-Examination

The *Globe* was more sedate:

DEFENSE IN 'PUBLIC GARDEN SHOOTING'
CASE TURNS TABLES ON PROSECUTION;
Sharp Exchanges In Cross-Examination
Of Alleged Victim.

On Barry Lindstrom's call-in show, reaction to Jack's testimony was fierce and divided. "What you think of this yuppie angst, folks? Isn't this something? I feel like Pontius Pilate tonight. 'Crucify him,' they're all yelling. Come on, people, so the guy gets a little skirt and then says bye-bye. Is this so unusual? Should he be shot for it?"

"I always knew you were a sexist pig, Lindstrom," a caller said. "Maybe we should take you out for some target practice in the Public Garden."

"Ma'am. Misses, Miss, or Ms., whatever you are, probably a lesbo, are you aware that using the telephones—" Click.

"She hung up. These are the kind of intellectual, rational discussions you have with the libbers, folks.

"My guest tonight is a man I'm sure you'll all recognize. Sidney Schlapman, adjunct professor of law at Harvard. Author of four books, including *I Fought the Law and I Won*. His latest book is *If the Law Is an Ass, What Am I?* Sidney. Professor. Welcome to the show."

"Happy to be here, Barry."

"We'll be taking your calls in just a few minutes, folks. Well, Professor, you're a veteran of these high-publicity cases. What do you think?"

"Defense counsel's doing an effective job. Her client's not sympathetic, so she has to attack the alleged victim."

"Do you hear that folks? The *alleged* victim. Don't you love the way lawyers talk? Go ahead, Professor. Sorry to interrupt."

"As I was saying, she's doing well. The prosecution seems to be bumbling around. At this point, I'd say she has a good chance of acquittal. But we shall see."

"Thank you. Our first call is from Betty from Brockton, hometown of Marvelous Marvin Hagler. The Night Owl here."

"Yeah. Hello? I just wanted to say ... I just want to say that girl shot him, and she should go jail."

"What about the presumption of innocence, ma'am?" the professor said.

"Presume *this*," Barry said.


"Fucking Harvard schmuck," Hurley said, listening to Schlapman. "Never did more than two or three trials in his life and thinks he's an expert."

Hurley was in his office with Julie. It was the night after Jack's cross-examination.

"Why'd you let Lee go on like that?" she asked. "She was hammering him."

"I got my reasons. One, Kaufman was letting it all in anyway. Two, I could see the guy was a lousy witness. Three, given points one and two—let me finish—I didn't want him to be too much our guy. Our guy the asshole up there. The guy's got 'guilt' written all over his face and his words are denying it. He thinks he's been a bad boy. Everybody thinks he looks bad, but he pretends nothing's wrong, so he looks worse. Our job is not to protect him, but to prosecute *her*."

He looked at her. "What do you think? You've been pretty quiet."

"This is harder than I thought it would be," Julie said.

"Oh, it was never going to be easy. Things happen in trials. Unexpected things. Sure, it'll be a battle. Klein's a good lawyer. Everything depends on the defendant. There's certain things she can't explain away. The gun, for example. What's the feeling around here?"

Julie shrugged, and he knew she was avoiding an unwelcome answer. "Don't think about it," he said. "Back-stabbing, Monday-morning quarterbacking's the name of the game in this place. You're new. You'll learn that people will step over bodies to get what they want."

"It's funny you should say that, because that's how Jack appears. Too ambitious. People cringe at that. I know I did."

"Then I'm glad you're at counsel table and not in the jury box."


In the morning, Hurley began rehabilitating Jack. He'd been through this before. The success of the case didn't depend on Jack's sincerity or likability. Hurley merely wanted to bring out the South Boston origins, the relative innocence, how Jack was naive when it came to women. Still, a bumbling innocent was one thing, a calculating son of a bitch was another, and Hurley had to redeem, at least in part, Jack's character.

Soon the focus would shift anyway. Alison was the crucial witness. This paper tiger of a defense could be easily ripped apart. Already, internally, Hurley was rehearsing a closing argument that would say something like "Ladies and gentlemen of the jury, the defense would have you believe that the defendant was justified in shooting at Mr. Donnelly. We're all grown-ups here. If every time someone shot somebody over the breakup of a relationship, where would any of us be? Dead."


Hurley began his redirect. "I just have a few questions, Mr. Donnelly. When you first met the defendant, why were you attracted to her?"

"Well, it's like I said, or tried to say to Ms. Klein, I thought she was pretty. She was smart. I could see that."

"And you were infatuated with her?"

"Yes. I thought of her all the time. It wasn't mean or dirty."

"And you never intended to hurt her?"

"It was the furthest thing from my mind."

"Mr. Donnelly, did you break off your relationship with the defendant because she told you she was pregnant?"

"No, of course not. It's like I said, I just didn't want to see her anymore. I didn't want a serious relationship with her."

"Did you force her to have an abortion?"

"No."

"Did you encourage her to have an abortion?"

"No. It was her decision."

"At one time you thought you loved her, didn't you?"

"I didn't know what it was." Jack couldn't say what he thought, that it was all just desire, sexual desire, and the desire to have something seemingly unapproachable.

But Hurley thought this was a perfect answer. It summoned up the impression he wanted to convey: Jack was lost with these emotions, emotions that were more familiar to his assailant. Hurley let his testimony end with that.

Lee was up. "Just a few more questions, Mr. Donnelly. I know you're eager to leave."

"I have all the time in the world, Ms. Klein." He gave her a pained smile. "Your client has deprived me of my livelihood."

"Well, let's start with that. That's all you're concerned about, isn't it? Your career."

"My career is important to me, yes. I have not been allowed to return to my job since she shot me."

"Your career is more important than how you treated Alison? More important than your unborn child?"

"I didn't treat Alison badly. And I'm sorry that she became pregnant. I've worked all my life to be a lawyer and your client, she—Alison—she just took it all away. I never did anything to deserve that."

"Well, thank you for clarifying that for us. Just now you told Mr. Hurley that you did not encourage Alison to have the abortion, isn't that correct?"

"Yes."

"But when she told you she was pregnant, you told her, 'You're not going to keep it,' didn't you?"

"I don't remember my words, but it was her choice."

"What did you say, then?"

"I don't remember, except I was in shock that she was pregnant. At first I probably thought she was kidding."

"You were in shock because you didn't want her to have your child."

"I was in shock because of the fact, you know, that she was pregnant."

"And you didn't want her to have the baby?"

Jack knew he could not hedge forever, that his evasiveness was only making matters worse. "No, Ms. Klein, I didn't. Our relationship was over."

"Nothing further of this witness, Your Honor."


In the hallway leading to the witness room, Jack saw two members of the firm heading there too.

"Drew. Janice. Welcome to the zoo."

"We can't talk. Court order," Drew replied.

"You can say *hello*."

Drew responded with a harsh rasp. "I can't believe you put us through this. We're wasting valuable time."

Jack grabbed the lapel of his jacket, and Drew slapped his hand away.

"Me? It's not *my* fault."

"Well, it's sure not mine. You and she deserve each other."

"Don't screw me, Drew." Jack hated the pleading in his voice.

"The whole truth and nothing but the truth. So help me God."

Jack left the building. The cold air felt fresh, away from the oppressive warmth of the courtroom. On the plaza, the demonstrators stood in clumps talking among themselves. From behind, a microphone was thrust in his face and a babble of voices shouted questions.

"No comment," he said. He pushed through the reporters, but there was no escape route. A middle-aged man rushed toward him, a Bible in his hand, and spit in Jack's face. "Murderer. Repent, you murderer. Baby killer."

"Pig!" a voice yelled, and the remains of a bologna sandwich landed on Jack's coat. The man dogged him as he attempted to make his way across the plaza to the escalators. "Get away from me!" Jack shoved the man in the chest, then ran down the escalator steps and crossed the street.

He sat on the stone steps in the plaza next to City Hall, catching his breath. His body trembled with convulsions that centered in his chest. He began to sob. He covered his eyes to capture the tears before they rolled down his cheeks, but the salty taste hit his lips. He wiped his nose with the sleeve of his jacket. He found himself silently praying for relief, as people in times of distress do, but he stopped. That he could even dare to request help now was sickening. Faith is not something you could use at your whim.

All acts, finally, have consequences. If he'd learned anything from his Catholic upbringing, it was that. To think you could kill and not suffer. But why him? That was not his act. It was hers. Was *she* afflicted by it?

He used to walk out of the confessional, leaving his greatest sins unspoken, kneeling dutifully with his prescribed penance—the Hail Marys, Our Fathers—wondering, eyes fixed on Jesus, whether He knew he hadn't fully confessed. Could he go back in and revise his testimony? He had done poorly in court. He had left too much unspoken.

he defense's case began with Janice, who explained that Alison's lateral hiring had been viewed with suspicion and trepidation. She was immediately perceived as a threat to others' advancement in the firm. Jack became obsessed with her; they were an embarrassment to the firm, the way they mooned over each other. But Alison never made any effort to be accommodating or friendly to anybody else.

"Sure, we all tried to be nice at first, but she was a difficult person. It could've been shyness, yes, but it certainly didn't appear that way."

Drew seconded Janice, then focused on Jack. "He was hot after her. The first night he saw her, you could tell he wanted her bad. He had this glint in his eyes that guys get, you know, like they've seen their dream girl. He talked about her constantly. It was pretty sickening after a while. We all thought they were a match made in hell."

Lee thought Janice and Drew testified well for her; Hurley had no real way to cross-examine them. With their nice clothes and comfortable incomes, they appeared as selfish, too well-fed yuppies. Their testimony had accomplished a simple yet vital point: Alison had encountered a hostile work environment, where she was the outsider, viewed with suspicion, and Jack was her only friend.

Dr. Sutherland entered the courtroom. In his gray suit and red tie, holding a fedora in his hands, he gave the appearance, as Alison had said to Lee once, of an emeritus professor.

He began his testimony by listing his professional qualifications, his previous appearances as an expert witness, his practice as a psychologist, his scholarly work. He explained that he had often testified on issues regarding post-traumatic stress disorder in Vietnam veterans, incest victims, battered women.

"I completed a study of a number of women who had undergone abortions. I noticed a high degree of similarity between the symptomatology of post-traumatic stress and the post-abortion experience. The diagnostic criteria are: a stressor, that is, the abortion experience, an experience outside the range of normal human conduct; a reexperience of the abortion experience through flashbacks, dreams; avoidance of the external world by the patient, such as a feeling of alienation from others; other symptoms, like guilt, sleep disturbance. I call this disease post-abortion syndrome, or PAS for short."

"Now, Doctor, did you examine Alison Moore regarding this case?"

"Yes, I met with her. We discussed a number of things. She was very reluctant to discuss the abortion experience at first. This is not unusual. She denied that it bothered her. She denied feeling any guilt or shame over the incident. Often with these patients, it's best to start with the pre-abortion experience, to both get a context for the event and to ease into troubling areas of inquiry."

"What did you learn from Ms. Moore?"

"She explained to me about how she found out she was pregnant, and how she felt knowing that the father would not want the baby because he didn't love her. She didn't want to have the abortion. She said it was the only choice that he gave her. In addition, she told me about the atmosphere outside the clinic the day she went."

"How did that affect her?"

"It traumatized her further. One of the things that makes the abortion experience difficult is the presence of demonstrators. I've seen that quite a bit in my studies. She said at that point she thought of just walking away and coming back another day, but she knew that if she didn't go through with it then, she never would, that she might do something drastic."

"Did she say what she meant by doing something drastic?"

"Yes. She mentioned a self-induced abortion, or even suicide."

"Go on."

"I asked her to describe the procedure, and at first she said she couldn't remember anything once they got into the clinic. Eventually, I broke that denial down. She talked about the coldness of the room and the awful hum of the vacuum pump used to remove the fetus."

"Did she use that term, 'fetus'?"

"Oh, no. She said 'it' or she mocked the lingo of the clinic, calling it the 'product of conception.' That's part of the problem. The people involved in the process employ euphemisms that can add to the trauma. Women know it's a life they're extinguishing."

"Objection, Your Honor," Hurley said. He wondered if Sutherland was helping or hurting Lee's case, but he wanted the jury to understand that by no means was he endorsing the abortion decision. "Could we move on to more relevant events?" he continued. "This is nothing but narrative."

"Break it up a little, Ms. Klein," the judge said.

"Dr. Sutherland, could you just briefly summarize for the jury your findings regarding Ms. Moore and the abortion experience."

"I'll try," he said. "It's not really subject to the quick sound bite."

"Try your best, Doctor," Judge Kaufman said.

"Okay. Ms. Moore frequently reexperiences the abortion through flashbacks. She said she would be reminded of it when she'd see a baby in a stroller or a pregnant woman. She said it made her physically ill. She told me this dream she had of the baby—"

"Your Honor, please, *dreams*?" Hurley said. "Can we have some conformity with the rules of evidence?"

"Mr. Hurley, the court is quite familiar with the rules of evidence."

"I didn't mean to insult the court, Your Honor."

"Your lack of intent is noted for the record. Ms. Klein, continue."

"Any other symptoms, Doctor?"

"In general, she still cannot adequately recount the events of that day. Only under intense questioning can she even remember some facts. You have to pull them out of her. She has emotional outbursts after being asked any personal questions. She has trouble sleeping."

"Doctor, as an expert in this field, do you have an opinion about whether Alison suffers from PAS?"

"Yes, I do."

"What is your opinion?"

"She certainly does. She certainly did that day."

---

Hurley began his cross-examination. "Doctor, this supposed disorder you're describing, it's not recognized by the American Psychiatric Association, is it?"

"Post-traumatic stress disorder is. This is a subspecies."

"In your opinion. Isn't it true, PAS is not specifically recognized?"

"No. Not by the establishment."

"In fact, all respected medical opinion, from the American Medical Association to the American Psychiatric Association to the Surgeon General of the United States, have discounted PAS, haven't they?"

"That doesn't make them right."

"Bravo, Doctor," Hurley said. "You're the lone wolf."

"I'm not the only one who believes in it."

"There isn't a single respected medical or psychiatric authority who agrees with you, isn't that correct?"

"Define your terms. Respectable to whom?"

"You admit, then, that your theory is not well-recognized as valid?"

"I admit it's not popular."

"Fine. Now, it's possible, isn't it, that Ms. Moore was suffering some trauma unrelated to her pregnancy, but prior to it?"

"Yes."

"Yet you meet with her for just a couple of hours and you can tell us to a reasonable degree of medical certainty that the abortion caused her to shoot—strike that—that she suffers post-traumatic stress due solely to the abortion?"

"I didn't say solely."

"So, you admit the possibility that there are other reasons, such as past personal problems or disappointments, that made the defendant shoot Mr. Donnelly?"

"They may have contributed, but she wouldn't have done what she did without the abortion experience."

"Now, Doctor, this denial you talked about. It could be the defendant isn't suffering at all, and you choose to call it denial?"

"That's highly unlikely."

"Is it? You didn't know the defendant prior to your retention as an expert, did you?"

"No."

"Did you examine her medical history?"

"No."

"Were you aware that the defendant had sought counseling in the past?"

"Yes, certainly. She told me she had."

"Did you consult with that doctor?"

"No. I based my opinion on my own experience and observations."

"Did you examine any of the clinic's records from the day of the abortion?"

"No."

"You didn't think they were important."

"They were not necessary for my diagnosis."

"So, you ignored all the available records, and yet you purport to know whether the defendant is suffering denial."

"We all suffer denial in some degree over something."

"In other words, we're all sick."

"In some degree."

"Thank you."

Hurley walked behind counsel table, pivoted toward the jury, then turned back to Sutherland.

"Isn't it true, Doctor, that you were convicted of disorderly conduct in Brookline in nineteen eighty-six?"

"Objection!" Lee said. This was the first she'd heard of it. She was overruled.

Hurley grinned. A little careless, Lee, he thought.

"Should I answer?" Sutherland asked. The judge nodded.

"Yes, I was."

"That was at an anti-abortion demonstration, was it not?"

"My diagnosis is not prejudiced by my politics. It's a scientific study."

"That wasn't my question. Were you arrested for blocking Beacon Street as part of an anti-abortion protest?"

"Yes."

"You are personally opposed to abortion, aren't you?"

"Yes, but that has nothing to do with—"

"Thank you. Now, Doctor, are you saying Ms. Moore was temporarily insane at the time of the shooting?"

"No, not insane. I'm saying the trauma induced her actions."

"Are you saying she didn't understand what she was doing?"

"She was traumatized."

"But she understood?"

"As far as I know."

"All you are saying is she had some traumatic event—whatever it was—and she acted the way she did because of it. That doesn't excuse it, does it?"

"That's for the jury to decide, Mr. Hurley. I'm just giving my opinion."

"And how much have you been paid for that opinion?"

"Nothing. I told Ms. Klein I'd do it for free."

"Out of the goodness of your heart? Isn't it true, Doctor, that you are currently working on a book about this alleged syndrome?"

"As a matter of fact, I am."

"You don't have a publisher for it, do you?"

"Not yet."

"And it would be fair to say your testimony here today may sway some publisher out there?"

"I don't pretend to know the publishing business."

"Well, it won't hurt, will it?"

Lee stood. "Your Honor, I object. Dr. Sutherland has already stated—"

"Sustained. Move on, Mr. Hurley. You've made your point."

"And your opinion in this case, Doctor, is directly affected by your religious beliefs, isn't it?"

"My religious beliefs are not relevant. I'm here in my position as a trained psychologist. Religion should not be injected in here."

"Okay, let's skip religion. Your political interests, Doctor, as evidenced by your pro-life activities—"

"Again, I must say, they have not affected my analysis."

"So, a person's biases, family history, et cetera, are not relevant to this issue?"

"They're certainly relevant to a determination of whether PAS exists, but not for my opinion."

"You're free from political, religious, or even a purely monetary bias in judging the defendant's condition?"

"That's correct."

"You're quite extraordinary then, Doctor. I have nothing further."

Lee had made a mistake, she realized, in not probing further Dr. Sutherland's possible bias. It never occurred to her to ask if he had any prior criminal record. He told her he had no hidden agenda, but he did. Hurley had clearly hurt him with those questions. All Lee could do on redirect was ask Sutherland if his pro-life activities, his possible publishing contract, affected his judgment in this case. He reiterated that they had not.

**36**

UBLIC GARDEN DEFEN-
DANT TO TESTIFY;
WOMAN ACCUSED OF SHOOT-
ING BOYFRIEND TO TELL HER
STORY FROM WITNESS STAND.

As Alison was sworn in she remembered Garrett's advice: Think of it as another part. She knew this was the most crucial moment in the case, in her life. People who tell you be yourself don't know what it's like under the bright lights. She saw herself back on a stage at that first audition, the klieg lights on her. She had been knock-kneed like a grade-schooler delivering a speech, and she remembered thinking, Why do I have to go through all this for a nonspeaking part?

She felt just as adolescent now, dressed in the outfit Lee recommended: a high-necked white blouse, a gray wool jacket, a long pleated skirt, a pearl necklace. The virginal look. Even eyeliner was taboo to Lee; only a light touch of rouge was permitted.

Direct examination began with background material: Alison told of her childhood in Indiana, spoke about her father, a distinguished history professor. Attending Wellesley. Meeting Jerry. Law school. D.C. How Jerry slept around and finally, "I had to stand up for myself. I had no self-worth left. I came back to Boston."

"And you accepted a job with Adelman and Kaplan?"

"Yes. It is a well-respected firm. I joined their litigation department."

"Could you explain to the jury what a lateral hire is?"

"Yes, a lateral is someone who is hired from another firm at the same level. That was my situation."

"Laterals don't start from the ground up, then?"

"No. Most laterals are brought in because they can improve the client base or maybe they fill a specific need in the firm. It's not that uncommon these days. The law has become a business like any other."

"But still, is it fair to say it's often resented by people who are already at the firm?"

"Well, you're treated as an outsider. You know, an interloper."

"And did you feel some of that when you came aboard?"

"Oh, yes, most definitely. It was clear I was resented. Nobody, besides Jack, of course, was ever really friendly to me. I tried, but they never warmed up to me. Except for one time. I was never included in any of their parties or drinks after work. Nobody asked me to lunch or anything. I could tell it was going to be rough sledding from the first day I arrived."

"That's when you met Mr. Donnelly, is that correct?"

"Yes, at Sevens on Charles Street. The litigation group went there regularly."

"And what were your impressions of Mr. Donnelly?"

"Oh, he seemed nice. Very welcoming. Friendly. He was the only one who seemed glad I was there. I certainly didn't think there was any sexual content, though."

"What did you and Mr. Donnelly talk about?"

"I don't remember the specifics, just general things like how are you settling in, how do you like Boston, where'd you go to school. He seemed very interested in that."

"What do you mean?"

"Jack has a chip on his shoulder about not being Ivy League. He always asked where a person went to school. It was that important to him."

"Go on."

"We were just talking. It was real loud in the bar, and it's not like you could have a serious discussion. Just a friendly getting-to-know-you chat."

"Did anything else happen that night?"

"No." She pursed her lips together, as if pondering an answer. "He walked me to the T-stop."

"When you left that night, did you think you wanted to have a relationship with him?"

"No." She laughed. "That's the last thing I would've wanted. I had just moved back to town and was reeling from my relationship with Jerry. No, I thought maybe he'd be a work friend."

"He's an attractive man. It might've crossed your mind?"

"No, it didn't."

"Still, the relationship changed?"

"Yes, but not because of me. It became obvious after a while that he was interested in me on more than a friendly basis. He paid a lot of attention to me at work. You know, during meetings he'd make a point of asking my opinion, and he looked at me in a way that made me realize he thought I was attractive. We had frequent lunches, conversations in the office, and sometimes we'd have a drink or two. We'd talk about our lives and some of the conversations were quite personal. We were becoming good friends, I thought."

"Who initiated these contacts between you two?"

"Jack always did. He'd maybe come down to my office and suggest we go someplace. Don't get me wrong. It was very nice. Being new in town, it was good to have a friend."

"And then you went to New York together."

"Yes." She smoothed her skirt.

"What happened on that trip?"

"It was a business trip. We were there to do a deposition. The first week of May. The deposition was scheduled for the sixth, a Friday. I thought we could stretch it into a long weekend. I always liked New York."

"Did you plan on having sex with Mr. Donnelly that weekend?"

"No. I looked forward to a weekend of theater, shopping, restaurants. But it was apparent he had more in mind. As I said, I knew he liked me beyond being just friends. He paid a lot of attention. We'd kissed once or twice, I think, before that, but I didn't think we were going to sleep together. I mean, I figured he was interested, but if the issue came up, I could prevent it from happening. But I did bring my diaphragm with me, just to be safe."

Alison was offering too much too quickly, Lee thought. Hurley had thus far not objected. Was it going badly? It was hard to be objective standing in the middle of the courtroom. Lee poured a cup of water from the silver pitcher at counsel table. Witness examinations were a matter of rhythm and texture. Lee sipped from the cup and snuck a glance at Hurley. He was absorbed with writing on his legal pad.

"But you had sex for the first time there in New York?"

"Yes. We'd seen this great play, and I was excited about it. We ordered some champagne, and we made love."

"How did he react?"

"He seemed so sad about the whole thing, I mean beforehand. I felt sorry for him. He didn't really like the play, and I'd thought I'd ruined his weekend because all we did was things that I enjoyed. I had sex to please him."

"And was he pleased?"

"No. I couldn't understand it. He was morose. I tried to brighten him up, but he seemed upset."

"Did you ever ask him what he was feeling that night?"

"I tried, but he wasn't exactly a big talker where his emotions were involved. I think he felt guilty—"

"Move to strike, Your Honor. Speculation," Hurley interrupted.

"No, we never talked about it directly," Alison said.

"What happened after you got back to the office?"

"It was awkward at first. You could tell people suspected something had gone on in New York. And the women, including Sally, his secretary, just hated the idea of it. They were like mother hens or acted like they were his sisters. But we came out of the closet, so to speak, eventually and had a regular relationship for a while."

"For a while?"

"Yes. He lost interest quickly. I was getting closer to him and he moved away."

"Did he ever acknowledge that fact?"

"No. When I brought it up, he brushed it off. He said I was always too busy, so we never saw each other much. He was busy, too. I said, People make time if they want to. I tried to make the time. And then poof! I told him I was pregnant, and he totally changed. He began to treat me like I was some one-night stand he wanted to get rid of."

"How so?"

"He'd get annoyed at the slightest thing. He said he needed his space, but we hardly saw each other."

"How did that make you feel?"

"Empty inside." She began to cry.

"Do you need a few minutes?" Lee asked. She was astounded at Alison's sudden emotion. There seemed to be no warning. "I know this is painful for you."

"Your Honor," Hurley said, disgusted.

"It's stricken," the judge said. "The jury is to disregard the improper remark by defense counsel. It's not evidence in this case. It's for you to decide what pain Ms. Moore may or may not have suffered. Bailiff, get the witness a glass of water, would you, please."

"Thank you," Alison said upon receiving the glass. The courtroom was quietly watching her, as if she were a magician about to perform some sleight of hand with the liquid.

"Okay?" Lee said. Alison nodded. "You were talking about how you felt when Mr. Donnelly lost interest."

"Dead. I felt like a part of me died. You give yourself to a person and they slap you in the face. You feel naked and raw."

Lee hesitated, allowing the words to linger.

"When was the last time you saw Mr. Donnelly before you became pregnant?"

"Well, as I said, we'd seen less of each other. Then one night, sometime in August I believe—I just remember it was real hot and humid—he showed up late, about two in the morning, at my apartment. He had this withered rose in his hand and he was drunk. He was saying how much he missed me and wanted me, and I don't know, I felt so lonely that I let him in."

Alison described how cold and indifferent Jack was when they lay down on her bed. "It was like a form of rape. He made me feel like a whore. Just walking out after we'd made love. But I still had some hope. He'd come back to me. He clearly missed me. He said he did. But, but . . ."

"Then you learned you were pregnant?"

Neither Lee nor Alison was sure if she was pregnant before that night, but to lessen the impact of the abortion, the fact that Alison might have gotten pregnant as the result of a "form of rape" was an effective point.

"Yes. It was horrible being pregnant with a child from a man who didn't love me. I paced around my apartment, biting my nails down to nothing, pulling out clumps of my hair. I thought of not telling him, but I had to. It was his baby, too."

"So, you told him you were pregnant. How did he react when you said you were carrying his child?"

" 'Are you sure it's mine?' he said. I wanted to just slap him for that, but I started crying. He stood up, and I thought he was going to come over and comfort me, but he just stared out the window."

"What happened then?"

"He acted like it was all my fault. I don't know how I expected him to act. How should he have reacted? Not like that. 'We'll meet later,' he said. He said, 'I have to think about this. I mean you're not going to keep it, are you?'"

"How did you feel when he said that?"

"That hit me like a rock. It sounded so awful the way he said it, like the baby was something we just had to get rid of. He said it like a gangster ordering a hit. It was that affectless, that unemotional."

"Did you discuss the issue any further?"

"No, not really. We met, but the issue was already decided. It was just a matter of when."

"Why did you decide to buy a gun?"

"I took a day off work and wandered the streets. I walked down to Washington Street and went inside a pawn shop. I felt so trapped. I was so depressed and so angry. I was angry at myself. I thought, God, I've gotten myself into this and there's no way out. I hated myself and Jack, too. I don't know what I planned on doing. I've never done anything violent before. I was so overwhelmed. I mean, I didn't know anything about guns. It's like that pawn shop man said. I really didn't know why I was in there."

"But you bought the gun."

"Yes. Mr. Bruno recommended one. I didn't know what kind it was. It was cold and heavy. I just stuck it in my bag. The world felt like metal and steel closing in on me." She began to cry again, and the judge gestured to the bailiff. A box of Kleenex was set on the shelf. She withdrew a tissue.

"Then you went for the abortion?"

"You never imagine yourself faced with this decision. It wasn't easy. I made an appointment with a clinic on Beacon Street. I knew they could do it.

"I took the day off work. I looked awful and felt sick. My eyes were all puffed. I stayed in bed all morning staring at the cracks in the ceiling. I had these horrible pains in my stomach. I wondered if the fetus was moving inside me, but I knew that wasn't possible. I was becoming hysterical. The hours seemed to drag by.

"I said to myself that it would soon be over and maybe we'd be back to normal. Of course, I recovered myself emotionally enough to realize what foolishness this thought was. It was over for him. I'd become some burden to him, a reminder of what he wanted to forget."

"How did Jack act when he met you at Park Street?"

"Like nothing special was happening. I knew he was going only out of guilt."

Hurley objected.

"I mean, I realize it wasn't a pleasant experience. Neither one of us wanted to do it, but he wasn't sympathetic at all. I didn't tell him to come with me."

"Did he make any attempts to comfort you?"

"He tried to touch me and I kind of flinched. I actually thought he was going to hit me, and then I hoped he would, give me a big smack, and I'd fall on the ground and lose the baby. It would be easier. I was thinking, God, just let this be over. It felt clandestine and sordid, like we were committing some crime."

"What happened at the clinic?"

"What I remember most that day was the crush of people. All that sweat and quiet violence. Numb faces on the subway. There was a breakdown, so the platform was filled with people. And then outside, when we got off the train, the roar of the riots. It was like the world was going crazy."

"Why didn't you just turn around and come back another day? Or make arrangements to go someplace else?"

"I just wanted to get it over with. It took so much for me to get up that day, I didn't know if I could do it again, and I didn't want to wait. Jack asked if I wanted to go someplace else, but I didn't know where. I was only going there because I didn't want anybody to know, like my gynecologist, nobody who would recognize me. Neither of us was interested in telling anybody. Now everybody knows. It's awful."

"Your Honor," Hurley objected. "Could the witness be admonished to not editorialize? This is becoming a narrative. A well-coached one, I might add."

"Mr. Hurley, there's no need to poison the atmosphere by casting aspersions on opposing counsel. If you're trying to provoke a mistrial, you're failing miserably."

"I'm not afraid of the evidence, Your Honor."

"Then cut the cheap shots. And Ms. Klein, instruct your client to just answer the questions. Let's keep to the usual format, shall we? There's been enough posturing."

"Please continue, Alison. After you arrived at the clinic, what happened?"

"Jack handed me his share of the money. I felt like a cheap whore who was being bought off."

"What were you thinking about after the abortion?"

"How it was just so terrible that I had to do it. That I had gotten myself into the situation and Jack didn't care a whit for me. I felt cold and lonely. I wasn't thinking clearly. I was woozy. I started walking down the street, disoriented.

"We got off the train at Arlington Street. I wanted to walk him by the Public Garden, to remind him of all his broken promises to me, like the ride on the swan boats. He said he'd take me there once. He said a lot of things he didn't mean. When we walked to the bridge, I thought I heard children's voices in the distance, feeding the ducks maybe. I was thinking of the children's book, *Make Way for Ducklings*, set in the Public Garden. I read it when I was a little girl. Thinking of the book reminded me of how I'd screwed up my life, that I'd never done anything but fail. And it was always a man who was causing my troubles. This man. Jack.

"We leaned against the guardrail. His mouth and cheeks were blue with cold. I'd thought he was such a good-hearted person once. I was thinking about how he was so cruel to me. He turned toward me and expected me to hug him. I put a hand in my purse. I told myself I was just looking for a Kleenex, but I touched the gun instead. I knew it was there, and that I was going to use it now, but I didn't know how. I pulled it out. He looked so scared. He was afraid. I wanted him to fear me.

"That's why I'd bought it, I finally admitted to myself. To use on him. The gun was shaking in my hand. It was so heavy. I pointed the gun away to the side. I was angry, but I didn't want to kill him. I just wanted him to hurt. I pulled the trigger. Then he was down on the ground. I was hit from behind and a man was on top of me. He was hurting me. I could feel the blood from the abortion coming out of me. I screamed.

"Jack just didn't care. It was like he was just going to toss me away, without a second thought. And now he was bleeding like I was bleeding."

Tears streamed down her face. "Do you need some time?" Kaufman asked.

"Oh, brother," Hurley muttered. "Why doesn't he just offer her a shoulder to cry on?"

Alison retook the stand. She spoke of the trauma she experienced afterward, her fits of insomnia, the flashbacks to her lying on the table in the clinic. One night in her apartment she was struck with terror, clutching her bedspread as a vacuum cleaner hummed upstairs, that sound reverberating in her ear. She knew the abortion was for the best, that there was no other possibility, that she would not have been able to keep the baby, but it didn't make it any easier. "There was something living inside me and I had killed it. There was no way getting around that. You couldn't sugarcoat it."

"We're almost through, Alison. I only have one more question. Did you intend to kill Mr. Donnelly?"

"No, I can safely say it now, no. It was really an accident."


"Good afternoon, Ms. Moore," Hurley said, grinning at her. "Let's go over some of your testimony one more time. There are certain things I don't understand. Let's begin not at the beginning, but near the end. Now, you testified that you remember buying the gun. It was some weeks before you shot Mr. Donnelly, isn't that correct?"

"Yes," Alison said. She had watched Jack wither under Lee's cross-examination, and she was conscious of not repeating his mistakes. He had been too defensive. Alison wanted to keep her voice at the same modulation, to avoid fits of hysteria. Lee drilled that instruction into her, and she knew now why: There was a world of difference between the hypothetical grilling Lee had given her and this.

"And you bought the gun without knowing how you would use it?"

"I was confused, scared, and angry. No, I didn't know what I would do with it."

"So, your first reaction when you're, quote, confused and, quote, scared is to purchase a weapon?"

"No."

"Well, let's see what you were scared of," Hurley said. "Have you ever been threatened or accosted?"

"No."

"Were there any disturbances in your building?"

"No."

"Any robberies?"

"No."

"Murders?"

"Not that I'm aware of."

"Rapes?"

"No."

"In fact, you live in a very safe building in a very safe neighborhood, the Back Bay."

"No neighborhood is safe these days."

"C'mon, Ms. Moore, you had nothing to fear."

"I didn't feel scared of the neighborhood. It was my life that was frightening me."

"Ms. Moore, you never used that gun for any purpose except to shoot Mr. Donnelly, isn't that correct?"

"I didn't buy it for that purpose."

"You never *used* that gun for any other purpose *except* to shoot Mr. Donnelly, did you?"

"No, I never used it."

"It was whim, then. You just woke up one morning and said, 'Gee, I think I'll buy a gun that fits into my purse'?"

"I told you it wasn't like that."

"Did you carry it with you every day?"

"No, I guess not. It was in my black bag, and I didn't change it, so I wouldn't have, no."

"So, you didn't carry it with you when you went to work every day?"

"It was a short walk. I didn't have a permit anyway."

"And you knew it was a crime to carry a concealed weapon, didn't you?"

"I guess so. I didn't carry it. It was still in the bag I had when I bought it. It's a casual bag. I don't use it for work."

"And your only use for the gun was to shoot your boyfriend?"

"No. I already said no. That wasn't the reason I bought it."

"You admitted you were angry, right?"

"Yes."

"You thought he was being unkind to you."

"At the end, yes."

"You thought he was mean, vicious, cruel, cold. All those fancy words you used on direct examination. So you planned to shoot him, didn't you?"

"I didn't mean for anything like this to happen. You've got to believe me!"

Hurley snorted. "There's been quite a lot of publicity about this case, hasn't there, Ms. Moore?"

"Yes."

"And you've benefited from it?"

"I don't see how. I'm on trial here."

"Well, haven't television shows and tabloids and movie people extended offers to you?"

"I've been approached."

"Various women's groups have supported you. They've made you feel victimized. And you like that feeling."

"Nobody likes to be a victim, sir."

"You haven't shied away from the publicity, though. It must be quite a heady experience for you. You've always craved the limelight, haven't you, Ms. Moore?"

"You think I want to go through this?"

"I don't know what you want. I suppose you didn't think of the consequences before you shot Mr. Donnelly. Now, you mentioned in passing your time as an actress. You've performed many roles since high school, haven't you?"

"Not as many as I would've liked." It maddened her to think of the news stories calling her a failed actress. She hadn't failed. She had given up.

"It would be fair to say you've played many characters during your stage career?"

"A few."

"And when you have these roles, you inhabit the character you're playing?"

"You try. That's the ideal."

"You have had a lot of time to prepare for the role you're playing today, haven't you?"

"I'm not playing a role. I'm just telling the truth, sir."

"Come on, Ms. Moore, you're telling us that a woman of your sophistication and experience was so hurt by Mr. Donnelly that you didn't know what you were doing?"

"I didn't say that exactly."

"It's true, isn't it, that you didn't think you were traumatized by the abortion until Dr. Sutherland told you his theory?"

"Dr. Sutherland didn't make up what happened to me. I told him my experiences. He put a label on them."

"Now, you're a lawyer, and you knew your case was hopeless. You'd been caught red-handed in the shooting, and you needed to invent an excuse."

"I didn't invent anything. It's not an excuse. I'm just explaining to you what happened. What I remember."

"You had a relationship with a man in Indiana who you said beat you. You lived with a man in Washington who slept around. And then there's Mr. Donnelly, who, according to you, scorned you. It would be fair to say, wouldn't it, that you have built up a lot of anger toward men, that it was boiling inside you ready to explode at any minute?"

"Any anger I may have had was way in the past and dealt with."

"Well, it has been now," Hurley muttered. He moved into the weekend in New York and asked Alison if she wasn't planning on sex that weekend why she brought her diaphragm along.

"I've always carried it in my purse."

"Just in case? But you're saying he stalked you like some prey?"

"I did not say that. I said he pursued me. Ardently."

"Not like an animal? You were interested in having sex with him, weren't you?"

"I had sex with him, yes. I'm not denying it."

"This was just another casual relationship for you, wasn't it? Sleeping with him was no big deal."

"It's always a big deal when you sleep with someone, Mr. Hurley."

"Oh, is it? So, you were in love with him?"

"No. Not actually."

"And you didn't like him?"

"I did like him."

"So, you didn't love him? Yet you had sex with him anyway."

"You don't have to love someone to have sex with him."

"So, the standard's fairly low. Come on, sleeping with him was no big deal, was it?"

"Asked and answered," Lee interrupted.

"Move on, Mr. Hurley," Kaufman said.

"You have a great memory for certain details and not for others. You can't remember why you purchased the gun. You can't say why you shot him. But you can remember every time you had sex and every time you thought he was mean to you."

"I don't know about that," she said.

"Does everybody hate you? You testified that everybody at the firm was out to get you."

"I didn't say that. I felt like an outsider. Mr. Kaplan and Jack were nice to me."

"But Mr. Donnelly was out to get you, isn't that correct? He was just as bad as everybody else. So the whole world is against you. We have a word for that, don't we, Ms. Moore?"

"I'm not paranoid. It's true what I'm telling you."

"And you were so paranoid and angry, seeking revenge, that you wanted to kill Mr. Donnelly?"

"No. No!"

"You thought you killed your baby and now you wanted to kill him."

"That's not true!"

"We'll let the jury decide that, *Ms.* Moore."

She was rescued by the judge's gavel, and the close of the trial for the day.

urley heard the shuffle of feet outside his office door.

"Come in." He didn't look up.

His visitor was Assistant District Attorney Mike Rogers, six-year veteran of the office. "Rough day?"

"Who's asking?"

"I sat in awhile today. You want to know my impressions?"

"You're going to tell me anyway. It's always easy from the peanut gallery."

"Hey. Hey." Rogers put up his hands in protest. "I'm not going to criticize anything. The case is a bitch. Just a few observations."

"Yeah, yeah."

"One. Klein looks great in a skirt."

"I hadn't noticed."

"Well, that's scary. Two, I'm amazed how puritanical everybody is. Jury of her peers, my ass. You old folks don't understand the ways of the world. You're playing to an audience that might not exist. There's nothing weird about what happened to them."

"That's the difference between my generation and yours," Hurley said. "We didn't think abortions and shootings were normal."

"The point is Klein's turned this into a morality play and Donnelly's the bad guy."

"Yeah, who would've thought? At first, the moral angle was all on my side. In the courtroom, I can feel the shift to Moore's."

"I don't get it," Rogers said. "So he knocks her up. What's he supposed to do? Klein's made him out to be the devil and Moore the Virgin Mary. Then, of course, you're dealing with the big dick, King Kaufman."

"Well, that's to be expected. The guy's a real beaut. He's always hated this office. The guy thinks he's the great civil libertarian, but he's a buffoon. No self-respecting judge would let Klein get that shit in."

"Yeah," Rogers said. "Anyway, I have to catch the T. Knock 'em dead tomorrow."

The hum of the building resurfaced. He'd been sanguine when the case began; now he was plagued with uncertainty. It was a familiar pattern: Every case had a momentum of its own. He came back to the basics: Nothing Moore said could detract from the fact that she had shot Donnelly in cold blood, that she only could have intended to maim him seriously or kill him, and all Jack's indifference to her could not excuse her conduct. As for PAS: total nonsense.

The silence made him edgy, and he left the office and went to a submarine shop near the Capitol. He ordered his usual late-night snack during trials, an Italian meat sandwich, and thought sourly of how the world had changed. He didn't fit in well with the finely coiffed young men in their double-breasted suits, with their fancy colognes, designer gym bags, and trim, well-toned bodies. He was a throwback to something they could ridicule. There were few career prosecutors anymore. His job was merely a stepping-stone to the big bucks. Yet here Hurley was, after fifteen years of the grind, of seeing the worst humanity had to offer, belching up Coke and provolone.

What's happened to the notion of public service? he thought. There would be little solace for Hurley if he didn't bag Alison. Nothing less than total victory—conviction on the attempted murder charge—would redeem the case in his eyes.

r. Donnelly never hit you," Hurley began his line of attack the next morning. "He was never abusive."

"Not physically."

"He never hit you, right?"

"No."

"He never screamed at you or abused you verbally, did he?"

"That depends on what you mean by abuse. I thought he was abusive by not saying anything, by being indifferent."

"You're telling us that you felt abused, but Mr. Donnelly didn't do anything to make you feel that way, that he was, if anything, reserved."

"More like smoldering. He had lots of anger."

"Oh, so now it's resentment. He was jealous of you because you're so successful and perfect, so you were free to shoot him."

"Badgering, Your Honor," Lee said. "He's badgering the witness."

Of course, Hurley thought. He had been barely able to penetrate Alison's veneer, and he was beginning to beat up on her out of frustration. He would be careful.

"Now, Ms. Moore, you're well educated. You have degrees from Wellesley and Harvard Law. You've had many advantages in life. Yet you come in here and testify that you've been treated badly by men and that should excuse you."

"I'm not really saying that."

"Your defense is that you were traumatized, that somehow the combination of the abortion experience and the relationship with Mr. Donnelly and other bad men means you're not responsible for your actions."

"We're all responsible for our actions, sir. Whether they're legally criminal or not is another question."

"They teach those fine distinctions at Hah-vad and Wellesley?"

She didn't respond. It was a rhetorical question.

"You would have shot him without the abortion, isn't that correct? You were just waiting for your moment to strike. It could've been then; it could've been some other day. The day you bought the gun you were conceiving your plan. The abortion gave you your excuse."

"I wasn't looking for an excuse. I already told you I didn't mean it."

"You're lying, aren't you? This whole thing's one big act."

"Your Honor!" Lee shouted. Hurley kept on talking.

"This is just one big con job. You think you can take potshots at people when you're unhappy and then have everyone feel sorry for you."

"I do not." Alison struggled to contain the mounting anger. She knew it was Hurley's intent to provoke her, to cause her to lash out, and she steeled herself. "I'm not asking people to feel sorry. Just to understand."

"Well, let's try to understand, as you say. You pointed the gun at Mr. Donnelly, isn't that correct?"

"Yes."

"You remember pulling the trigger, don't you?"

"Now I do, yes. At the time, I wasn't thinking clearly."

"You did pull the trigger. You saw the video, didn't you?"

"Yes. Obviously I pulled the trigger."

"You shot at him, didn't you?"

"Yes, I admit that, but it's not what you think."

"Yet you think you can just walk away from this without paying the consequences." Hurley glared at her from the podium. "Ms. Moore," he began, then quickly ceased. "I have nothing further, Your Honor."


Lee rose from her chair and addressed Judge Kaufman. "No redirect, Your Honor. The defense rests."

"Any rebuttal for the Commonwealth, Mr. Hurley?"

"No, Your Honor."

"Closings at nine A.M.," Kaufman said.

## HE WAS A BRUTE;
## DUMPED HER WHEN SHE BECAME PREGNANT;
### PUBLIC GARDEN DEFENDANT TELLS TALE.
### COURTROOM HUSHED BY RIVETING TESTIMONY.

What the bullet couldn't accomplish, her testimony did. He was through. Jack saw the headline on the *Herald* outside the door of his neighbors' apartment. His head was cloudy with fatigue; he was on his way to get something to help him sleep. The paper sunk his spirits further, but less than it would have only a few weeks before. He heard his neighbor shuffle toward the door and made a quick retreat to his apartment.

## 39

A number of Hurley's colleagues were in the courtroom the morning of closing arguments. Hurley was renowned for his closings. But it wasn't just respect for his forensic skills that brought his fellow D.A.s there: They wanted to see whether he could rescue the case from disaster. The rumor floating through the office was that he was on a downward arc. If a defendant takes the stand, the prosecutor has to destroy her. Alison Moore had survived.

"Let's look at the facts," Hurley began his summation, inserting Ray Ballard's tape into the videocassette recorder and remaining silent while it played on the television screen. Afterward he said, "Those are the facts. This is a simple case. Draw on your experiences. Use your common sense. She buys the gun. She hides it in her purse. There can be only one purpose for her buying the gun, but she comes in here now pretending she can't remember why she bought it. It's a very selective memory she has. Remember that video. Pictures don't lie. It's the clearest evidence you have. That's what you should remember. This was no accident. This was an act of violence, planned and deliberate."

Hurley stood directly in front of the jury box.

"This is not a case about whether abortion is or is not immoral. This is not a case about when life begins or whether a woman has the right to terminate her pregnancy. This is a case about attempted murder. What is this PAS? It's an excuse cooked up by the defense. Dr. Sutherland comes in here with his own agenda and tries to bamboozle you. You know better. Ms. Moore was not a religious person *forced* to undergo the abortion in contravention of her beliefs. Nobody put a gun to *her* head, as she did to Mr. Donnelly.

"Nobody is saying Mr. Donnelly's a choir boy, but he's certainly not the monster the defendant tried to portray. In contemporary society, whether we like it or not, young people have casual sexual encounters. Ms. Moore herself admitted that she was not in love with Mr. Donnelly and did not anticipate a long-term relationship.

"What did her testimony really display? No remorse. She's shown absolutely no remorse for what she's done. It is mere luck, to use her word, an accident, that Mr. Donnelly was not more severely injured. You think she'd come in here and say, 'I'm sorry, I didn't mean it.' But she's not sorry and she did mean it. There is no other logical way to look at the evidence in this case.

"Oh, Ms. Moore and her very able counsel have put up a smoke screen with their so-called expert, their emotional crying, their attempts to put Mr. Donnelly, the victim, on trial. We were treated to quite an entertaining performance. But Ms. Moore can't act her way out of the facts. Drama isn't evidence. Facts are evidence. And the evidence, the only real evidence in this case is crystal clear. Alison Moore goes to a pawn shop down in the dregs of Washington Street. She doesn't go to a sporting goods store or another reputable establishment that sells firearms, but to a pawn shop, where they sell the weapons to criminals, petty crooks, drug addicts. 'Not the usual type,' you remember the pawn shop man, Mr. Bruno, testify. Remember, she already knows she's pregnant at this point. She and Mr. Donnelly aren't on the best of terms. In fact, she said, in her typically melodramatic style, that she felt raped by him. So they meet and she decides to have an abortion. It's the only option. Much as we may not like it, it was. She had originally planned on the baby being orphaned of its father.

"She's got her gun with her when they meet at Park Street. She's got a big black bag, one of those commodious ones that carries everything, so the outline of the gun is disguised. What's she thinking? She's thinking about the gun in her purse and how she wants to kill him for the way he's treated her. She's talked herself into this feeling of being abused and abandoned by a man she *admits* meant little to her, was just a casual lover for a few months.

"So, they get outside the clinic, and it's havoc. Mr. Donnelly suggests they go somewhere else or come back another day. So, does she do the sensible thing? Does she decide to leave? No! It doesn't fit in with her plans! She wants this over with now. She can't wait another day. She has her gun. She knows what she's going to do.

"When they leave the clinic, they get back on the subway. They get off at Arlington Street. She asks him to walk with her. She's got a plan. They walk across to the bridge and lean against it. And she finally speaks. She says to him, 'Remember the swan boats, Jack,' and he thinks this is some conciliatory gesture, some reference to their former happy times. He moves away from the railing because he thinks maybe they are going to embrace in recognition of what they've gone through together, and he wants to offer her comfort. But that's not what she has in mind."

He stopped his flow of words and moved closer to the jury. "Not what she has in mind at all." He leaned his upper torso over the edge of the jury box, near enough to see the wrinkled hands of juror number six. "As close as this, she was. As close as I am to you right now. She reaches into her purse, for what she's been waiting to do is this, that's all she's really been thinking about, this one moment when he will pay."

Hurley removed his hand from his jacket pocket and formed it into the shape of a pistol. With his free hand, he slammed on the top of the jury box. *"Bang!*

"That's what happened, ladies and gentlemen. As simple as that. You saw it yourselves! The defendant is guilty of the crimes charged. It is the only verdict you can render in this case."

Hurley's hands were clammy. He hoped that the summation would compensate for his woeful cross-examination of Alison. It seemed to have the desired effect. After he sat back down, Julie leaned over and spoke in his ear. "Great job."

Over at the defense table, Lee took a last quick glance at the notes she made when Hurley was speaking, patted Alison affectionately on her unnaturally cold hand, and stood, ready to deliver her response.

"You know, ladies and gentlemen, I listened to Mr. Hurley just now, and I was thinking about the gap between what he thinks went on in this trial and what went on between these two people. I heard, and I hope you did too, the discrepancies. The miscommunication.

"This is a tragedy about two people. Mr. Hurley exhibited a

lot of anger when he stood up here and spoke to you just now. But it's not anger you should feel. It's sadness. This is a sad story. We all like to think when boy and girl, man and woman, meet, that it will end in romance, permanence, marriage. Sadly, that's not what happens most times. We have here two bright, intelligent people, anticipating promising careers as lawyers. Now the future is not as bright for either one of them. We can all look back and think, Couldn't they see this coming? Why did this have to happen? But that would be speculation. We have to look at the facts we have.

"Mr. Hurley is wrong. He doesn't want you to look at the human beings involved, the human dimensions, how people— normal, average people—make mistakes and take actions they wished they could take back. I'm sure even Mr. Donnelly would say he would do things differently somehow. If he had known, if he had been sensitive to Alison's feelings. But he wasn't. He didn't know better, he says. He's evading the facts as well.

"I want you to look closely at Alison, put yourself in her shoes for a moment, while you sit here, while you deliberate on her fate. Think of her finding herself back in Boston, ready to begin a new life after her unfortunate experience in Washington. She's fresh and happy with new horizons to explore. You heard her testify. She wasn't interested in having a boyfriend. It was Mr. *Donnelly* who incessantly, almost obsessively, pursued *her*. Then he got what he wanted—and we all know, no matter how unpleasant that may be, what that was." She paused. "Sex. Then he casually, brutally, dumps her. Ignores her. Pretends she doesn't exist. After she's given herself emotionally and physically to him, snap, he's gone. She's a memory, a conquest. Except that she is pregnant with *his* child. And he wanted to be rid of her because that child will affect *his* career."

Lee walked over to the defense table and stood alongside Alison.

"You can't isolate an experience into one single moment like Mr. Hurley wants you to do. He wants to talk about the Public Garden. You should think about the whole *worlds* of these two people, about the events leading up to the Public Garden. These are facts, too.

"The Commonwealth has not proven that Alison intended to cause injury to Mr. Donnelly. It's mere conjecture. You heard her testify. You know she's not lying. Sometimes unforeseen things happen. She was distraught, traumatized over the demise of their relationship, the abortion she really didn't want to have. Although we all may think that abortion is sometimes a grim necessity, that doesn't mean it's easy or that people take it lightly. Mr. Hurley makes much of the fact that she went to a pawn shop. Precisely. She doesn't know what she's doing. Remember Mr. Bruno said she didn't know the first thing about guns. A person like Alison doesn't know where to buy a gun. She wasn't hiding anything. She didn't use a false name. It's a red herring."

That was the best Lee thought she could do with the facts: Lightly touch on the gun issue and move on.

"All you need is a reasonable doubt. Remember that. A reasonable doubt. Keep coming back to that. The kind of doubt that would make you hesitate in making the most important decision of your life. That kind of doubt certainly exists here. Ask yourself, Do I think Alison might not have meant to shoot him? Do I think she was so distraught over the abortion that she was traumatized? Do I think someone can be so emotionally on edge that she isn't thinking clearly? Do I really know why she bought the gun? She was depressed when she bought it. She'd just found out she was pregnant. Mr. Donnelly didn't care what happened to her. We can all understand how she felt. Mr. Hurley says use your common sense. Doesn't common sense tell you that could happen? I suggest to you that there are reasonable doubts.

"Mr. Hurley doesn't want you to focus on the person—Alison Moore—because it's not favorable to his case. He doesn't want you to sympathize. To empathize. We all can be depressed sometimes about how our lives are going. But not all of us suffer the sudden upheavals Alison went through. Lonely as she watches the blue spot appear in the pregnancy test. Lonely because the baby's father seemingly hates her. Lonely because he wants nothing to do with her now. She's an impediment to his career. She's going to ruin it for him! How dare she, he thinks. She must abort the baby. She can't go through with the pregnancy.

"Mr. Hurley makes much of the fact that Alison is well-educated. But Harvard Law doesn't guarantee anything about a person's character or how they will respond in a crisis. A good education doesn't make someone well-mannered or a nice person. Mr. Donnelly, for all *his* education, wasn't nice to Alison. He wasn't a gentleman. He treated her shabbily. You have to put yourself in her mind, understand what *she* was going through."

Lee went to the edge of the jury box.

"When I first was retained by Alison, I thought, How could she explain herself? She must be guilty, right? It's a trap we all fall into, forgetting the presumption of innocence. How what appears so simple and clear on the surface is often quite murky. Think of your-self watching the TV news and hearing a story about a woman who shoots her husband. They show her sobbing and admitting her crime. What we don't know oftentimes is what led her to the act. How she might have been abused. How she might have exercised self-defense. We haven't heard the whole story.

"Well, you have now heard the whole story of Alison and Jack. It's not a pleasant story. It's not a fairy tale where the girl meets the handsome prince. But it's a true story. A story of a mis-matched couple, two people who never should have come together. Just think what could have been if they never did. We wouldn't be here today. So your sadness should be tinged with pity. Pity for both of them, yes, but Alison is the only one who sits before you today, awaiting your judgment. There is a reasonable doubt. There are reasonable doubts. The Commonwealth has simply not proven its case. You must find Alison not guilty of the crimes charged."

The courtroom cleared out quickly. There was a dash to the exits by reporters preparing their stories or setting up for spots outside. The closing arguments had ended soon enough for live reports on the first edition of local news and for feeds to the national networks. A reporter read snippets of the closings into a camera. "The jury has the case," she continued. "Neither side offered any estimate of how long the jury would be out, but both sides expressed confidence. Mr. Hurley, representing the Commonwealth, stated that the case was clear cut. Ms. Klein, representing Ms. Moore, offered nothing for attribution. As you can see behind me, various groups are or-ganizing an impromptu rally. Ms. Moore has had a wide range of supporters throughout the trial . . ."

ack at Lee's office, Alison paced, too nervous to sit down. "What do you think?" she asked, sniffling, as if she had become allergic to the air in the courtroom.

"You never can tell," Lee said. "We did as much as we could."

"What does it mean if they're out long?"

"Depends. In this case, I think it favors us. A quick verdict, with these facts, favors the prosecution."

"Oh, God."

Peter had gone down the street to buy them sandwiches and drinks. He had called their parents from the phone in Lee's outer office and informed them that they were waiting for the verdict. Alison was glad her parents weren't there. She preferred to suffer without their accusatory glares. She turned from the window and saw Lee writing.

"What are you doing?"

"Other work," Lee said without looking up. "It's good to keep busy."

Alison stared back out the window onto Milk Street. Tourists circled around the Old State House. She wondered why they would come to gray, cold Boston in the middle of winter.

"You don't have to stay here," Lee said. "I can call you at home when the jury comes in."

"You think they'll decide tonight? Oh, yeah, you said. Who knows?" Alison removed herself from the window and plopped down on the sofa across from Lee's desk. "I'm a wreck. I think I'll go home when Peter gets back. Home. What am I saying? The hotel. My room."

"It'll soon be over," Lee said.

"Either way."

"Yes. Try to remain calm."


The next morning, just after nine o'clock, Lee was in the lawyers' lounge in the courthouse. The room was filled with unmatched furniture, rejects from government offices—steno chairs, lime-green couches, tattered recliners, art deco ashtrays. On a rickety bookshelf was an outdated edition of the Massachusetts General Laws.

Lee was the only woman in the room. She had arisen an hour earlier than usual for her morning run, and she was tired. She gazed without concentration or comprehension at a deposition transcript on her lap for an employment discrimination case set for trial in federal court in three weeks. She imagined herself in a café in Italy. For years, she'd promised herself she would take a break and travel. At forty, the years started to fly by.

"This is the worst time, isn't it?" a lawyer said to her. "No matter how many times we've been through it. Waiting. Waiting's the worst. You did a bang-up job in there. Not an easy case." He rubbed the folds of his fat chin. She feared he was about to offer a criticism or a war story on some great defense he'd waged in the past.

She was surprised the jury was out so long, and she thought it was, on balance, a good sign.

A serious young lawyer strode in dressed in a blue pinstripe suit. He seemed put off by the others in the room, and when he saw the telephones were all in use, he turned on his heels.

"Smart-asses these days. Think their shit don't stink," one attorney said from an adjoining chair.

She was at the point of leaving when the bailiff came in.

"Verdict," he said.

She called the hotel and told Peter to bring Alison down.

# 41

endy Thomas delivered news of the verdict from a "stunned and hushed courtroom" while Jack sat at a restaurant lounge in the North End, watching her on television. "The case that began with a shot ringing out in the Public Garden ended in shocked silence today as the jury convicted Alison Moore of only the least serious charge brought against her, possession of an unregistered weapon. She was found innocent on the other charges, attempted murder and assault with a deadly weapon. An emotional Ms. Moore hugged her lawyer outside the courthouse steps and praised her for her efforts." The cameras cut to a shot of Alison clutching a bouquet of red roses. She looked like the winner of a beauty contest.

Jack walked through the neighborhood, sidewalks crowded with tourists on their way to the Old North Church. He fell in behind a group moving into the vestibule of the church and took a seat in the white pillbox-shaped pews. A pocket in the front of Jack's pew held a black covered hymnal with gold-leafed pages. The tour guide explained that they were in the oldest standing church in America. Jack noticed the simplicity of the church. No crucified Jesus, no madonna, no confessionals. These people must have been confident of their salvation.

The jury had said he deserved to be shot, that Alison was justified in her actions. Maybe she was, he thought. This is my punishment, the lack of justice. He kneeled down and prepared to recite a penance, but none came to him.


Peter, Alison, and Lee celebrated back in Alison's hotel room. Channel 4 News broadcast a special report on the aftermath of the trial. The station replayed the videotape of the shooting and assembled a panel to discuss the implications of the case. Peter sat on the edge of the bed, listening to the opinions of a Harvard Law professor, a criminologist, and the media critic for the *Globe*.

Alison was flush with excitement and relief. She lay sprawled on the bed in a white terry-cloth bathrobe, sipping the champagne Peter had ordered, her hair wrapped in a towel.

"It's finally over, isn't it?" she asked Lee.

"Yes, except for sentencing, but you should get probation on the gun charge." Lee, standing in her stockinged feet, looked out the hotel window at Copley Square. Her arches were weary and painful; a blister had formed on one of her toes from standing so long in heels. The trial had consumed her energy the last few months, and she was forlorn.

"It feels weird, doesn't it?" Alison said. "Eerie, like we're in some time gap or warp."

Lee nodded.

"Anticipation, I guess. We won't know what's going to happen next. What *is* going to happen?"

"That's your business. I hope you'll straighten out your life."

Alison's shoulders shrugged underneath the robe. "Thank you so much for everything. And don't worry about me. I'll land on my feet."

arry Lindstrom let out a screech that night when he opened the show. "What can I say, folks? The feminazis have chalked up another victory. Wake up, America! Soon they'll be on the streets, little bands of girls shooting at every male chauvinist pig, perceived or real. Nobody listened to me! I warned you all. The dykes and fairies are ruling our lives. I can't go on. I must go on. Screw the censors. I'm serious. No calls tonight, folks. The lines are down. Down in mourning. In mourning for our lost civilization. Nobody is out there crying for the dead baby. They feel sorry for that murderous bitch. I can't believe it. Nobody's crying for poor Jack. What about him?"

A week after the trial, the video wing of the Contemporary Museum of Art opened its exhibition of the work of Raymond C. Ballard, avatar of a new art genre, the cinema verité videocassette. His work caught the immediacy of contemporary life, it was said by certain segments of the art world, although there were others who said it wasn't art.

In the foyer of the museum on opening night, patrons celebrated the exhibition at a white wine and cheese reception. Ray was surrounded by a coterie of artists and benefactors. Behind him was a black screen with a black-and-white image of a homeless man pawing through a garbage can in front of the Ritz Carlton. Ray's name was superimposed on the image.

Natalie Goodman hung on Ray's arm. She and Ray had just recently become lovers. Her hair was a dark red now and styled in a pixie, with a bow on top. She wore black eye shadow and similarly painted nails. Ray wished Natalie was better looking in a more conventional sense, but she was hip enough. She now said she found merit in his work.

"You're a smash, darling," Natalie whispered in Ray's ear.

Wendy Thomas was a distant memory by now. Ray saw her debut as the weekend anchor and he felt no lust, no passion, just anger. He was responsible for her rise to the top, and she was either an ungrateful bitch or blissfully unconscious. She actually thought she had made it on her merits.

Chagrined, Hurley went back to regular duty. His initial claim that a great injustice had occurred was ignored. His colleagues offered excuses for the inexplicable defeat. Juries were unpredictable. Alison Moore was simply a great actress. Hurley, finding nothing he would have done differently, decided on a sociological explanation.

"We live in a time when people are willing to excuse any behavior, however barbaric, on the theory that we are not responsible for our actions, that there is an excuse for everything." But his words rang hollow to the others.

For the first time, Hurley considered a move into the private sector. It was clear that at least for a few years his name would be identified with the Public Garden case. A former law school classmate, Jim Donahue, had a two-person firm on the South Shore in Braintree and invited him aboard. The financial remuneration was attractive and Hurley was seriously contemplating the change.

Two weeks after the verdict, Hurley gave a lecture to the Benevolent Order of Police on the latest decisions on search-and-seizure law, but his exegesis was frequently interrupted by hoots from the audience. This was his type of crowd, or should have been: veterans, mostly Irish, who liked his pugilistic tactics in the courtroom and appreciated his unwavering support for law enforcement. But Hurley realized how little credibility he had left. The next day, he announced his resignation from the District Attorney's office. At a reception in the Parker House, he was feted for his spirited public service and presented with a gold plaque.

There was a sense of relief at Adelman and Kaplan. The trial had been difficult, but the recruiting committee reported a larger-than-average number of new candidates applying and interviewing. Notoriety intrigued the graduates from NYU to Yale to Georgetown, from Michigan to Chicago, even a few from Stanford and Berkeley.

In the first few weeks after the trial, however, the firm continued to debate its lessons. The gossip focused on the litigation group and the poor decisions of the recruitment committee. There were even intimations that Martin Kaplan was slipping in his skills, that it was time for him to move aside, to accept an "of counsel" position. Kaplan felt shunned even at the Barclay Club, his usual lunch spot, where he had been a member for over ten years, a club where he'd broken the Jewish barrier. But people were greatly mistaken if they thought the departure of two associates was going to bring him down.

"I knew she'd get off," Drew said.

"I never believed he could be such a jerk," Janice added.

Drew believed his partnership chances were affected by the specter of Jack and Alison. The firm had announced that decisions on partnership would be deferred another six months. Some litigation group associates actively sought employment in other firms or corporations throughout town.

Adelman and Kaplan had issued a memo to all personnel discouraging fraternization between employees. "Although the firm recognizes it cannot dictate personal lifestyle, recent events have shown the dangers of such relationships. Sensitivity training will be offered to all interested employees."

"Sounds like some New Age thing," Janice said. "Like codependency. Being tied to your coworker as self-destructive. I guess that'll eliminate a lot of the extramarital events we've come to expect as one of the perks of partnership."

"You turning into a feminist on us?" Drew said.

"What's that got do with feminism? Marital fidelity's not a matter of sexual politics."

Andy, most closely identified as a genuine friend of Jack's, did not offer excuses for Jack's behavior and didn't defend him. Larry was still suspicious of his relationship with Maggie. She had gone into a depression after the trial, as if she'd lost the eye of a secret admirer. Larry wished everybody would forget about the trial. But how could they? Alison was a fixture on the talk shows.

"Did you see her on 'A.M. Boston'?" Janice said. "It was gross. She thinks she's Joan of Arc."

Over time, Jack and Alison's tale became part of the folklore of the firm. In restaurants and bars it became a badge of honor to be associated with such an infamous event. The Boys' Club continued meeting at Sevens on Thursday nights. They hoisted their glasses in a toast to their former member, Jack, "Victim of a Piece of Twat," and vowed to never make the same mistake.

# 43

ecisions. Decisions," Brian said.

Lee was packing for a trip to Florida. She had been offered the use of a house by a friend. "Well," she said, "I don't exactly know what the weather will be like this time of year. God, I need to get away. The winter is getting me down. But it's a bad time."

"You always say that. Don't feel so guilty about leaving. The law will still be here when you get back, and so will I. You think you're indispensable."

"I do not. I just have responsibilities."

"Unlike yours truly, the vagabond."

"Exactly. How come these summer clothes feel like they've been in mothballs for ages? When was summer?"

"How would you know? You lock yourself in the office. When's the last time you were even at the Cape?"

Brian was working on a book about the trial. He hoped to finish it by late spring, before others beat him to it. Lee's practice had been building exponentially since the celebrated trial. After her vacation, she thought she might take on an associate to ease the load.

Lee had declined all requests for interviews on the case and would not appear on television with Alison.

"I want you to be my technical adviser on this book," Brian said. "You'll come back, won't you?"

"Don't write a schlocky book. You know, cheap true crime."

"I'm offended. This will be my bold statement on American culture."

"Uh-huh. You won't forget to water the plants?"

She fastened the clasps on her bags. A taxi horn sounded outside her window on the street below.

"I'm off," she said. He helped her down the stairs with her luggage.

44

D o you know me? My acting career had an unusual trajectory. You could say I shot my way to the top." Alison emerged from dark shadows on the stage, Ray's video-tape freeze-framed and matted behind her. There was a news photograph of her below the headline: ALISON WALKS.

"And bullshit sells," she said. "Lucky for me, my aim wasn't true. Annie Oakley, thankfully, I'm not. But my shooting days are over. I've hung up the old holster. I'm a pacifist now."

Garrett Walker's production of *My Life as a Femme Fatale*, Alison's autobiographical monologue, premiered at the Colonial Theater in the middle of December.

Reviews were mixed. One critic labeled it a "feminist diatribe masking as art" (*Herald*), and another "a searing portrait of contemporary women" (*Globe*). "She comes off as a cross between Spalding Gray and a Catskills comic" (*Aurora*). Ticket sales were brisk.

Alison was an emerging, not an ephemeral star. She became a regular on "A.M. Boston," and said she hoped to be an inspiration to all women. She announced that she had sold her story to a publisher.

"Are you bitter?" a member of the studio audience asked.

"Bitter, no. I feel sorry for him. I really do."

She had been sentenced to two years' probation for the only charge she was convicted of, possession of an unregistered weapon.

For her community service, she would volunteer at a battered women's shelter.

When she had time in her schedule of appearances before women's groups and spots on talk shows, Alison had fleeting images of Jack. She felt no anger toward him. Who, after all, was he? She had no true memory of him anymore—their meeting, their sex, all those events you swear will remain vivid when they are happening.

She moved to a refurbished loft in a former manufacturing plant in Chelsea. The apartment consisted of an expansive front room and a kitchen area. The walls were painted a bright white. Her possessions were unsettled, scattered in cardboard boxes. One box was filled with notices on her performance and clippings from the trial, including the cover story in *Them* magazine. Her mother had even sent articles about her from the Wallace *Courant*, along with a handwritten note: *Thought you might like these. Love, Mother.*

After he helped her unload her things in the new apartment, Peter took off for Newport. He was playing for an AIDS benefit, his first public performance in years.

She found the place a haven. At night, she would take a bottle of wine from the refrigerator and sit in a rocking chair, relaxing. The quiet was soothing after the tumult of public attention. A folded script of Sam Shepard's *Fool for Love* lay on her lap. She was auditioning for the Somerville Theatre's upcoming production. She had to develop a repertory, move beyond the public role she had carved for herself. She was serious about this. From now on, she would have nobody to blame but herself if things didn't work out.

45

ack found himself on Boylston Street late one afternoon, walking through the Theater District. In the glass windows bordering its entrance, the Colonial Theater displayed posters of Alison. It was quiet outside the theater, mid-performance of a matinee. While he stood there, intermission arrived and the audience filled the lobby.

Jack thought of heading into Chinatown for a beer. Maybe he'd get good and drunk. No, he just didn't have the energy. Besides, he could see the danger signs coming. Alcohol wasn't going to lift his spirits.

Adelman and Kaplan had sent him a letter officially informing him of his termination. Given the circumstances, the letter said, it was best for all parties concerned that they end their relationship. The firm wished him every success in finding employment elsewhere.

He had to regroup. He would send his resumé out to other firms, but the legal market in the Northeast was tight. He would have to consider moving out of his apartment on Beacon Hill and explore Somerville or even Jamaica Plain. His savings and severance pay would soon be depleted.

The first week or so after the trial, as the media trumpeted Alison's acquittal, there was no escape. How could he continue to live in Boston, in this disgrace? At the grocery store and in the subway, he was recognized. In a bank line, the teller recognized him. "You're somebody famous, aren't you?" she said. He grabbed his money and left the bank quickly. He'd have to find a new place.

As he walked along now, snow fell steadily throughout the city. Traffic was heavy, stalled in the gray slush. As of yet, he was unsure of his direction or what lesson he could glean from the experience. In the end, Jack thought, we live as we die. Alone. He'd known it all his life. He remembered how his father had died, on the couch listening to Sinatra, in a vacant house. Now Jack could summon up, finally, pity for his father, victim of the fates. The world, he saw and always knew, belonged to the winners.

Sitting on a bench in the Common, he stretched out his legs, plunged his hands in his pockets, and watched the snow fall. Tree branches waved with the wind and dropped a thin mist of snow. He dozed off. When he awoke, the air was colder. He reached for a cigarette, but his pockets were empty. All he had was a light.